wreck me

THE MADISON RIDGE SERIES: HOMECOMING

ELIZA PEAKE

CAFFEINATED WORDS PUBLISHING, LLC

WRECK ME

By Eliza Peake

Cover design by Julianne Fangmann at Heart to Cover

Editing by: Happily Editing Anns

www.elizapeake.com

❀ Created with Vellum

about this book

He's the grumpy, broody, sheriff who knows how to use handcuffs.

She's the sunshine, hot mess express wrecking havoc in his town and his life.

Sharing a bed with her wasn't part of the plan...

Aidan Reynolds' life is simple. Orderly. Just the way he likes it.

As interim sheriff with a woefully understaffed force, he doesn't have time for Megan Gentry, the beautiful, big city stranger who just caused a traffic jam in the town square.

He's just doing his job making sure her car gets towed. It's the right thing to do, escorting an injured woman to the town doc.

He's just being a decent guy by offering her a temporary place to stay. His mama raised him right, after all.

Besides, he can keep his hands to himself.

Maybe.

How does a man pass up his favorite pie made from scratch, even if she destroys his kitchen? Or resist unexpected, mind blowing kisses in the dark?

With Megan, he's breaking all his rules, consequences be damned.

She believes in love and he gave up on that emotion a long time ago.

When it's her time to leave Madison Ridge, he'll watch her drive away.

Even if it wrecks his heart in the process.

WRECK ME is a super steamy interconnected stand-alone small town romance. It has an HEA, no cheating, and scorching chemistry. Wreck Me is the third book in the Madison Ridge: Homecoming series set in the fictional Georgia town, Madison Ridge.

CHAPTER ONE
crash into me

AFTER PULLING AN ALL-NIGHTER, Aidan Reynolds was exhausted.

Thankfully, the good citizens of Madison Ridge had managed to behave most of the day, a relief after he and a couple of other deputies had broken up a bonfire get-together gone sideways. Of course, the Brewster brothers had never done anything quietly—even when they were all back in grade school together—especially when they'd tied one on…maybe even two. Aidan's bad shoulder throbbed from where one of them had taken a cheap shot at it.

It wasn't the first time he'd had to haul in the two knuckleheads for fighting, and he figured it wouldn't be his last.

But damn, at thirty-two, they were all getting too old for that kind of stupid shit.

He circled through the square, headed for the station, where a mountain of paperwork waited for him. With Sheriff Thompkins only working part-time due to his cancer treatments, Aidan had been picking up a lot of slack as Deputy Sheriff. Part of that slack included hiring some new staff, especially with the fall festival in a couple of weeks and the holiday season coming up.

Their small town would swell in population for the next few

months. As would the number of calls for crime and accidents from the influx of tourists who seemed to forget the laws of the road when visiting. It would tax their already woefully understaffed department.

At least he had the next day off. He could get some much needed sleep and work on the paperwork from the comfort of his cabin.

If he ever got there. There was some sort of traffic jam in the usually free flowing square. It's why they'd put in the roundabout thing, to keep traffic moving. Aidan peered out the windshield to see the bottleneck was coming from the circle. Turning on the lights and siren, he maneuvered the SUV along the edge of the one way street through the town square, cars moving off to the side however they could.

The cause of the traffic jam sat in the middle of the curve where a red late-model sedan looked like it had failed to yield to an old turquoise-colored sportster. Unfortunately, the coupe looked like it got the worse end of the deal.

That was a shame. It'd been years since he'd seen a Karmann Ghia on the road. And because it had been a while, he didn't have to look at the plates to know that they weren't local.

He made a U-turn in the middle of the road, blocking it off to traffic until he could ascertain what went down. A woman with dark hair was talking to the other driver through the driver's window, but started to walk his way when he parked.

Aidan slid on his glasses and got out, meeting her halfway in the middle of the road. "Ma'am, I'm Deputy Aidan Reynolds. Are you okay?"

She blinked, full pink lips parted. "Um, yes?"

"You're not sure?" He ran his gaze over her, the professional in him looking for injuries, the man in him taking in the curves that her hip-length sweater tried but failed to cover.

He gestured to her forehead where a bright red gash marred the pale skin. "You're bleeding."

"Oh…" A hand went to her hairline and when she pulled it away, she frowned. "I didn't notice."

"Shock. Why don't you walk over here with me to the sidewalk, and I'll get you something to stop the bleeding. Then you can tell me what happened."

She nodded and winced, sending concern skittering around his chest, especially when her eyes seemed to glass over.

"Ma'am?" He waved a hand in front of her face, but she didn't react. "Can you hear me?"

"Yes...I..."

Her eyes fluttered closed and her knees buckled.

"Shit," he muttered, but moved fast, catching her as she fell. He picked her up and carried her to the bench, laying her flat and elevating her feet on the back of it.

"Hey, Aid. Need some help?"

He glanced up to see his sister Charley jogging toward him. "Where'd you come from?"

She lifted the cup and bag that was looped over her wrist. "I was picking up my lunch over at the deli. Saw her go down. Nice catch, by the way."

"Can you sit with her while I go check the rest of the scene?"

Charley waved him off. "Yep, go ahead. I got this."

"There's a first aid kit in my cruiser. Get some gauze for her head."

"Aidan, I got this. Go."

For some inexplicable reason, he didn't want to leave the woman, even though he trusted his sister. Something in her hazel-colored eyes made his gut tighten, and he itched to protect her.

But he had a job to do and he didn't need any distractions.

He jogged over to where a smattering of onlookers talked to a young girl. "How's everything..." he trailed off when the girl turned to him. "Damn it. Again, Ashley?"

When the girl broke into tears, Aidan blew out a breath, wanting to kick his own ass for making her cry. Maggie, an older lady who owned the local diner, wrapped an arm around her and shot him a look. He held up his hands in a silent apology. "Ashley, are you okay? Any bumps, bruises?"

She shook her head against Maggie's shoulder. "No," she squeaked out through tears.

"Okay, good. Can you tell me what happened?"

Ashley hiccupped through a short explanation of how she was making a right turn but never saw the car she hit.

Aidan nodded. "Did you call your dad yet?"

She shook her head and Aidan frowned. "I hate to do this, but you know we have to call him, right?"

Tears coursed down her face, but she nodded and swiped them away. "Yeah, I know. But I don't know where my phone ended up. It was in my hand when…" She stopped and her mouth formed an O.

Busted. Aidan dropped his head and shook it. He pulled his phone out of his back pocket and handed it to her. "Call your dad, Ashley."

While Ashley made a phone call Aidan didn't envy, he took pictures of the scene from several angles for his report. Maggie brought his phone back to him and could only shake her head with a grim smile.

"Not good, huh?" he asked.

"Nope. We may not see Ashley much this year. Or next. Sounds like she might be grounded for the rest of her teenage years."

"Thanks for staying with her, Maggie."

"No problem, son. Come by for breakfast soon and tell your mama I said hi." Her eyes crinkled at the corners when she smiled and patted her beehive hair, a style she'd had since he was a kid and probably before that.

"Will do."

He called a tow truck, since it looked like the sporty little coupe wasn't going anywhere on its own, and walked over to the bench, where the woman was awake and sitting up. Charley ran a hand over her back in a way that reminded him of their mother. The woman's head bent forward, holding the bandage to her head with one hand and a bottle of water in the other. The gauze had a bright red spot that was stark against her increasingly pale skin. He squatted down to catch her gaze.

"Hey, feeling any better? Did I need to call 911 for you?"

"There's no need for all of that. I'll be fine." Her voice was low and barely a rasp over the sounds of the birds chirping and the cars and activity in the square behind them.

"What's your name?"

She lifted her head and closed her eyes as she leaned back against the bench. The movement made her wince before she answered. "Megan."

"Okay, Megan." He stood and shoved his hands into the back pockets of his tactical pants. "Can you tell me what happened?"

She opened her eyes and looked up at him. Fuck. Those eyes. Grayish green with gold flecks and a brown ring circled her slightly dilated pupils. He supposed they would be called hazel. He called them incredible.

Something in his gut confirmed that she was going to be nothing but trouble for him. It was time to get this wrapped up and move her along. He didn't have time for any sort of entanglements, but especially a woman with eyes that had the power to take a man out at the knees.

Megan cleared her throat. "I was driving through the square and came upon the roundabout there. I was in the circle, headed this way. I saw the red car coming from the side street and thought they'd yield. By the time I realized they weren't, I had no time to stop."

Aidan nodded. "Yeah, she said she never saw you. She admitted she was looking at her phone."

"Well, that's just great." Megan sighed deeply and chuckled without humor. She grimaced and put a hand to her forehead.

"Listen, I need to write up my report and try to get the vehicles moved out of traffic. You be okay here?"

"Yeah, I'll be fine. I've got Charley here to keep me company." She leaned over and gave his sister's shoulder a friendly bump and tried to smile, but it ended up morphing into a frown that marred her lips and caused a crease between her big hazel eyes.

"Insurance and registration in your car?"

"Yeah."

"I've got a tow truck on the way. Anything you need to get out of it?"

Megan rubbed her temples. "Yeah. Everything." She dropped her hands and looked over at her car. "I was headed to Florida to see my brother. So all my luggage, my purse."

She looked so dejected that he wished he could pull the car apart and fix it for her. But there wasn't a whole lot he could do about any of it. Other than find out what happened and get the scene moving along.

Aidan made notes and drawings of the accident, writing up each party's account of the accident and his determination. He wrote out a couple of tickets for Ashley—her father stood next to her, stoic, when he handed them over to her. Ashley's car was still mobile and soon they drove away.

He was glad he wouldn't be in that household tonight.

When the tow truck showed up, he chatted with the driver a minute and then retrieved Megan's luggage and personal items, putting the stuff in the back of his SUV. She had a couple of suitcases and overnight bags, a toiletry bag, a laptop bag, and an unlabeled box. He glanced over to where she sat with Charley.

How long was she visiting her brother? Why didn't she just fly? The address on her license was in Nashville. He didn't know where in Florida her brother lived, but judging by the fact that she landed in Madison Ridge, she wasn't headed to the Panhandle. Anywhere else in the Sunshine State was not a quick trip.

He shook his head as though to rid himself of the thoughts. It wasn't any of his business as to what Megan Gentry was doing. All he needed to do was his job and that was to wrap up this accident scene, drop her wherever she found a place to stay, and head back to the station.

While the tow truck hooked up Megan's car, Aidan walked back over to her and Charley. He studied Megan's face, not liking what he saw.

"You really should let me call an ambulance. Or take you to the clinic. You look a little green around the gills. And you need to get that gash looked at."

"I'm a little nauseous, but it'll pass. Oh…the world is tilting," Megan said, her voice slurring slightly. She held her arms out as though trying to find her balance, even though she was sitting down.

Aidan moved forward and wrapped one arm around her back and the other underneath her knees. "Okay, time for the doctor."

That snapped Megan awake. "What? No. I'm fine. I don't need a doctor. I swear I'm good."

He lifted up with her in his arms again—no, it wasn't an excuse to touch her again—though she made it more difficult to keep ahold of her by squirming in his arms. Charley stood and moved ahead of him to open the passenger side front door. He set Megan gently in the seat, and though she continued to protest, she was starting to lose the fight for consciousness, which was enough in Aidan's mind to get her over to the clinic.

"I don't need a doctor. I'm okay. I just need my stuff and some sleep."

"I've got your stuff in my cruiser. But I can't let you go to sleep. You need to see a doctor."

She looked over at him, her eyes bright with pain and shadowed with shame. "I can't afford a doctor."

He raised an arm and leaned against the doorframe. "Don't worry about that right now. We'll figure it out. I know your head hurts, I see it in your eyes. You probably have a concussion, and that cut needs stitches." He smiled. "And you don't want me doing the stitches for you. Not on your face. So let's go to the clinic, okay?"

She rolled her teeth over her full bottom lip and looked out the wide windshield of the SUV.

Something flared in his gut, hot and primal. What the hell was that shit? It wasn't like she was the first beautiful woman he'd ever come across in his line of work and on duty.

But there was something about this one…

Nope. No way, man. Abort mission. Don't even think about it.

After several seconds, she whispered, "Okay."

So much for aborting the mission.

concussions and inner bitches

MEGAN'S HEAD THROBBED. Damn, she'd really whacked her head hard on the window.

With a sigh, she closed her eyes, trying to figure out what to do next. But the more she thought about it, the worse her head pounded.

She should have known that this trek wouldn't be easy, but she was hoping her luck would turn around. After five years of mingling with Nashville's elite and old money, Megan had escaped hell—disguised as a McMansion with an open floor plan, a fenced in yard for the dog and kids she never had, and in a neighborhood that would make Pleasantville look downtrodden.

At thirty-two, she hadn't planned on being in a place in her life where she had a divorce under her belt and could fit everything she owned in the trunk of her car.

But starting over she was, and thanks to her brother, she had a job waiting for her in Florida. As long as she could get there sooner than later, which was looking like a long shot now.

She turned her aching head toward where the wrecker was driving away with Beatrix. Damn, she'd loved that little car. Before the ink was dry on her divorce papers, she'd traded in the BMW roadster that she'd always hated for an almost fifty-year-old, pristine-condition Karmann Ghia. It was cute, sporty, and ran well.

It may have lacked Bluetooth and electric windows, but it had air conditioning and was bought and paid for. It was all hers and she loved it.

Now it was crumpled and sad looking on the flatbed of a tow truck.

When officer hottie—Aidan—got in the SUV, the police radio went off, sending a bolt of pain through her brain. He reached over and turned it down. "Sorry about that. You okay?"

She turned toward the side window and closed her eyes, trying to fight back the nausea. "As good as I can be with a marching band stomping through my head."

"The clinic is just around the corner. We'll be there in a minute."

Silence filled the cabin as he made a U-turn in the middle of the road to take them back toward the square. Now that things had calmed down, she studied him. Really looked at him.

She'd noticed he was attractive before, but she must have really hit her head hard because her vision had to be playing tricks on her. The man sitting next to her looked like he belonged in Hollywood or on the pages of *GQ* magazine. She had no clue men that looked like him actually existed in real life outside of La La Land.

And the tactical gear uniform he wore upped the hot factor another notch. Yep, he looked like that hot captain dude in the *Transformer* movies. Josh something.

With his height and broad shoulders that looked like they could carry the weight of the world without breaking a sweat, he wore the uniform well. Sunglasses covered his eyes, and the black baseball cap with "Sheriff" written in yellow across the front cast a shadow over his face, but the jaw was strong and covered in dark stubble.

Shit, she was a sucker for guys with the right amount of stubble.

She bit back a sigh and looked out the window while they sat in a short line of traffic at a stop sign, watching the town bustle around.

From the historic courthouse in the center of the square that looked like it was the overlord watching the town move about its day to the brick buildings housing everything from a general store to a law office, she'd been instantly charmed by the small town that looked like it belonged in a Hallmark movie.

And she adored there wasn't a chain or big box store or lodging in sight.

Her hands itched for the camera she'd had to pawn before leaving Nashville.

With the exception of the accident—and she was still trying to figure out what to do next—her stop in Madison Ridge had been enjoyable. She glanced over at the man sitting next to her.

The scenery was some of the best she'd ever seen.

"So you were headed to Florida to visit your brother?"

"Yeah. Well, actually, I'm moving there from Nashville."

"Moving? In a Karmann Ghia?"

"Yep. Just me and Beatrix."

Aidan's brow furrowed. "Who's Beatrix?"

"My car."

"You named your car Beatrix?"

"Yeah. You know, from *Kill Bill*."

Aidan shook his head, but one side of his mouth lifted. "All right then."

"Don't you like *Kill Bill*?"

"Sure. Uma Thurman is a badass, and Tarentino is in his own league. I just wasn't expecting that answer." He turned to watch for oncoming traffic and pulled out smoothly at an opening before continuing. "So you're moving everything you own to Florida in a fifty-year-old Volkswagen."

"Yep. I was ready for a change from Nashville. So once my divorce was final, I started making plans, and Nate—that's my brother—said he'd help me."

Aidan maneuvered the SUV through the small streets quietly before speaking again. "I'm sorry about your divorce."

"I'm not. It was long past time." A wave of nausea hit her again, harder than before, and she closed her eyes. She inhaled deeply, hoping to not make a fool of herself. When she did, the smell of Aidan's cologne wafted to her, and in spite of the nausea, she wanted to bury her nose in his chest.

"Are you okay? You're looking green again."

She laid a hand over her stomach and took deep breaths. Drank some water. "Yeah, I think so," she said as she capped the water bottle and leaned her head back against the seat. "I just keep getting these waves of nausea."

"Definite concussion."

"Do you moonlight as a doctor, officer?" *Wow, Megan, bitchy much?*

"Deputy."

"What?"

He slowed down and turned on his blinker. "I'm a sheriff's deputy, not a police officer. But to answer your question, no. But I've seen my fair share of concussions, even had one myself. And I guarantee you need stitches."

She raised a hand to the bandage that was stuck to the gash on her head. When her fingers brushed it, it stung. "Oh yeah. I'd almost forgotten about it. This headache has had a way of blocking everything else out."

"Well, we're here."

She sighed in relief and hated the shame that burned her cheeks.

Aidan pulled into a parking spot right in front of the red brick building that housed the clinic and other doctors' offices.

"Is there someone I can call for you?" he asked after parking. His voice was deep, gravelly, and warm like a shot of whiskey. He slid the glasses off his face, and the bluest pair of eyes she'd ever seen made the breath in her lungs stop.

In spite of the pounding in her brain, her skin flushed under her clothes and her mouth went dry. His glance had only lasted milliseconds, but Megan felt like she'd been set on fire.

She licked her lips, trying to gather her thoughts. Between the accident and his gaze tying her tongue in knots, she was a hot mess. "Um, I need to let my brother know what's going on. But I'll call him later."

Aidan's brows drew down. "No parents? Other siblings? Cousins? Friends?"

"Nope. No one else. Not that counts anyway."

Aidan blew out a breath and nodded. "Okay. Let's get you in to see Doc."

"Wait," she said as he started to get out of the car.

He looked back with one brow lifted, and she swallowed hard. "I'm sorry if I'm a bit bitchy. It's no excuse, but my head is killing me."

One side of his mouth quirked up in a slight smile. "It's okay. You're in pain. You're allowed some leeway to be bitchy."

"Right. Thank you for your help."

"You're welcome. Now let's get you inside."

He came around to her side of the SUV and helped her out. "Put your arm around my shoulders," he said, meeting her gaze. "It's okay. You can lean on me."

Oh, she wanted to lean on him. The man smelled like heaven. Like a virile man, mixed with an expensive cologne, and…sex.

Okay, maybe that last one was her imagination. Because it had been a long time.

She was far from being in the market for a man of any sort right now. But she was still a flesh and blood woman, and his looks alone would tempt a saint. Add in the fact that he was in the business of protecting others. She wondered how he was still single.

Yeah, she'd checked the all-important ring finger.

She leaned on him because she really had no choice. Her feet acted like they were encased in cinder blocks and her legs were jellylike. At that moment, she totally understood how a new foal felt trying to gain their footing after being thrust into the world.

When Aidan opened the front door, warmth greeted them, along with the slightest bite of antiseptic in the air. He guided her toward the door to her left, opening it and helping her through.

Megan frowned. While she may have liked being tucked up against the broad chest of the hot man in uniform, the damsel in distress vibe wasn't her. At the same time, her head felt like it was going to roll off her shoulders at any given moment.

The waiting room was comfy and inviting with its plush chairs and small loveseats, and luckily, empty. He guided her to the nearest chair, and she sank down onto it with a small sigh.

Why did everything take such an effort?

And how the hell was she going to pay for this? She didn't have health insurance anymore and her funds were limited. Just thinking about how she was going to deal with the car made her head pound harder and her stomach turn.

The frosted glass partition closing off the office staff from the waiting room opened. "Well, hey there, Aidan. I wasn't expecting you today. Did you have an appointment for something?"

"Hey, Wilma. No, I'm not here for me. I've got an accident victim. I think she's got a concussion. Definitely has a gash that'll need some stitches."

An older woman peered around the glass, using a pencil to scratch her head. "Oh, goodness. Well, let me get Doc and we'll get her right in."

"Thanks, Wilma."

"Sure thing, hon." She and the pencil disappeared back behind the glass.

Aidan walked back over to her and squatted down on his haunches. He turned his baseball cap around so it sat backwards on his head. "Need a bucket or anything? Cold cloth?"

Those blue eyes were like looking at the bright blue sky. They stood out against his tanned skin and dark stubble. Good God, he really was gorgeous. It was a surreal sort of thing for her. And she'd been around her fair share of celebrities working high-end bars in Nashville. Being around the rich and beautiful didn't really faze her anymore.

But this guy? There had been some extra effort put into the looks department of this one. He was a little on the serious side, but that was probably an occupational hazard. She had to admit though, if she was going to have a car accident and knock the hell out of her head, she couldn't ask for a better chaperone.

"I'm just peachy keen, officer. Sorry, deputy." Her words had a sarcastic edge to them when a slice of pain ran through her head. Damn it, she hated when inner bitch came out to play, even for a second. "Again, I'm sorry. Headaches always make me..."

"Bitchy?" Aidan supplied with a grin that made her panties want to spontaneously combust.

She smiled back. "I call her my inner bitch."

"You mean you didn't name her after a *Kill Bill* character like your car? I think Elle would be fitting."

Megan nearly swooned. "That sounded suspiciously like a joke."

He smiled, and Megan couldn't tell if the turning in her gut was the concussion—she had to agree with deputy hottie on that—or the fact that the man had a smile that was a lethal weapon.

"Well, just relax. Doc will get you squared away."

"You don't have to stay. I'm sure you've got more crime to fight. Or accidents to tend to."

"It's fine. I'm not the only deputy on duty. We have a whole department, you know." His lips twitched in a smile.

"Hey, you made another joke. You're on fire."

"I can be a funny guy."

"Whatever you say, Deputy Reynolds."

He stood and crossed his arms over his chest, looking out the window behind her.

She lifted a brow, her gaze raking over him. Holy hell, he really was tall. Standing there, legs hip width apart, his jaw set, the protective vibe came off of him in waves. Whatever woman ended up with this man was going to be the luckiest bitch on the planet.

"You don't look like any sheriff I've ever seen before."

Wait. What was she doing flirting? Sure, he was hot as hades, but she had no business flirting with him. This concussion was really messing with her.

He grinned again, and her dusty lady parts woke up. "Seen a lot of sheriffs in your day?"

"No, but I always think of *The Andy Griffith Show* when I think of sheriffs. And you don't look anything like that."

For the love of God, shut up, Megan!

What did it say about her that even in the midst of having a concussion, all she could think about was how his hands and lips would feel on her skin? She wasn't normal.

Maybe her ex was right. She *was* weird. Or maybe she'd hit her head harder than she thought and this was all some whacked-out dream.

Before he could respond to the ridiculousness that she continued to spout, the woman from the front desk opened the door leading to the patient rooms.

"Hey there. Y'all can come on back."

we have rules, remember?

HE'D JUST MET this woman and already she'd made him want to throw out his rule book on more than one occasion.

Including the ones where he'd taken an oath. To protect and serve took on a whole new meaning when she licked her lips and flirted with him in her quirky little way. Aidan didn't date, and he certainly didn't take women he did meet for a night of no-strings-attached sex back to his house.

But he could see Megan spread out in his bed, and he liked the vision just a little too much. So much that his hands actually tingled with the need to touch her in any way he could, even when she probably could have walked on her own.

She was messing with his head, and he needed to shut that shit down quick. This banter between them that lightened his heart, where he actually teased a female that wasn't his sisters? Yeah, that couldn't keep happening.

He needed to keep space between them so he wouldn't be enticed by the vanilla and whatever kind of flower she smelled like. It was driving him crazy in ways that he had no time or inclination for. That lasted all of about two seconds when she tried to get up and wobbled. He grabbed her arms to steady her. "You okay?"

"Yeah." But she didn't sound confident about it as she looked at her shoes. When he started to let go, she looked up at him, worry flashing in her eyes. "Will you come back with me?"

Those job requisites didn't stand a chance against Megan's pleading look.

"Of course."

"Good." Her smile was one of relief, and her shoulders relaxed.

She walked ahead of him, slowly, and he couldn't help but admire the sway of her hips. He couldn't touch, but he may as well enjoy the view while he could.

Wilma led them back to an exam room, promising Doc would be in soon. Not thirty seconds of tense silence later, Doc came in the room.

"Aidan, how's it going, son?" Doc reached out and they shook hands.

"Good."

With a comforting smile, Doc pulled the rolling seat toward the exam table where Megan sat. "So, what we got going on?"

Aidan stood on the other side of the room, leaning against the wall. Megan explained what happened, and little by little, as Doc asked questions, her shoulders finally stopped meeting her ears. His uncle had that gift of making his patients feel relaxed even when they came in feeling anything but relaxed.

"Aidan?"

Doc's deep voice pulled him out of his thoughts. "Yeah?"

"We're going to take Megan to get a CT. You sticking around?"

"Uh, yeah. I'll just wait out in the waiting room." He pushed off the wall and addressed Megan. "I'll call and make sure your car made it to the shop."

Her nod was small. "Thank you."

In the waiting room, he called Henderson's shop and confirmed her car made it and then checked in with his cousin Landon, who was one of his deputies. When it appeared all was handled—except for the mounting paperwork on his desk—he flipped mindlessly through faded magazines and wondered about the woman down the hall.

Nah, man. We have rules, remember? You have plenty of people to protect and serve. You don't need to fixate on one out-of-towner. No matter how gorgeous she may be or how hard her smile hits you in the gut.

Finally, Doc and Megan came through the door and into the waiting room. Megan's gash on her head had been stitched, and she had some paperwork in hand.

Aidan stood and slid his phone in his back pocket. "Everything look okay?"

"Yeah, we just had some paperwork to go over." Doc turned slightly to Megan. "Mind if I share with Aidan?"

"It's fine."

Aidan had two older brothers, but he was surrounded by sisters in the sibling birth order, making him well versed in what it really meant when a woman says "I'm fine."

Megan was anything but fine.

"She definitely has a concussion. My recommendation for the next forty-eight hours is rest, no screen time, no television, no driving, nothing that requires brain stimulation. Taking a light walk is fine, as long as symptoms don't return. Tylenol, no aspirin. And she shouldn't be alone for the next forty-eight hours." He turned back to Megan. "And I'd like to see you back in three days."

Aidan's gaze shot to Megan. The poor woman looked like she was about to cry. Every cell in Aidan's body screamed at him to shield her from everything.

He held out his hand to his uncle. "Okay, thanks, Doc."

Doc returned the shake. "How's the shoulder?"

"It's fine. A little sore today after taking a shot from Robbie Brewster, but I'll live."

Doc rolled his eyes. "Those two…well, let me know if you have any trouble." He turned to Megan. "You have my cell. If you have any questions, don't hesitate to call me. And I'll talk with Wilma about the other issue we spoke about. Okay?"

"Thanks, Doc."

Once they were situated back in his SUV, she turned to him. "Thank you for helping me with all that. I hate to put you out further but do you know a place where I can stay for a few days? Just until I figure out my next move?"

He pushed the start/stop button and the SUV cranked on. "There's a couple of places around here. But I know a place where I can get you a deal."

For the first time since he'd met her, her smile lit up her face, and it was like staring into the sun. "That would be great. Thank you, Aidan. Oh, what did you find out about my car?"

"It's at the shop. Henderson said if you want to come by he can give you a timeline and estimate." His hands gripped the wheel, and he tapped his thumb. "You know, Doc said you shouldn't be alone for the next two days."

"I'll be fine. I'm a big girl. Like I said, I just need a place to stay for a few nights until I figure out my next move."

Against his better judgment, Aidan let it go. He had no claim on this woman and couldn't make her be sensible, even if every cell in his body wanted to make her see reason.

He dropped the SUV into gear. "Okay, let's go find you a room."

The smell of lemon, wood, and beeswax made the wide room of the Historic Square Inn feel more like the living room in a family home than the lobby of a place where strangers laid their heads. Aidan knew for a fact that the furniture was expensive, family antiques that were anything but comfortable, but the large rugs on the floor and the raging fire in the fireplace in the middle of the room gave it a cozy, warm feeling.

He and Megan walked toward the vacant check-in desk at the back of the room. "Hello?" he called out.

His mother, Stella, came through a doorway off to the side. "Aidan, why are you hollering? Don't you know you're supposed to ring the bell?" Her tone was teasing, and the smile on her face made her blue eyes light up. "What's up, baby?"

"Hey, Mom. Where's Aunt Linds?"

"Her day off." His mom folded her arms over the desk and leaned forward. "Aidan, don't be rude. Introduce me to your friend."

"She's not...never mind." He sighed and stepped aside so that

Megan could step forward. "This is Megan. Megan, this is my mom, Stella Reynolds. Megan was passing through town and had a fender bender this morning. She needs a room for a few days."

Stella's eyes were wide as she studied Megan. "Ouch. Took a shot to the head, huh?"

"She's got a concussion," Aidan supplied.

"I can still talk though," Megan muttered, glaring at him and lifting a hand to the bandage on her forehead. She gave his mom a smile. "It's been a rough day. But it's nice to meet you. This is a beautiful place."

Stella returned the smile. "Thanks. My sister-in-law has been running it for decades. She bought it a couple of years back. I fill in on her day off." She stepped over to the computer and shook the mouse. "Let's see what we can find. I know the rooms on the east side of the second floor are unavailable due to a busted water pipe."

She clicked the mouse a couple of times and lowered the reading glasses from on top of her head to her face. She typed in a few things and then looked over the rims at Megan.

"You know, if you've got a concussion, you shouldn't be alone. You should be monitored for forty-eight hours."

Aidan crossed his arms over his chest and dropped his chin. He didn't think Megan would appreciate a smug "I told you so" and at the same time a thought crossed his mind. Guilt settled in for not saying it out loud.

But it would go against so many of his rules.

Megan's smile was weak. "You sound like Doc."

Stella smiled. "It happens with siblings."

"I thought you might be related. But I'll be fine. I'm going to sleep it off. Just need a bed."

Aidan's hand fisted against his chest. Why didn't this woman take her concussion seriously? He glanced over at her just in time to see her sway. His arms shot around her to keep her steady. "Easy now."

Stella came around the desk. "Aidan, sit her down before she passes out. I'll get some water."

Aidan kept Megan against his side and led her to a nearby chair, easing her into it. It took everything he had in him not to sniff her hair or think about how her body fit against his like it was made for it.

Damn, dude, get it together. She's injured, you perv. "Let's take a seat." He crouched down once she was settled in the chair.

A moment later, Stella came out with a glass of water, a cool washcloth, and Tylenol. Megan popped the pills in her mouth, and Aidan raised a brow when she drank the water like she'd been stuck in the desert for a year. When she'd downed half the bottle, she slumped against the back of the wingback chair.

"Better?" Stella asked.

"Yes, thank you."

Stella crossed her arms and looked down at Megan. "So, I have a room available for tonight and tomorrow. But I really think you need someone to stay with you. Do you have anyone—"

"No," Megan and Aidan answered in unison.

Stella looked back and forth between them a moment before speaking. "Okay…"

"Thank you for being so kind," Megan said with a smile. "But I can take care of myself."

Shit. Son of a bitch. Damn it all to hell. Fuck.

Aidan closed his eyes and pinched the bridge of his nose.

He had no desire to play babysitter for the next two days, his only days off for the next seven. No two ways about it, he was going to be sorry for what he was about to say. He didn't know how or why just yet, but all he knew was that he was about to take a headfirst dive into a steaming pile of shit. And it wasn't going to end well for him.

But his mouth didn't get the memo of what a monumental bad idea this was, otherwise he would have never uttered the words…

"You can stay with me."

can't win for losing

MEGAN TURNED her head to meet Aidan's gaze. "What?"

Aidan huffed out a breath as though pained he had to repeat himself. "I said, you can stay with me. I'm off the next two days and I can monitor you."

"I can't do that, Aidan."

"Why not?" he asked.

"Because"—she blew out a breath and met his gaze—"I know how tight-knit communities work, okay? The sheriff taking in a strange, injured woman into his home? And they're alone?" She scoffed and looked away, taking in the charming little town outside the front window. "People will talk. I'm leaving soon so I can leave the gossip behind, but you live here."

She set her shoulders the best she could in her weakened state and looked him in the eye. "I won't besmirch your reputation that way."

Stella raised a brow and glanced over at Aidan, as though she were waiting to see how her son was going to handle that one. Not for the first time, Megan wondered how often a woman said no to him. Her guess was not often.

His lips pursed before he spoke. "I won't deny the town will talk. But first, I don't care. And second, you know what would really put them in a tizzy? They'd ask how I, of all people, could dump you off at a room and make you fend for yourself when you need to be monitored."

"So what you're saying is there's no winning?"

"Basically," Aidan and Stella said in unison.

She continued to stare at him. Why would he do this? He just said he didn't care if they talked, so he could ignore the wagging tongues. But he didn't know her. And while he might be law enforcement, this seemed a little extreme on the "to protect and serve" front.

Aidan sighed, his wide chest expanding and contracting. "Look, I have a guest room that's ready to go. I live alone so it will be quiet for you to recover. If it would make you feel better, I can call one of my sisters to come over and play chaperone. After the forty-eight hours, you can find a room somewhere else."

Megan wanted to trust him, and even though her gut told her she could, she'd been burned one too many times before. She'd trusted people that should have protected her and they'd turned out to be the wrong people.

"No. I can't."

He stood up and moved next to his mother, jamming his hands on his hips. A V formed between his brows that she wanted to smooth away, and his lips turned down in a frown.

Was it bad that in the middle of the chaos that continued to plague her life, she couldn't quit looking at his mouth and wondering what it felt like?

Mother and son looked down at her, identical blue eyes studying her, waiting for her to tell them why she couldn't stay alone with a strange man who looked like an Adonis.

What was it with this family and their eyes? They were so sharp, like they saw everything.

Stella finally spoke. "I understand your hesitation. You're in a strange town and banged up. And this guy is offering to take care of you." Her eyes moved back and forth between Megan's. "Not something you're used to, is it?"

Megan swallowed back the tears that threatened to form. She

wanted to lie, wanted to tell this woman with the beautiful smile and kindness in every movement to mind her own damn business.

But for the life of her, she couldn't. There was a moment of understanding that passed between them, and a glimpse of a feeling that had been foreign in Megan's life for so long appeared. Trust.

Megan shook her head before whispering. "No."

Stella's smile was sad. "I know. And while Aidan is my son and I love him, I can tell you this without bias. You don't have to worry about anything with him. He'll take care of you. He's one of the good ones."

She pointed a finger at Aidan. "And if you tell your brothers I said that, I'll deny it."

A hint of a smile that Megan had seen a couple of times—which wasn't nearly enough in her opinion—tugged at Aidan's mouth.

Megan smiled and met Aidan's eyes. They were steady, not backing down from her stare. She couldn't read all the emotions there, but one thing she didn't see was lying eyes. And she'd learned pretty quickly what those looked like.

He did appear to be one of the good ones, much like her brother. Nate was the only person she trusted in her life. But it looked like she was going to have to trust the man that currently towered over her as well.

"Okay, I'll stay with you."

"Excellent." Stella smiled and stepped back. "Aid, get this girl home so she can start healing."

Before she took her next breath, Aidan was by her side and helping her from the chair. Stella opened the door to the inn and then the passenger door of the SUV, and within moments, Megan was strapped in.

"Take care, Megan. I hope you feel better soon," Stella said before closing the door.

"I will, thanks." All she could do was close her eyes and lean her head back. God, why was the sun so freaking bright? She groaned and covered her eyes with her hand.

A moment later, Aidan slid in on the other side and started the vehicle. "Did you want to check on your car before we head to my house?"

What she wanted was to curl up into a ball and lay her head down. But she needed to check on her car and call her brother once she found out how long she'd be stuck in Madison Ridge.

"Yeah, that would be great. Thanks."

They didn't speak for the next few moments it took for Aidan to pull into Henderson's Auto and Body Shop.

Before Aidan could get out of the car, Megan laid a hand on his arm to get his attention. Instantly, she wished she could take it back because the warmth of his skin radiated from under the fabric of his long-sleeved shirt. It gave her system an unexpected jolt.

It had been a few years since she'd really felt anything resembling desire for a man. Sure, she'd been married, but the sex with her ex hadn't been driven by desire. At least not on her part.

"Thank you."

His bright blue eyes met hers, and the air around them grew thick. He cleared his throat and leaned back slightly. "You're welcome."

The deep timbre of his voice made her belly jump and warmth spread through her blood. She stared back at him, unable to look away.

"You've been awfully kind."

"Just doing my job."

Right. That's all this was. His job. He was a nice guy and he may have been going out of his way, but it wasn't because he was interested in her. And she was a fool to even think otherwise.

Besides, she wasn't in the market for a man, and she needed to remember that. She was starting life anew. New job, new town, new Megan without a man.

She was also going to get a new car by the sounds of it.

According to Henderson, it was going to take at least two weeks for the shop to fix her car—as long as they could get all the parts in. In her old life, she would have called the insurance company for them to handle it all. But she was just getting her footing back, and insurance claims weren't something she wanted to contend with. Hell, she didn't even have a home address anymore. So cash it was.

But even using aftermarket parts on her older car, the estimate was enough to make her eyes pop and the pounding in her head to nearly blind her.

Dejected and unsure of what to do next, she closed her eyes and leaned her head back as Aidan drove them to his house. She swiped the tears that leaked from the edges of her eyes.

It seemed like just a few seconds had passed when Aidan opened her door. "Where are we?"

"My house." He held out a pair of sunglasses. "Here, put these on. It'll help keep you from squinting. Just makes the headache worse."

"Thank you." She slid the sunglasses over her eyes and moved to the edge of the car seat.

He wrapped an arm around her shoulder. "Lean on me."

They made their way up the sidewalk with his arm loosely wrapped around her waist. She didn't mind the weight of his arm on her a bit, actually. It was…comforting.

While he unlocked the door, Megan leaned against the wall. She hoped there was a bed in her near future. She needed to lay her head down in the worst way.

Warm air greeted them as Aidan swung open the door and held out his arm for her to go in ahead of him. Thankfully it was dimmer in the house than outside, and she sighed in relief, lifting the glasses to the top of her head.

She walked farther into the foyer, her steps slow because with every move she made, her head pounded. Her gaze roamed around his house, looking over the comfortable brown leather sofa and recliner in the living room. On the wall hung a flat screen television that she was sure astronauts could see from the International Space Station. Other than the TV remote, a copy of *Car and Driver*, and an empty glass, the coffee table was clean and clear of clutter. A charcoal-gray blanket thrown haphazardly on the back of the sofa looked soft, and Megan wanted to rub her cheek over it. A rug covered a large area of the hardwoods in the living room, adding warmth to the room.

A few framed pictures sat on the fireplace mantel, and she wanted to check them out, see if they would tell her anything about the man who'd taken care of her today, but it was too much effort to walk over there and look.

"I'm going to put your things in the garage. What do you need brought in here?"

"The big purple suitcase and the toiletry bag for now. You know, you don't need to take everything out. I'm only going to be here for a few days."

He shrugged. "You won't be able to keep all that in a hotel room though. You can just store it here until you leave town."

This man. He just kept doing things for her. "You sure?"

"Yep. I'll be back in a bit. Will you be okay for a few minutes?"

She smiled. "I'll be fine."

"I'm not going to find you on the floor when I come back, am I?"

Her chuckle was soft as she shook her head. "No. I'll be vertical. I promise. I'm going to sit down and call my brother."

He nodded and then walked out the front door. A moment later the garage door opened. Megan crossed to the sofa and sat in the corner of it, grabbing the blanket and wrapping it around her. It smelled like her favorite fabric softener and was just as soft as she had imagined.

Once comfortable, she pulled her phone out of her purse and called her brother.

"Hey, Meg-pie. How's the trip going?" Nate's deep voice came through the phone, and she closed her eyes against tears. She'd really missed him.

"Well, that's why I'm calling. I've hit a snag of sorts."

"Are you okay?" Concern colored his voice.

"Yeah. Mostly."

"Mostly? Megan, what's going on?"

Oh shit. He only called her Megan when he was serious. Like the way her parents had done.

"Okay, I'm going to tell you but you have to keep quiet until I'm done. Okay?"

He sighed on the other end. "Fine."

"You have to promise, Nate."

"I promise. Jesus. Just tell me already. Wait, hold on." There was a muffled noise and then some tapping. "Okay. I needed to tell Angie to move my meeting a few minutes."

"Oh, shit. I'm sorry. You should have told me."

"It's fine. But you need to tell me what's going on."

She sighed. "Okay, I had a car accident."

"You what?" His voice rose, and she pulled the phone away from her ear with a wince.

"Please, stop. You promised to be quiet, and I have a concussion." He was quiet but she could practically hear the steam coming from his ears.

She told him the rest, including the fact that she'd be staying with Aidan. Even though she really didn't want to tell him, they'd never had secrets from each other. Her brother was the only person she trusted absolutely.

"Are you done?" he asked when she stopped talking.

"Yes, but remember to keep it down. Concussed here."

"I'll charter a plane for you. Is there an airport nearby there?"

She rubbed her forehead. "I don't know and no. You're not sending a plane for me."

"Why the hell not? The team uses one that I can pay for."

"No. I'm not letting you do that."

"Then let me pay for a room for you or pay for the car."

"Nate, no. You've done enough. I love you, but I'm trying to do this on my own in some way. You've already sent me money, plus you're giving me a job and a place to stay. I don't want anything else."

"I'm not giving you a job. You earned it. You're a great bartender, and I need someone that can run a bar. You know how, so you have the job."

"Well, thank you. But still, you've done enough. No more. I'll sort all this out on my own. Okay?" She sighed. "Look, I know this puts the opening of the bar back a bit and I'm sorry—"

"Don't worry about it, Meg-pie. It actually works out. Renovations got behind and I have some wiggle room for the opening. And I'll be around now that I'm retired." There was a wistful tone in his voice.

Her brother had been the catcher for the Florida Seabirds major league baseball team and the home run king of the majors. The Seabirds had made it all the way to the National League playoffs before getting booted. Nate had been in the majors for over a decade, and his body had finally decided enough was enough.

Megan chuckled softly to keep her head from hurting. "Oh, you know you're okay with it."

He sighed. "Yeah, maybe. I know it got harder each year to recover. Anyway, do what you need to do to get well with that concussion. We'll figure out what to do with the car."

"Uh, we're going to get the car fixed. I can't leave without Beatrix."

"You and that damn car." Humor tinged his voice. "Okay, I gotta go. I've kept the sponsors waiting long enough. Love you, Meg-pie."

"Love you too." She hung up and closed her eyes.

The sound of rolling wheels scraped across the floor before they stopped. Aidan's boots made a soft shuffling sound across the dark hardwood floor as he made his way into the living room.

"Can I get you anything?" he asked, crouching down next to her.

She cleared her throat. "A bed. I need to lay my head down."

"Right, follow me." He closed his hand around hers so she had no choice but to follow him through the living room and kitchen area and down a short hall. He opened the door on the left. "I'm giving you my room."

She stopped at the doorway. "No. No way. I'm not taking your room."

"Well, the only other bed in this house is in the loft."

"I'll do that. I'm not taking your bed."

He shook his head. "I don't think so. The only way to access it is by a ladder. You're not climbing a ladder in your condition and risking further injury."

She sighed. He wasn't wrong. There was no way she was climbing a ladder of any sort. "Fine. You win."

The room was minimal but comfy, just like the rest of the house she'd seen thus far. She walked in and sat on the edge of the bed, bouncing a little on it. "Comfortable bed."

He slid his hands into his back pockets. "I'll get your suitcase then leave you to rest."

Before she could thank him, he was out the door, so she laid her head down with a moan. She couldn't remember the last time laying her head down felt so damn good. She sniffed the pillow, and the scent of fabric softener made her smile. There might not be much more than the bed in his room, but it was soft and cozy and she wanted to sleep for a hundred years.

Megan opened her eyes when Aidan came through the door. She wanted to sit up and thank him, but she just didn't have the energy to do it.

"Here you go," he said, lifting the luggage and putting it on a bench at the end of the bed. "Need anything else?"

"No, I'm great now that I've laid my head down. Thank you so much, Aidan. I really appreciate it."

He nodded. "Let me know if you need anything."

"Mmm…" She closed her eyes again, and the fabric rubbed against her face as she nodded.

As darkness took over, her mind wandered to the man with bright sky-blue eyes, and she wished she'd met him before her self-induced man hiatus.

midnight questions

MEGAN WOKE IN STAGES. The first thing she registered was the soft, clean-smelling sheets. She opened her eyes, or at least she thought she did. The room was too dark to tell.

Where was she? The comforter rustled as she sat up before blinding pain stopped her cold.

"Ow, shit." Her hand flew to her head where her fingers brushed against gauze. What the hell?

Bits of memories played in her head like a disjointed movie. A charming small town and a tall, sexy guy. A cop, sheriff, whatever. Was there something about her car?

The puzzle pieces fell into place. Poor Beatrix. The accident, the concussion, Aidan. And the fact she was in his bed. She ran a hand across the sheet, her fingertips tingling, unable to stop thinking about the fact that his skin had touched these sheets before her. It made her head light and that had nothing to do with her concussion.

Her phone lit up next to her on the nightstand. God, it was bright. She reached over and turned on the lamp, the light causing her to squint and hold her head again. Her stomach decided to get in on the action as well and sent up a small protest. "Son of a bitch."

There was a glass of water next to her phone, and she took a sip.

The cool water relieved her parched, dry mouth. She picked up her phone and the screen read 1:30 a.m.

"You're not supposed to be looking at that."

Megan let out a small yelp and her phone went flying. A flash of pain seared through her head and she gripped it with both hands. "Oh my God. Don't scare me like that."

Aidan leaned against the doorjamb, his eyes watchful.

She didn't want to notice how the black T-shirt was taut against his wide chest, or the way his folded arms showed off strong forearms and biceps. And she really didn't want to notice that he was wearing gray sweatpants that hung low on his narrow hips.

Her mouth watered and she swiped at her chin. Nope, not drooling. Yet.

"I didn't mean to scare you. It's been a while since I checked on you. Saw the light underneath the door." He frowned and that V between his brows showed up. "I suppose I should have knocked first."

"Hmmm..." She didn't quite know what to say to that. She had taken over his bedroom after all. "Well, I'm fine. Thanks for the water. My mouth felt like I ate a bag of cotton balls."

His lips quirked into a slight smile. "You're welcome. Need anything else?"

At that moment, her stomach growled loud enough that it seemed to echo around the room. Aidan raised a brow.

Megan laid a hand over her stomach and smiled. "I think I'm hungry."

"I've got some soup left from dinner. I can bring you a bowl."

She rubbed a hand over her thigh, soreness beginning to set in. "Actually, I'd like to come out there. I need to move some. But I need to change."

"Sure."

When she pushed back the covers and swung her legs to the side of the bed, the room started to spin. Aidan moved to the side of the bed and held out his hands. "Easy, basher. Go slow or it'll make the pain worse."

She blew out a breath, then looked up at him, her eyes narrowed. "Did you just call me...basher?"

"If the shoe fits."

"Hey, that accident wasn't my fault."

"I know." Aidan chuckled and pushed a lock of hair behind her ear. The movement was oddly intimate and tender, causing a lump to form in her throat. "Take it easy, Megan. Now, take my hands."

"I got it. I'm fine."

Did the man just growl at her? "Take my hands, Gentry."

"Fine." She huffed out a breath, unhappy that she needed him to help her up. But at the moment, if she stood without assistance, she might faceplant on the floor.

Her hands slid into his large ones, and he helped her stand. When she swayed, her hands landed flat on his chest. His arm banded around her waist, bringing them close together.

"You okay?" His deep voice was a raspy whisper in her ear.

Desire lit up her body like a Christmas tree. Her fingers curled inward, taking some of the fabric of his shirt with them. His body was hard under that shirt, and damn, he smelled good. It was like leather, soap, and man. If she could bottle it somehow, she'd make a fortune.

The hand on the small of her back applied more pressure, and she wanted to just sink into him. It had been so long since she'd felt the touch of a man that set her soul on fire. Had there ever been a man to do that? If the feeling she had right now was any indication, the answer was no.

When she looked up at him, those bright blue eyes were dark with a hint of gray. They reminded her of storm clouds on the horizon. Something deep in her gut told her that Aidan Reynolds would be amazing in bed. Probably ruin her for the rest of her life.

But that was something she was never going to find out. Her head was a little fuzzy, but one thing she knew was that she had a new life waiting for her in Florida. Not in a little mountain town in Georgia.

And she definitely wasn't getting involved with anyone right now. She was done with love for now. For as long as she could remember, she'd always had a man. It was time to figure out who Megan was without a man by her side.

No matter how good of a guy Aidan was, she wasn't sticking around, and even if she were, she wasn't ready to go down any road where she'd be hurt again.

That thought was enough to put the brakes on the desire that whipped through her body. She tore her gaze from his and lifted her hands from his chest. "I-I'm sorry."

Oh perfect, now she was stammering.

"It's okay."

Carefully, and unable to look into his eyes again, she stepped back and he let his hand fall away from her back. He kept a hold of her hand, but loosened his grip.

"Soup sounds good," she said to the floor. "I'll change and be out there in a minute."

"Steady?"

Not really, but she'd have to be. "Yep. I'm fine."

He left the room without another word. All of the oxygen in the room went with him when he closed the door with a soft click. She blew out a breath and turned to the bench at the end of the bed where her suitcase sat.

Damn it, he was a thoughtful one. She didn't want him to be thoughtful or kind.

She changed into a pair of pajama pants and a long sleeve T-shirt. It took her longer than it normally would have since she had to pause a couple of times to let the room stop spinning. But she'd managed to get changed and even use the bathroom connected to the bedroom.

The fact that he'd put her toiletry bag in the bathroom for her was almost too much. Who the hell was this guy? Was he for real? Stella had raised him well.

She padded out into the kitchen, following the smell of chicken noodle soup. When she rounded the corner, she came to a stop like she'd hit a wall.

No microwave reheating for this one. Aidan stood in front of the stove, his back to her, stirring the soup in a large red pot. Megan tilted her head, unable to do anything more than watch him. The man had an amazing ass, which the baggy pants didn't detract from. How was that even possible?

He put the lid back on the pot and ran a large hand through his hair. As he turned, he noticed her standing there and motioned toward the long peninsula. "Come on over to the bar. It'll be ready in a minute." He moved toward the coffeepot. "I have some tea. Want any?"

"Yeah, tea sounds good. And some water if it isn't too much trouble," she said, making her way to a long expanse of granite countertop.

He went to a door on the other side of the kitchen that opened into a walk-in pantry. "I've got green tea and some of that herbal sleepy stuff," he called out.

Megan smiled and slid onto a barstool. "Herbal, please."

He walked out, turning off the light behind him all in one fluid motion. Watching Aidan move was like an erotic, alpha male dance. His motions were smooth, economical, but unhurried. Her sex-starved brain wondered how his body moved in bed.

She closed her eyes and dropped her forehead to her hand. No, no, no. There would be no more thinking of this man in any way sexual. What was wrong with her?

She blamed the concussion.

"Megan, are you okay?"

God, how many times had he asked her that today? He had to be tired of it already. She was. She lifted her head and met his concerned eyes as he stood in front of her with a box of tea in one hand.

"Yeah, I'm fine." She cleared her throat and gestured to the box of tea with her head. "You like your Sleepytime tea?" she teased.

He looked down at the box in his hand as though he wondered how it got there. "Oh. No. I don't drink tea unless it's cold and full of sugar. My sister Grace is always bringing teas over and leaving them here. I humor her and let her."

"Well, that's sweet of you."

He shrugged a shoulder as he filled the kettle with water. "My mom and sisters like their tea, and they like to drop by to make sure I haven't turned into a caveman, I guess."

"How many sisters do you have exactly?"

"Three." He set the kettle on the stove. The burner clicked for a few seconds before the flame lit up. "Charley, who you met today, Grace, and Amelia."

"Did your mom say something about brothers or did I dream that?"

"I have two older brothers."

"Wow. A big family." Her heart twisted a little at the old pain of never having much family. "So, I take it you were born and raised here. Do all of your siblings live here?"

"Yeah, for now. But I think Charley wants to get out of town. She graduated from college last year. And she hasn't really figured out what she wants from life just yet. My brother Del moved back earlier this year."

"I bet your parents are happy about that."

A shadow crossed his eyes just before he looked away to open a cupboard and reach for a bowl and mug. "It's just my mom. My father died when I was thirteen."

She looked down into the bowl of soup he'd just slid in front of her. "I'm sorry."

What was she doing? She didn't need to know all these things about him. No, as soon as she was cleared to stay on her own, she was moving into the inn until her car was ready. And then she was out.

"No need to be sorry. It was a fair question. Do you want some crackers?"

"No, thanks. This is good." She picked up the spoon he'd set out and stirred the fragrant broth. "You know, you don't have to do all of this. I'm sure you have better things to do. Like sleep or something."

He leaned back against the counter and picked up a mug next to him. "Not a problem. I was up anyway."

The mug was standard sized, but the way his hand wrapped around it, it seemed small. She couldn't help but wonder how those hands would feel skating over her body.

Her eyes flicked up to his as he sipped from the cup, eyes watchful over the rim.

"You going to eat the soup or just stir it the whole time?" The smile on his lips softened the words.

"Hmm...I was just waiting for it to cool."

She ate the best damn chicken noodle soup she'd ever put in her mouth and sipped tea while he cleaned and put away the dishes he'd used.

"Don't you sleep? Or are you one of those people who exist on coffee and adrenaline?" It appeared her mouth wasn't going to stop playing twenty questions.

He went back to what she'd thought of as his place in the kitchen, leaning against the counter, arms crossed over his broad chest. One thing was for sure. It gave her a nice view.

He shook his head and looked at the floor. "I just don't sleep much. When I do, I don't sleep well."

"Is it because of your job?"

"That might be part of it, since I'm always waiting for a call. But it started when I was in the military actually."

"What branch did you serve in?"

"Army. Ranger. Three tours in Afghanistan."

"Wow, that must have been rough."

"It was hard being away from home." He nodded toward her. "If you're done, I'll take your bowl."

Unlike other men she'd known, Aidan was adept at deflecting the conversation from him. It made him all the more intriguing and pushed her to ask more questions than she should. But she was a stranger in this man's house who was doing her a solid. It was really none of her business, and she just needed to shut up.

"Yes, I'm done." Megan pushed the bowl and mug away and sat back. "Thank you, that was delicious. Best chicken noodle I've had. Did you make it?"

"Yeah, Mom's recipe." He reached over the bar and took her dishes before rinsing them in the sink. "Sure I can't get you anything else?"

"No, I'm good. Thank you, though. You've been great."

"My mom would kick my ass into next week if she knew I'd been inhospitable."

More questions were on the tip of her tongue. But her head started to get fuzzy again, and going back to bed sounded like heaven.

She slid slowly off the stool, trying to make sure her stomach didn't protest too loudly. Slow movements. So far, so good.

"I'm going to get back to bed." She lifted a hand to the side of her head. "My head's starting to pound again. I really appreciate you helping me, Aidan."

"You're welcome." He pushed off the counter and came up behind her. When she turned to look up at him, he smiled. "Just here to make sure you don't fall down." He ran a fingertip down her cheek, his eyes clouded with concern. "You look pale again."

It wasn't much contact, but that slight touch from him sped up her pulse and made her breath come a bit faster. She swallowed hard and looked away from the stare that captivated her. "Th-thank you."

Shit, stammering. Again.

She turned and walked down the short hall, back to his bedroom. He stopped at the doorway and leaned against it. Grateful he didn't come any closer, she slid under the covers and pulled them up to her chin.

"Let me know if you need anything," he said, reaching in and shutting off the lamp.

She nodded. "Good night, Aidan."

"Good night, Megan."

When the door closed with a soft thump, she let out a sigh. This was so not part of the plan. She could only hope her head would heal quickly, her car repairs would be swift, and she could get the hell out of Madison Ridge before she lost anything else.

Because the more she was around Aidan, the more she found she did have something to lose.

CHAPTER SIX

no vacancy

HE WAS IN DEEP SHIT.

With a heavy sigh, he kicked his sock-covered feet up along the deck railing, pushing off to make the chair rock. He sipped his coffee and let the silence of the air settle around him. The cool October mountain air was a welcome feeling. At least he had that going for him.

Nothing since he met Megan had gone as planned. There was something about her that he just couldn't say no to. Obviously, since he barely knew the woman and she was sleeping in his bed. Actually sleeping. No sex involved.

And wasn't that just the irony of it all? He wouldn't call himself a ladies' man. He didn't have women throwing themselves at him like his brother Del did, and after some of the crazy things he'd seen, he was thankful for it. But he'd also never had a problem getting a woman between the sheets when he wanted one.

Lately, he hadn't wanted one. At least, none that were in this town.

Unfortunately, now that he had no time to pay attention to a woman, one had snagged his attention and wouldn't let go. If he didn't start watching the way his dick got in on the thinking process, he'd be in some serious shit. He couldn't be interim part-time sheriff during one of the town's peak seasons and let his libido run the show.

The sunlight began to peek over the mountains out along the horizon. Aidan watched the sunrise every morning since he was always up before it, whether he needed to be or not. It was comforting to watch though, in spite of the riot of emotions running around in his head. The burst of sunlight turned the green of the mountains into an emerald sea.

A few minutes into the show by Mother Nature and a couple of deep breaths later—he'd never let his mother know he was using her meditation techniques—his mind began to quiet. Another twenty-four hours and he could get back to normal. Megan would move into the inn and finish out her time there while her car was fixed. And then she'd be on her way to Florida and whatever life she was headed to. Madison Ridge would be a distant memory.

Feeling a bit more settled that he'd be back to being solo again soon, he stood and walked inside. When he closed the back door, movement came from the kitchen. He blew out a breath, his pulse racing.

See? This is why he was looking forward to her moving on as soon as she was feeling better.

He walked through the living room and into the kitchen, where the fridge door was open with Megan bending over. All he could see was her ass. And it was a fine ass.

Fuck. He didn't want to scare her but he also couldn't just stand there ogling her ass.

He cleared his throat so as not to startle her like he had the night before. At the sound, she lifted up and whirled around. He was grateful she didn't smack her head on the fridge door before spinning around.

"Good morning," he said, moving farther into the kitchen. "Something I can help you find?"

"Um, I was just looking to see if you had creamer."

Aidan walked closer to her and pulled the carton from the door, holding it up for her.

She mimicked smacking herself in the head. "Helps if you look on more than just one shelf."

She was a funny one. "Half and half work for you?"

"Yes, thank you." She took the carton from him, where the tips of her fingers brushed his briefly before taking it from his hand. She walked over to the bar where a cup of steaming coffee sat.

"How are you feeling?" he asked, refilling his cup then leaning back against the counter.

"Better." She capped the carton and put it back in the fridge. "A lot better than I thought given I didn't sleep longer than just a few hours."

He tilted his head. "That's because you did sleep longer than a few hours."

Her brows drew down and she pursed her lips. "I wasn't super great at math but I know I was up at one thirty and it's after seven now. That's not super long by my calculation. I usually need seven hours or better to feel decent."

Damn it, didn't she remember the couple of times she woke up yesterday when he gave her Tylenol? "Megan, today's Wednesday. Your accident was on Monday. You slept all day yesterday."

With each word he spoke, her eyes widened. "Oh my God. Are you serious? I lost a whole freaking day?"

"Afraid so."

"Shit." She patted her hips as though checking pockets before it dawned on her she didn't have pockets. "Where's my phone? Oh!" She started to head out of the room, but he stopped her.

"I've got it on the bar over here. It was almost dead and I thought you might need to have it charged when you woke up."

Megan stopped midstride and did an about-face. "You charged my phone for me?"

"Yeah. You kept getting calls from Nate. I figured you might need to get in touch with him when you woke up."

"Oh." She ran a hand over her flat belly. With her hair piled on top of her head and the snug long-sleeved T-shirt paired with plaid pajama pants, she shouldn't look sexy, but damned if she didn't make his blood burn just a bit. "Thank you."

"You're welcome."

She went to the bar and retrieved her phone. "I'll be back. I need to make a call."

He motioned with his hand that held his coffee cup. "Do whatever you need, Megan."

She stood there a moment staring at him. An emotion he couldn't quite decipher flashed in her eyes before she turned and walked away.

Huh, what was that all about? It didn't matter. He didn't have the time or inclination to find out.

After Aidan had fielded a few calls from work and answered a few emails, Megan came out to the living room where he was sitting.

"Hey, everything okay?"

She nodded. "Yeah, but I need a favor. And I feel really bad about asking because you've done so much for me already, and I'm sure you have your own life. You know, like work and probably a girlfriend. I mean, just look at you…"

Her eyes widened and then darted away. A blush crept into her cheeks, and it was fucking adorable. She was fucking adorable, and he was pissed off that he'd noticed. But how could he not?

A small smile touched his lips. "It's fine. I'm off today and I don't mind helping you. What's up?"

She wrung her hands but moved forward to sit down on the recliner next to the sofa. "Doc called me while I was on the phone. He wants to see me today to check my stitches and concussion. He said anytime today."

He nodded and leaned forward, dropping his phone on the coffee table. "I'll take you."

Her hazel eyes watched him for a moment before she shook her head with a smile, wisps of her dark hair falling around her face. "What are you, Aidan, some kind of saint?"

If she only knew the dirty thoughts he had where she was the star. "No. But you need help, right?" He shrugged. "I have the time, I can help." His nonchalant tone betrayed the churning in his gut that told him he needed to tread carefully with his offers of help.

"You don't have anything you need to do? You know, work or something…someone else?"

"Nothing else. No one else."

She shook her head again and stood. "Okay, give me a few minutes to change and we can go. If that's okay with you."

"Take your time."

She bit her lip and fidgeted. "Would you mind if I took a shower?"

Hell yeah, he minded because he didn't need the images of her naked in his shower tumbling around in his head. But he cleared his throat and said, "Megan. Take your time. It's fine, okay?"

She nodded and hightailed it out of the room. A little while later, she came out into the living room in a colorful sweater that hugged curves her T-shirt and pajamas pants had done their damnedest to hide from him, and a pair of leggings that clung to shapely, long legs. Her freshly washed and dried hair fell in waves down her back, and her lips were glossy.

It didn't bode well for him that covered from head to toe, with no makeup, she made his blood thrum under his skin.

"Okay," she said, slinging a small bag over her shoulder, "I'm ready."

He cleared his throat and stood from the couch. "Let's go." His voice came out a bit gruffer than he'd intended. If it bothered Megan, she didn't let on.

She trailed behind him out to the garage, where he opened the door. When the sun lit up the garage, Megan gasped.

"Wow, this car is beautiful."

Aidan nodded. "She's my girl. And I haven't driven her in about a week. Thought we'd take her out, stretch her legs."

The royal-blue '69 Mustang gleamed in the sunlight, ready to hit the road. They slid in, and Megan looked around the front and backseat. "It's in pristine condition."

Aidan started the engine, which roared to life and then idled to a purr. "Yeah, I finished the restoration on it a few years back after I got home from the service."

They rode in silence for a couple of moments before Aidan shifted his glance over to her. Her hands were in her lap, fingers twisted together. "Want to go by Henderson's and see if they have an update on the estimate for your car?"

She turned her head to him, and a small smile curved one side of her full mouth. "I'd appreciate that. But you've done enough, Aidan. I know you didn't sign up to be my nursemaid and taxi."

He shrugged a shoulder, one hand draped over the steering wheel. "It's not a problem. We're going right by there."

"Okay, then. I do need to get an update."

They pulled into a spot in front of Doc's office, and when he put the car in park, she laid her hand over his that gripped the gear shifter. "Aidan, thank you so much for your help. If the doctor gives me the all clear, I'd like to go ahead and move to the inn so you can have your house back."

"You're fine, Megan." Again, his tone came out with a snap that made him want to saw his tongue in half when her eyes widened and she pulled back her hand as though he'd scalded her.

Fuck.

When Megan put a hand on the door handle and pushed it open, he stopped her. "Wait. I'm sorry. I didn't mean to snap at you. I just..." She turned back and looked at him, the lightness and smile on her face from earlier gone.

And he'd done that. Damn it. He ran a hand through his hair. "I just meant you don't need to keep thanking me."

She looked down at the seat between them for a moment before meeting his gaze with a smile that didn't make it to her eyes. "Apology accepted."

He tilted his head, not quite believing her. "We're good?"

She nodded, but it was stiff. "We're good."

Without another word, she got out of the car and hightailed it into the office before he could catch up with her.

As he opened the door that led to the waiting room, Wilma was leading Megan back with a smile. When she noticed him standing in the doorway, her smile grew. "Hey, Aidan. She shouldn't be long."

All he could do was nod and take a seat. He stretched his legs out in front of him with a sigh.

He was an asshole. What was so wrong with her thanking him, anyway? It wasn't her fault that he couldn't keep from thinking of her or that it took all the discipline in his arsenal to keep his hands to himself. Hopefully, she'd be cleared and she could get herself a place at the inn. He didn't mind helping her, but at the same time, he needed to be alone.

Yep, that's all it was.

So why did the thought of not seeing her, possibly ever again, give him chest pains? He'd have to have his uncle check on that. Maybe he needed to watch his diet better.

He rubbed his chest and dropped his head back against the wall and closed his eyes. Clearing his mind of all things Megan, he began to run down the list of items he'd need to go into the office and do in spite of it being his day off. He had an interview later this afternoon and another two new deputies starting tomorrow. He'd need to get Landon going on that.

Aidan stood when Wilma opened the door and Megan walked out. She carried a folded paper in her hand and a smile.

"Megan, let us know if anything changes. Y'all have a great day." Wilma waved before heading back down the hall.

He opened the door for Megan, his hand finding the small of her back as she brushed past him. It was an innocent gesture, one he'd done without thinking. Megan didn't seem to notice, but the warmth of her skin radiated through her sweater and into his palm. He pulled his hand back casually, not wanting to call attention to it.

He cleared his throat and pulled out his keys. "So, off to Henderson's?"

She nodded and slid inside when he unlocked and opened the car door.

He pursed his lips as he shut the door for her. The silent treatment. Okay, maybe he deserved that.

Henderson's was just a street over, and with no traffic in town at that moment—he needed to mark down the date and time of that little anomaly—Aidan parked the Mustang in front of one of the four bays less than five minutes later.

Again, Megan stepped out and walked into the office before he could catch up to her. He sighed and rubbed the back of his neck before joining her in the small lobby area.

The shoebox size waiting area hadn't changed since he was a kid and had come in with his dad when it was time to service the family vehicles.

The walls were painted in a blue that made him think of a popular

American carmaker logo. Pictures of former champion race car drivers hung on the walls, along with posters of old muscle cars and one discussing the importance of timely oil changes. The smell of motor oil hung permanently in the air.

Jake Henderson—the third generation of Henderson men to run the shop—walked in a side door. The sound of rock music mingled with masculine shouts and an air drill followed him in, then muffled when the door shut behind him. He wiped his hands on a rag and smiled at them.

"Ms. Gentry, how are you?"

She smiled. "Please, call me Megan."

Jake smiled, a flirtatious gleam in his eye. "Sure, Megan."

"Just get on with it, Henderson." Aidan's voice brooked no argument and bordered on a growl.

Jake looked at him and chuckled. "Sure." He turned his focus to Megan. "Okay, so we were able to find some of the parts…"

The more Henderson talked, the paler Megan became and the more doom built in Aidan's chest.

When they walked out of the body shop, she walked toward the car in a daze. He stepped in front of her, causing her to stop short, and took her by the shoulders. It was dangerous for him to touch her. But she looked like she needed to be brought out of her haze. "Hey, you okay?"

She nodded, but she looked around like she was lost. "Yeah. I just… wow. It's going to take a month and be so much more expensive than I'd thought."

"I know." He glanced over her shoulder toward the shop before looking back at her. "I wish I could tell you that he was raking you over the coals. But Henderson is as honest as they come, and if he could move faster or give you a better price, he would."

She looked away. "I'm sure. Well, I guess I should go by the inn and see if I can get a room for a month." Her shoulders slumped under his palms, and he briefly wondered if her skin was as soft as her sweater.

Aidan pulled his hands off her shoulders and stuffed them in his pockets. He didn't like where his thoughts were headed or what that weird feeling was in his chest when he thought of her leaving.

"Sure, I'll take you by there."

Things went further downhill from there. The burst pipe issue at the inn was taking longer than expected and the rest of the inn was booked. The news at the other inns in town wasn't any better. October in Madison Ridge was the start of the busy season, and with all the festivals in town, the fall foliage, and nearby wineries, lodging was at a premium. The one room they'd managed to find brought tears to her eyes when she was quoted a month-long price.

The short ride back to his house was quiet, punctuated with sniffles here and there from the passenger seat.

The lost look on her face as she gazed around his house nearly did him in. He didn't want to get caught up with this woman. Any woman for that matter. But definitely not this one who seemed to pull at his protective streak and his baser instincts simultaneously.

His phone pinged in his pocket and Megan spun around. "Is that your cousin?" Her hands were under her chin like she was begging. Maybe she was at this point.

He'd sent his cousin Emma a text while he waited for Megan at the Mountain Lodge. Emma and her fiancé owned a bed and breakfast in Madison Ridge that was connected to her fiancé's winery. His company had bought her family's old house, and they'd renovated it back to its former glory. But he also knew they'd been booked up with weddings since September.

Emma: Hey, Aid. We're booked solid through the end of the year. I wish I could help.

Well, shit. Aidan sighed and started typing.

Aidan: Well, that's great news about business. I appreciate your help. Can you let me know if you have any cancellations?

Emma: Absolutely.

Aidan: Okay. Tell Shane I said hello.

Emma: Will do.

"Well? What did she say?" Megan walked up to him, hope blooming in her hazel eyes.

Aidan slid his phone back into his pocket and looked down at her. "They're booked solid through the holidays just like I thought."

She blew out a breath and walked away. "Damn it." She paced his living room, swiping tears from her eyes. She mumbled under her breath before she finally said aloud, "What the hell am I going to do for a month? I can't afford anywhere around here even if they had a place to stay. Hell, I can't even sleep in my damn car!"

She plopped down on the couch and leaned back, staring into space.

He pulled on the back of his neck. Shit, this was a bad idea. No good could come of it. A night or two was one thing. But a month?

And yet he walked over to the couch and sat down next to her. And couldn't believe the words that came out of his mouth for the second time in as many days.

"You can stay with me."

CHAPTER SEVEN
thai and pie

MEGAN BLINKED at the sunbeams dancing across the ceiling of Aidan's bedroom.

Not the inn guest room that was part of her original plan.

Her skin flushed when she thought back to the way Aidan's eyes had darkened when he'd said she could stay with him. That raspy, deep voice that held a twinge of southern drawl had danced across her skin, giving her goosebumps even now. The electricity in the air crackled between them.

Or so she'd thought.

But then he'd said he would talk to his mother and sisters to see if they knew anyone that had a room for her. Like a pin to a balloon, the spell she'd started to fall under popped, leaving her mortified.

Instead of answering him, she'd feigned a headache and fled to the bedroom. A glance at her phone on the nightstand told her that had been hours ago.

She ran both hands through her hair, holding it away from her face, and blew out a breath. Outside the window across the room, leaves colored the golds and oranges of the season blew around the backyard that stretched out behind the house. Aidan's house.

Once again, the man put up with her when she knew he'd prefer to be alone. Not that he'd been rude to her. In fact, he'd been nothing but gracious—even patient. But something in his mannerisms told Megan that Aidan preferred the solitude and quiet compared to her somewhat chatty ways and games of twenty questions.

The fact was, she didn't want to feel indebted to him. She didn't want to be indebted to anyone. She'd gotten a nasty taste of that medicine when she was married to her ex. The way his family was always involved in everything they did—from the type of house they bought and where they bought it, to the kind of clothes they should wear, and the schools their future kids would attend all so that they could "maintain" the family name.

Megan often wondered if she'd married into the royal family and didn't know it.

Although the shit that had gone down surrounding her divorce was ugly, Megan was relieved to be out of there. Even if it meant she was starting over nearly penniless. It was bad enough that her brother had given her money *and* a job. But he was her brother. It was easier to take from him. She was grateful, but she wanted to be like she once was—independent. Her own woman.

Which led her back to her current situation. With a sigh, she kicked her legs to the side of the bed and stood, straightening her clothes and hair. When she walked out into the main living area of the house, it was quiet. Too quiet. She ambled into the kitchen and found a note on the counter.

Went to work for a few hours. I'll bring home some dinner. Make yourself at home.

- Aidan

She balled up the note in her fist, trying to ignore the jump in her belly at the almost intimate tone to the note. Her mind was reaching for something that wasn't there, and she needed to get over it. Aidan was just a nice guy.

Megan almost wished he'd be an asshole on some level to make it easier for her to leave. As it was, he was too nice and making it diffi-cult for her to *want* to leave.

If she was going to stay here, she needed to pull her own weight. Since he was bringing dinner and she wasn't much of a cook anyway, she would bake something. It wasn't much but it would give her some-thing to do.

She was rummaging through his pantry when the doorbell rang. In the doorway of the pantry, a can of mushrooms in her hand, she wondered if she should answer it. It was late in the afternoon. He was a hot—really hot—single guy. He was sure to have women on retainer for sex, right? What if it was one looking for a booty call?

When it rang again, followed by a knock on the door and a "Megan, are you there?" she sighed and leaned against the doorway. That would have been awkward.

She rushed out of the kitchen and opened the front door.

Charley smiled at her. "Hey, you are here."

Megan smiled back. "Yeah. Um, Aidan's at work."

His sister waved a hand. "I can see that cranky ass anytime. I'm here to see you."

"Me?"

"Yep." She paused and raised a brow, her lips quirked in a half smile. "Can I come in?"

Megan blinked and stepped back, opening the door farther. "I'm so sorry, please come in."

"I came to check and make sure my brother was treating you okay," Charley said, crossing to the couch and plopping down on it like she owned it.

Megan smiled. "Aidan is being a perfect gentleman. He took me to the doctor this morning for my follow-up and has made sure that I eat and sleep."

"How's the head?"

Megan raised a hand to her head. "Better. I've still got a little bit of a headache."

Charley nodded her head to Megan's hand with a grin. "I've heard that 'shrooms can have an effect on your head, but I'm not sure how they are for curing concussions. Plan to use those?"

Megan looked down at the small can of mushrooms she still held. "Oh." A chuckle slipped past her lips and she looked up at Charley. "You know that was a pretty lame joke, right?"

"Hey, you're the one carrying around a can of mushrooms like a security blanket."

Megan laughed and then sighed. "As far as your brother is concerned, he's been great. Has he asked you anything about a room?"

Charley frowned. "No. Why?"

"Well, according to Henderson's my car isn't going to be ready for about a month. There was more damage than they thought, and getting parts for a car like mine isn't exactly easy. Or cheap for that matter."

She blew out a breath. "And it looks like all the inns and hotels around are booked for the month or not available for one reason or another. Know anyone who might have a room I can rent for cheap for the next month?"

Charley tilted her head. "Aren't you staying here? At least that's what Aidan mentioned when I saw him about an hour ago."

"Oh." Megan drew back, confusion circling in her mind. Hadn't he said he was going to talk to his sisters and ask around? "Well, I thought he was going to ask around. But admittedly my head still gets fuzzy at times, so I may have misunderstood him."

Charley pursed her lips. "Well, I can check around for you. Talk to Mom, Amelia, Grace. I'd offer you a room, but I don't live in my own place yet."

Megan ran the small can in a rolling motion down the side of her thigh. "I'd appreciate it. And I know Aidan would as well." She looked around his living room that had all the creature comforts for a guy but in a minimalist sort of way. "He seems to be one who likes his routine."

Charley nodded. "Oh yeah. It's his military training, I think. But he's always been more stoic than my other brothers." She tapped a finger on her chin. "Well, Noah can be pretty stoic too."

"My brother can be that way too."

"Noah's the oldest. Always been so serious." Charley pulled her legs up into her chest and wrapped her arms around her knees. "Of course, we aren't very close. I was an oops baby. Noah and I are twelve years apart. But Aidan?" She crossed her fingers. "We're tight. He's always looked after me. Especially after our dad died."

There was a twist in Megan's heart. "Aidan told me about that. I'm sorry."

Charley shrugged. "I was pretty young when my dad died. I don't remember a lot. But I do miss the idea of him."

Megan looked down at the can in her hand. She thought back to the loss of her own parents and when she and Nate became orphans. They'd been lucky to have family take them in, and their childhood had been pretty decent given their circumstances.

Which reminded her that she needed to call him again before he started to worry. And he would. He'd also send more money to pay for her car. Hell, he'd buy her a brand-new car if she'd let him. And there was no way. She needed to make some money somehow.

"I hate to keep imposing, but do you know somewhere I can work temporarily while I'm here? I need to make some money if I can. Not to mention, I'll go crazy if I don't have anything to do all day."

Charley's face lit up. "The Silver Moon Cafe—where I work—we need some help. Can you wait tables?"

Megan chuckled. If she only knew. "Waiting tables has kept me from starving many a times. That and bartending."

"Perfect!" Charley exclaimed with a clap of her hands. She tilted her head. "We actually need a bartender. One of our best guys—Wyatt —is taking some time off with his mom. She's got cancer and he's with her in Texas for treatments. So we're short handed. Marcus is going to be ecstatic. When can you start?"

"Um, Doc said I need another day of rest. So, maybe this weekend?"

"We could really use you by then."

"Then I should be ready."

"Cool. I'll talk to Marcus, see when he wants you to stop by to talk to him."

"Sounds good."

A few minutes later, after exchanging numbers and promises to get in touch, Megan leaned her back against the front door. With a smile, she let the little bit of hope that bloomed in her chest spread through her limbs.

The accident was a little setback, but she was hoping to turn her luck around while she was stuck in Madison Ridge. She couldn't ask for a better job here since that's exactly what she'd be doing in Cape Sands when she got there. She could brush up on her skills here with the temp job and go kill it once she got to Florida.

She went back into the kitchen and put the mushrooms away, looking at the other things he had in his pantry. He had all the items she needed to make one of her favorite recipes. She pulled out her phone to double-check the ingredients and got to work.

A couple of hours later, Megan wiped her forehead with the back of her hand and looked down at her cherry pie masterpiece. She was incredibly pleased with how the latticework had come out on the top, so golden brown. She'd even managed to make the lines straight. The filling wasn't homemade but since Aidan had a can of cherry pie filling in his cupboard—it was interesting the things he had in his cupboard and fridge for a guy—she hoped he liked it.

She set the pie on a rack in the middle of the long bar and turned to the mess on the island with a sigh. Bowls and utensils and flour were everywhere. This was the part she hated about baking.

The front door opened and closed as she started to gather the dishes and put them in the sink. When he turned into the kitchen, he stopped in his tracks as he took in the disarray, his brows raised in question.

God, he was gorgeous. His broad shoulders were covered by a black long-sleeved T-shirt with the sleeves pushed up to his elbows, showing off muscular forearms and a large silver watch wrapped around a thick, muscular wrist. She didn't need to see his chest and abs to know that the man worked out and his abs probably had abs.

Dark wash jeans covered his long, strong legs and brushed the tops of his black boots. She'd stolen a couple of glances earlier in the day and knew that the jeans hugged a fine ass. He wore his signature black baseball cap backwards so that his strong jaw and sharp cheekbones were prominently displayed. Bright blue eyes bounced around the kitchen before looking at her intently.

Her fingers itched for a camera in her hands. He'd make an amazing black and white portrait.

The man was built like a brick shithouse. Her thighs clenched trying to relieve the pressure that landed between her legs. Man, it had been a long, long time since she'd felt the weight of a man on her body. But she didn't want just any man, she wanted the one standing in front of her looking at his wrecked kitchen.

The man that was off-limits.

"Megan?"

The deep timbre of his voice brought her out of her dirty daydream. "I'm sorry, what?"

"I said it looks like a flour bomb went off in here."

"I know, and I'm cleaning it up. I swear." She ran the dishtowel through her hands. "I hope you don't mind. I did some baking. As a thank you."

He narrowed those dangerous-to-her-heart blue eyes. "You didn't overdo it, did you? You should probably still be resting."

"I'm fine, Aidan. I promise. I just wanted to thank you in some way."

"Okay…"

He sounded unsure as he looked at the floor. He bit his lip as though trying to hold back a smile and pointed to the floor behind her. "You know, it's a good thing you haven't committed a crime. You left behind some evidence."

She turned and glanced down. Several flour footprints dotted the floor where she'd walked around from the island to the fridge and to the oven. When had that happened? Her cheeks heated. "Oh no. I'm so sorry. Do you have a mop?"

"In the garage. I'll get it for you." He set two plastic bags she hadn't noticed looped over one of his wrists down on the table. "But let's eat first. I'm starving." He started to open the bags and stopped, looking at her with a frown. "I hope you like Thai food. I probably should have asked you."

She grinned. "I love Thai food. I haven't had it in a long time."

His lips curved into a smile. "Me either."

Together, they unloaded the bags and set out a variety of Thai dishes for them to share. They ate in silence for a few minutes before Megan cleared her throat. "This is delicious. I didn't know there was a Thai place here."

"Yeah, they also have Chinese dishes. But I was feeling like Thai." He looked at her with a smile. "I'm just glad you like it."

From there they talked about inconsequential things like the weather, and he told her about some of the festivals that were coming up over the next few weeks. It was no surprise that the lodging around stayed booked.

"Wow, I didn't realize so much could go on in a small town." She chewed and swallowed some flat noodles. "I've never lived in a small town like this. Suburbia is the closest I got. Even then we weren't too far out from the city."

"Your license said you were from Nashville."

"Yep. Lived there my whole life." She nodded her head side to side. "At least up to this point."

"Is your family still there? Well, besides your brother," Aidan asked before biting into some peanut chicken.

Megan looked down into her plate and swallowed hard before answering. Her parents had been dead for twenty years and yet the pain still seared in her heart. "No. My parents were killed in a car accident years ago."

"Oh shit. I'm sorry, Megan."

"It's okay. It happened a long time ago."

"Yeah, but that pain never goes away."

She looked up at him, seeing understanding in his eyes. "No. It really doesn't."

Tension between them grew thick until she couldn't stand it anymore and looked away. "Anyway, my aunt and uncle who raised us moved to Arizona a few years back when they retired to be near my cousins and the grandkids. So there's no one left there."

With all her family gone, the only memories left there were ones she'd rather bury deep and never let see the light of day.

"So you're headed to Florida?"

She nodded. "Yep. Nate's opening a bar and grill and wants me to run it. Oh!" she exclaimed. "That reminds me. Your sister got me a job while I'm here for the next month."

Aidan's gaze was wary. "Which sister?"

"Charley. She's going to talk to someone named Marcus about a bartending job while I'm here." She forked up some rice. "It will be nice to have something to do again and make some extra money so I can replace what I'll use on the car."

Aidan was silent before he said, "At the Silver Moon?"

"Yeah." She pointed at the carton in her hand with her fork. "You need to try this..." Her words died on her lips, as she held out the take-out carton at him. He chewed but looked at her with an intent stare. "What?" She swiped at her face with her free hand, almost poking herself in the eye with her fork. "Do I have something on my face?"

He shook his head. "No, your face is fine. Perfect, actually."

Butterflies took off in her belly, momentarily taking her breath away. "I..." She rolled her lips in to keep from talking. She didn't know what to say and really didn't want to babble in front of this man. He was way out of her league, and tongue-tied didn't begin to cover how she felt when he said something like that to her.

Aidan shook his head but took the carton from her, careful not to touch her fingers. "Let me try this." He took a bite of the chicken and noodles then nodded. "That is good," he said after swallowing. "When it comes to the Silver Moon, I'll tell you what I tell Charley. Just watch for the handsy ones. Especially the tourists. They seem to be the ones we get calls on the most."

Annndddd there she was in the friends-slash-sister zone again.

Her stomach sank and she berated herself for even thinking that there could or would be anything between them. He was simply a nice guy who'd gotten stuck with a chatty, sometimes awkward woman like herself.

Sure, maybe if he'd seen her before she'd opened her mouth, he'd want to take her to bed. It wasn't as though she hadn't been told she was beautiful a time or two. She knew she was pretty in a certain way and that guys found her attractive.

But guys who looked like Aidan? All chiseled and built and only had to smile to have droves of hot women lined up at his door? Not to mention he was a genuinely nice guy? Yeah, a man like him would never be with a woman like her. In spite of her somewhat positive outlook on life, Megan knew she was damaged goods. Only good for one thing to a man since she had no real breeding.

Her ex-husband's family had told her enough times.

She nodded and laid her fork on her plate before pushing it away. "Don't worry about me, Aidan. I can take care of myself. Not the first time I've ever worked in a bar with handsy men."

He leaned back in his chair, his gaze roaming over her in a way that made her skin spark underneath the fire of his blue eyes. His jaw tightened before he released it and started to stand. "Let me get that mop for you. I've got some paperwork to get to."

"Oh, wait." She jumped up, hitting her knee on the unforgiving wood table. "Ow, shit! That's gonna leave a mark." She rubbed her knee as her face warmed. She didn't need a mirror to know her face was as red as a cherry.

"Are you okay?" He moved toward her but she put up a hand like a stop sign.

"I'm fine. Fine." She'd only dislocated her knee cap or something equally stupid, but that would heal better than her ego at this point. "Don't leave yet. I have something for you."

His eyes roamed her face, his brows lowered, concern etched in his face. She smiled. "I swear I'm fine. Stay here. I'll clean up."

"Okay, but let me—" he started, picking up a couple of the cartons.

She took them from his hands and blew out a breath. She needed to gather her wits about her before she went off the rails and ended up doing something truly horrifying like hooking her foot on her chair and faceplanting onto the hardwood floor.

"Please. You've done a lot for me already. Let me do something for you. Just let me clean up. Okay?" She looked up at him and did her best not to sway closer to him when the scent of his cologne wrapped around her.

Her luck was that he'd think she was going to faint and tuck her into bed like a brother.

How humiliating.

He nodded and sat down, leaning back in the chair with those long legs kicked out in front of him. "Okay."

It was all he said and all she needed to hear.

Excitement bloomed in her chest, wanting to please him. It was a feeling she hadn't felt for a man in a long time.

CHAPTER EIGHT
moonlight walks & famous siblings

GOOD GOD, she was a fucking adorable mess.

Actually, she wasn't adorable at all. She was gorgeous and sexy but didn't seem to know it. Her actions told him she had no clue of the effect she had on him. Of course, he'd called on all the discipline training the military and academy had taught him to keep his hands off her.

Okay, except for when she needed to be steadied or something. She did have a concussion and all.

Who was he kidding?

It was just as well she didn't know. Madison Ridge wasn't her final destination in her journey, and he wasn't going to take advantage of a woman when she was down on her luck. And Megan Gentry seemed to have a good run of bad luck going for her.

He pulled his phone out of his back pocket under the guise of not watching every move she made. Aidan didn't want to notice the way her chestnut brown hair fell in a long curtain around her face when she leaned forward, gathering their empty dinner cartons. Or the way her hazel eyes alternated between sparks of confidence only to be chased away by shadows of self-doubt. It would do him no good to notice that she moved in economical movements and yet in such a way that she flowed around the room.

He really didn't need to see that she had some banging curves under those second-skin leggings and oversized sweater. Curves that he wanted to cruise his hands over followed by his mouth until she was a panting mess underneath him.

Aidan shifted in the chair, trying to make more room in the crotch of his suddenly too small jeans. And when had it gotten so fucking hot in the room? He rubbed the back of his neck and blew out a breath as she picked up the last of the trash and walked past him out of the room and back to the kitchen, leaving the scent of vanilla and lavender—he'd seen her shampoo bottle in the shower that morning and couldn't help but sniff it—in her wake.

The sounds of silverware moving around in the drawer came from behind him. And a few seconds later a small plate with a slice of cherry pie sat in front of him.

His favorite.

Something squeezed at his heart, a feeling he didn't recognize. Must have been that spicy sauce in that one Thai dish.

"You made cherry pie?"

She nodded as she sat with a plate in hand. "Oh,"—she snapped her fingers—"would you like some coffee? I can get you some." She rose and started to walk to the kitchen.

He reached out and snagged her wrist before she walked past him. "Hey, Megan. Stop. I don't need coffee and I don't need you to be a hostess. It's my damn house and you're my guest."

When she looked down at him, he couldn't make out what she was thinking. His words had come out a bit sharper than intended but it pissed him off that she felt like she had to serve him. He tugged on her wrist and tempered his tone. "Just sit down, okay? Eat some pie with me?"

"Sure."

When she sat back down and began to dig into her slice, Aidan took a bite and almost moaned. Holy shit, that was good. The cherries had the right amount of tartness and the crust was incredible. It was cooked perfectly, flaky and light.

"Did you make this crust?"

Megan nodded. "I can't cook, but I did learn to bake. My aunt—the one who raised Nate and me—was a whiz in the kitchen. We used to make cookies together and as I got older she taught me other things. So this recipe is hers."

"This is better than my mother's. But don't tell her I said that," he said around a bite he couldn't help but shovel in his piehole.

With a laugh, she covered her mouth and held up three fingers. "I won't say a word. Scout's honor." She shrugged a shoulder. "You already had the can of filling. I was surprised to see you had the other staples I needed."

He finished chewing the bite in his mouth before addressing her raised eyebrow. "Why does that surprise you?"

"Well, most single guys I know don't keep a ton in their kitchens. My brother has a stocked kitchen but only because he has people making sure he has the right food to stay in shape. I don't know. I was just pleasantly surprised."

First, he wondered what her brother did that he had people to keep his kitchen stocked. But on the heels of that, the clenching in his stomach when she mentioned other guys was not a welcome feeling.

They ate in silence for a few moments, and Aidan couldn't help his gaze wandering her direction. Every time that little pink tongue popped to lick her lips, his pants grew tighter in the crotch. It was pure torture sitting next to her with his palms itching to reach out and touch her.

Or to spread her out across the table and have *her* for dessert.

He coughed to cover a groan and shoveled more pie in his mouth.

When they finished, Aidan leaned back in his chair, a hand over his stomach. "That was amazing. Thank you for making that. It's been a while since I've had it."

Megan leaned forward on the table, dropping her chin into her hand. "I didn't know what else I could do to thank you for putting up with me. I can tell you're the type of guy who prefers to be alone with peace and quiet. And I've sort of crashed that party."

"I do like my solitude. It's peaceful after a day at work that can sometimes be trying. But I'm not going to let you be homeless, Megan.

You needed a place, I had a place." He shrugged. "I was happy to help."

Well, happy may not have been the best word at first. But even though it had only been a little over forty-eight hours, he'd already gotten used to having her in his cabin. He didn't know if he was more pissed off about getting used to her being there or not.

She rubbed her hands on the tops of her thighs and he did his best to keep his eyes from following their track up and down that long length of thigh. He swallowed hard and tapped his finger against the plate. "Let me help you clean all this up."

She stood and picked up her plate. "I got this. You said something about paperwork."

Oh yeah, he had said that.

"It can wait."

They worked in a comfortable silence as though they'd done the domestic chore of cleaning the kitchen together for years.

Megan dried her hands on a towel and turned to him, shifting her feet. "Well, I guess that's it."

He didn't want her to leave. The thought of their time being over for the night left him cold and—dare he say?—lonely. A sense of urgency washed over him when she turned toward the bedroom.

"Hey, want to take a walk down to the lake with me? We could take a couple of beers, enjoy the cool, night air." *And I'm not quite ready to let you go.*

The smile she gave him made him feel like a million bucks. "I'd love to. Mind if I get my phone? I'd love to take some photos of the moon."

"Sure. I'll grab the beers."

Aidan led her out to the back deck and down the gently sloping yard to the edge of the lake. The cool, autumn air surrounded them as they walked down the long dock that jutted out into the water. Out here, moonlight was their guide, making everything look like a black and white picture. It reflected off the smooth-as-glass water.

"Oh wow, it's beautiful out here." Megan stopped halfway down the dock and looked around. She pulled her phone out of the waistband of her leggings and began snapping a bunch of pictures. When she was done, she returned the phone to its place. Aidan turned away when he spied a sliver of the bare skin of her torso.

Was he so hard up that a flash of her pale smooth skin made his mouth resemble the Sahara?

He cleared his throat before he could speak. "I used to have some chairs out here, but they needed replacing and I just haven't gotten around to it."

She waved him off. "No worries. I can sit on the edge and dangle my feet."

And that's what they did. In the quiet night, they sat shoulder to shoulder and drank their beer, her feet swinging back and forth over the water.

She sighed and leaned her head back. "You know, this whole town is a photographer's dream. All of the colors with the leaves and historic buildings. Even the night sky out here over the water doesn't disappoint. The moonlight is just perfect."

"Have you done a lot of photography?"

"It was just a hobby that I really loved once. I was pretty good though. A couple of my photos made it into some regional magazines. I'd love it as a job, but I've never been able to make it work."

"You always use your phone?"

"These days, yeah. I had to sell my camera and equipment. But it's okay, these phones take damn good pictures actually. Still,"—she shrugged a slim shoulder—"I miss my fancy camera."

She turned her head to him and smiled. "So Charley told me today that you guys are pretty close."

Deflection. Her reasons for starting over were obviously still a sore subject for her. Since her shoulders had relaxed when she turned the question on him, he let it go and smiled. "Yeah. We were near the end in the lineup."

Megan paused. "And she's six years younger than you?"

He nodded and sipped his beer. "Yeah. It was almost like my parents took a break for a few years and then Charley came along."

"She said she was an oops baby."

"I don't know. Maybe. All I do know is that my dad loved the hell out of her."

A pain shot through his heart as memories of his parents came to the forefront of his mind. As a kid, he didn't get it, but he knew now why there were so many of them. His father had never been able to keep his hands off his mother. They'd had a love that Aidan had hoped he'd have one day, but it just wasn't in the cards. Not after his father died way too young.

She nudged his shoulder with hers. "You were the protective big brother to her, weren't you?"

"Yeah. Even with six years between us, I've always been pretty protective of Charley. She's the daredevil. She was only seven when our dad died and she needed someone to keep her grounded. That was my dad for her. So it became me."

She was quiet for a minute before she said. "I'm sorry about your dad. That must have been hard on your mom."

"Thanks. It's been a long time though. I've made peace with it." *Sort of.* "My mother is a force to be reckoned with, no doubt about it. She's the best person I know."

She turned her head with a soft smile on her face, her gaze on him. He looked at her out of the corner of his eye. "What?" he asked.

She sighed and shook her head before looking away. "Nothing." After a sip of beer, she continued. "So tell me about your other siblings. I'm intrigued by the fact that there's so many of you. You have two other brothers…"

"Yep."

"And who are they?"

"Noah and Del. They run the family construction business here in town."

He was careful to glide over the fact that his brother Del was a celebrity. Even though he didn't actively film a weekly show anymore, Del's old TV show, *Property Ace,* could be found at any given time in reruns. Not to mention that he did film specials here and there for the network.

Megan didn't strike him as the type that would go all stalker like on his brother, but people were weird when it came to stars sometimes. He'd had to lend Del a hand in an official capacity more than once in town when the tourists came to call.

"You met Charley, but there's also Grace and Amelia. They're like Irish twins, although they couldn't be more different." He smiled thinking of his sisters. "Grace is a kindergarten teacher at one of the local elementary schools. She's perfect for it. The calm during a storm."

"And Amelia?"

"Amelia owns the bakery in town, The Sweet Spot."

"Hey, I saw that the other day before my accident. I wanted so bad to go in, but I'd stuffed myself at the deli."

"I'll have to take you in. But fair warning, Amelia likes to ask a million questions and can be a ball-busting loudmouth if the mood strikes. But she's smart as hell and making a name for herself with the bakery. Not that she needs it. She used to be a chef at some fancy-pants restaurant in New York for a couple of years."

"Wow, really? What happened?" She closed her eyes and shook her head. "You know what? Don't answer that. It's none of my business. I'm sorry."

Even in the moonlight, the flush on her face was evident.

"It's okay. If you were to ask Amelia, she'd tell you. She burned out. Said she didn't want to live her life in that cutthroat world."

"I can understand that," Megan said, her voice barely above a whisper. She sipped her beer and looked up at the sky. "It's so beautiful out tonight. I haven't seen stars like this in years."

"Too much city living?"

Her mouth quirked up on one side. "You could say that. I can't remember the last time I was outside at night in such darkness for no reason other than to just be. Or hang out. If I was out during the evening, it was usually on the way to some sort of charity function or something."

His eyes slid over the pale curve of her neck, and his gut tightened watching her long, dark hair fall in a straight curtain down her back and brush across her ass.

Jesus, she was gorgeous.

And he couldn't stop the thoughts that flashed through his mind of wrapping all that hair in his fist while he took her from behind.

He sipped his beer to cool the fire raging in his blood. "So what does your brother do? You said he lined up a job for you?"

She rubbed a hand down a thigh. "He owns a sports bar in Cape Sands, Florida. And I'm going to run it."

The pieces started to click together. "Now I see why you're happy to work at the Silver Moon."

"I've worked in bars before as a server and a bartender. It's great money when you've got a good client base. I worked in some high-end bars in Nashville before I got married."

It didn't take a detective to put the puzzle pieces together. "He made you quit work?"

Her lips pursed before she looked at him with a smirk. "More like implied I should quit. My ex's family is old Southern money in the elite part of Nashville. Debutantes and all. My family was upper middle class, but his family was a whole other world. I turned out to be nothing but a pawn. He only married me to make his mother happy."

Aidan had many things he wanted to say as his blood boiled, but she wasn't deflecting anymore, so he kept his mouth shut. She sipped her beer before continuing. "Anyway, me being a bartender, even in the city's most exclusive club where drink tabs could run more than some people make in a month, was unseemly for the family name. So I quit, thinking that would get me in the good graces. Unfortunately—or maybe fortunately now—my ex didn't realize that he had to quit dating other women while he was married."

Her sigh was heavy before she continued. "The truth is I didn't love him. I was in love with a fantasy. That's always been my problem. I'm in love with love. So I constantly pick the wrong guys. Something Nate has always told me, but I didn't listen." She straightened her shoulders. "So now I'm determined to stay single for a while and give the whole love thing and guys a break. It's been nothing but trouble for me."

Shouldn't he be glad to hear that? Megan was off-limits anyway, so shouldn't the fact that she was on a guy hiatus bring him some relief? So why didn't it?

Shut that shit down, Reynolds. We've been over this.

"And that's why you're headed to Florida. For your fresh start."

"Yep." She looked out over the lake, her booted feet swinging over water. "I'm lucky Nate hasn't rubbed all this mess in my face too much and is giving me a chance at starting over."

Something tickled in his brain about the name. Why did his name sound familiar? "Do you and your brother have the same last name? Gentry?"

She leaned away from him and watched his face for a moment before frowning. "Shit. Let me guess. You watch baseball?"

He narrowed his eyes and nodded his head when it hit him as to why he knew the name. "Holy shit. Your brother is Nate Gentry?"

At her nod, he said, "Nate Gentry is your brother? He's had an amazing season. Even if they did get beat in the playoffs."

She sighed and swung her legs faster. "Yeah. I don't tell a lot of people because they get weird about it when they find out. But I should have known you'd pick up on it."

He held up his hands, one holding his beer bottle. "You don't have to explain it to me. I get it."

She sent him a look that said *yeah right.*

"My brother Del is Delaney Reynolds."

"Property Ace," they said at the same time. Her eyes went wide as saucers.

"Are you serious? I love him!"

Aidan chuckled and looked down. "Yeah. Most women do."

"I didn't even make the connection. See, this is why you're the lawman and I'm the...civilian or whatever." She laid a hand on his arm. "Wait, my brain's working now. He lives *here*?"

Okay, maybe he'd pegged Megan wrong. Maybe she would be a stalker chick.

"Yeah, with his fiancée, Addison."

Megan bounced and a hand covered her heart. "I saw that episode. Oh my God, it was so romantic. I'm not sure I'd want to get engaged on live television, but it was still one of the most romantic proposals ever." She sighed and hearts practically flew out of her eyes.

He rubbed the back of his neck. "Yeah, well. I'm just saying I get it. I understand the not wanting to tell people about your famous sibling. It's a pain in the ass."

She dropped her hand and laughed, all heart-eyed emojis gone. "It really is. My ex found out—I didn't tell him—and after he chewed me out for not telling him, he was always trying to hit Nate up for tickets. Ugh. He was such a douche."

"So why did you marry him?" Aidan barely got the words out before he laughed.

She wagged a finger at him. "Nah, nah. I'm having too nice of a time with you here to go into all of that. I don't want to ruin it."

Aidan's chest tightened at her words, but he kept the smile on his face. "Fair enough."

Megan clinked her almost empty bottle against his. "To beautiful moonlit nights and pain-in-the-ass famous siblings."

He lifted his bottle. "And not talking about douchey exes."

"Amen."

They settled into a comfortable silence that was broken by the far away sounds from the woods and the soft lapping of the water against the dock.

When Megan shivered, Aidan wrapped an arm around her shoulders and pulled her into him before he even thought about it. She stiffened for just a moment before relaxing against him. The scent that he was quickly beginning to associate with her, lavender and vanilla, wafted around him. Before he could get too far down that road of wanting something he couldn't have, he released her.

Hell, what was he thinking? He was already halfway down that road.

"Ready to go in?"

When she nodded, he got to his feet and held out a hand to help her up. His hand dwarfed her small, softer one, and he held on to it for longer than he should have before they walked down the long dock and back to dry land.

"Aidan, I just wanted to thank you again for putting up with me. I know I'm not always easy."

He raised a brow and shot her a sideways glance. "Your ex tell you that? You've been pretty easy to deal with so far. Outside of the mess you made in the kitchen,"—he grinned—"you've been pretty clean and you only talk a little too much at certain times."

She chuckled, wrapping one arm around her middle, the other at her side with the beer bottle dangling from her fingers. "You're not wrong. It drives Nate insane. He's pretty quiet. Like you."

Did she just put him in the brother zone?

It's right where you need to be, buddy. Focus on the conversation.

"Nate stays out of the spotlight, doesn't he?"

"As much as a man with his level of success and fans can. It's part of the reason he settled in a small beach town that's still under the radar."

He rubbed a hand over his chin. "Del's the same way. It's easier for him in some ways now that he's back home in a small town. Other times, he has nowhere to hide. But having family around and being back with Addison keeps him pretty grounded."

She sighed as they strolled up the hill to the cabin. "I wish my family had been bigger. I guess with them all living here, you see them pretty regularly."

"Yeah. Don't worry. You'll meet them all before you leave. My siblings and a few cousins are everywhere in this town."

"Cousins too?"

"Yep. My family was one of the town founding families. A Reynolds has lived in Madison Ridge for a couple of centuries now."

"Wow." She blew out a breath. "Well, I can't wait to meet them all then."

Something in Aidan's chest shifted that he ignored. "Well, you're here for a while. Which brings me to a question."

"What's that?"

They'd made it to the deck stairs, and she was a step ahead of him. When she turned back, they were eye to eye. The light from the cabin illuminated her eyes, making them appear to shine. He put a foot on the step where she stood, which brought him a little closer to her.

He needed to tread so carefully with this one. She made him want things, awakened not only his baser instincts but ones he'd never felt with another woman.

But it was crazy, right? He'd known her all of what? Two or three days? Things like that didn't happen in real life, but especially not for him.

Keep it light, Reynolds.

"Why a Karmann Ghia?"

Megan blinked at him for a moment before a beautiful smile lit up her face and she started laughing. She shifted her weight and leaned against the railing.

"Okay, don't laugh."

"I can't guarantee that since you haven't told me yet."

"Well, then I'm not telling you." She started to turn away, but he snagged her wrist and brought her back around.

"Okay, okay. I won't make fun of you," he said, unable to keep the laughter out of his voice.

"Promise?" Her eyes searched his.

"Promise."

"Okay." She blew out a breath like she was about to dive off the high board. "So you know how I told you I named my car Beatrix?"

He blinked. "Yeah…"

"Well, I always thought Beatrix Kiddo was such a badass. Not the killing people part because that's just…bad. But the part where she was able to focus on a singular goal like that. And who am I kidding? The fact she could kick so many asses like that is just short of amazing."

Where the hell was she going with this? "Okay…" He drew out the word into multiple syllables.

"Well, in the second movie, she drove a Karmann Ghia when she got to Mexico on her final leg to find Bill." She looked down. "After my divorce, I needed out of Nashville. But I was pretty broke. The ex took back all the gifts"—she did air quotes when she said that— "except my car. And frankly, I hated that car."

"What was it?"

"A BMW convertible."

"I can't picture you in a car like that."

"Right? It wasn't me at all. But anyway, I traded the BMW in and bought a car the biggest badass woman I could think of drove. It took me a couple of weeks, and Nate helped me out, but I found one." She raised her head and shrugged. "And that's how I ended up with a blue Karmann Ghia. I just hope they can fix it."

They watched each other for a few seconds, the air around them growing thick with tension. She bit her plump bottom lip and shoved a lock of hair behind her ear before looking away. At some point he'd shifted closer to her.

"Hey." He put a finger under her chin and brought her gaze to his. "I don't know what all you went through with your ex, but I admire your strength to start over."

She rolled her eyes. "Please. If it weren't for my brother, I'd be sitting in a cardboard box, singing for my next meal. And I don't sing, Aidan."

He grinned and rubbed his thumb along her jawline. "Be that as it may, you walked away from a bad scene. Even if it wasn't physical." His next thought stopped him cold. "He wasn't, was he?"

"No." She shook her head, her chin still in his grip. "He was never physical. Too lazy for that anyway. He got his rocks off with insults and infidelity."

In Aidan's mind, that was still abuse. The bruises were just on the inside. And those took longer to heal than the physical.

He'd seen it time and again in his line of work.

"Well," he cleared his throat. "Either way. It takes guts to walk away from a marriage. Even though your brother is helping you, you're making it." His thumb brushed over her lips. "Beatrix Kiddo's got nothing on you, Megan Gentry."

Her throat moved as she swallowed and looked at him, her eyes wide and searching. Fuck. She was messing with his head. Her scent, her warm, soft skin. He had no doubt she'd be warm and soft in other places he'd give his left nut to explore.

He wanted nothing more than to strip her bare and lay her down in his bed. Worship every curve and plane of her body.

Or shove her up against the side of his house and fuck her brains out.

It was toss-up as to which would win if he were that type of guy.

But he wasn't.

She was his guest. He was the interim town sheriff and all around standup guy. She wasn't here because she *wanted* to be so much as she was stuck here. He'd never had to take advantage of a woman before and he wouldn't start now. No matter how much his body ached to be inside her.

He dropped his hand and stepped away from her. "Um, I'm going to hang out here a little longer. So if you need to take a shower or whatever, feel free."

Megan blinked once. Twice. Then shook her head a little. "Right. Thanks. I think I'll do that." She stepped up another step, putting distance between them. "I enjoyed the walk. Thanks for the invite. And dinner."

"Thanks for the pie."

"You're welcome," she said with a smile. Damn, those smiles would be the death of him.

"Good night, Aidan."

"Night, Megan."

She left and Aidan blew out a breath. He waited a couple of minutes, hoping the air would cool him off before he went inside. His cabin wasn't all that large. He needed a breather from seeing her for a little while.

When he thought enough time had passed, he walked inside, locked up the cabin, and threw out his empty beer bottle. He climbed up the ladder stairs to the loft area he'd taken over when he'd given Megan his room. He changed into a pair of pajama pants, forgoing a shirt since he was still overheated.

He lay on the twin bed he was almost too tall for in the loft of his cabin, staring at the A-frame, pine slat ceiling above him, trying not to think of her in his bed for another night. He'd had a hard enough time trying not to think of her in his bed all day long today. Wondered if he went into his room, if her scent would be on his sheets. If he would see the indent of her head on his pillows.

When he heard the shower come on in the bathroom, he groaned and rubbed his eyes with the heels of his hands. What the fuck was wrong with him? He was a grown-ass man and yet here he was reacting like a damn teenager. He hardly knew this woman, but she'd done nothing but worm her way into his psyche all day and night.

All he could do was think of her in his shower, wet and naked, her hands drifting over the curve of her hips and up over her tits, where he just knew her nipples would be perfect and responsive. She'd lean back so she could wash all that long length of hair, hair that probably brushed the top of that amazing ass when it was wet and slick. The water running in rivers down the center of her belly headed straight for the promise land.

His cock went hard as steel. "Fuck." He squeezed his eyes shut and tried to think about something else. Anything else would do.

Maybe he just needed to rub one out and be done with it.

He slid a hand down and gripped his cock, stroking it, looking for relief. He closed his eyes and with the sound of the shower running in the background and images of Megan wet and slick, it didn't take long for his desire to end up all over his stomach.

After he cleaned up, he lay back down and tried for sleep. To his dismay, the relief he'd felt when he came was only temporary. As soon as he heard her moving around downstairs, his body tightened all over again.

His sigh was deep and heavy as he closed his eyes, willing his brain —and his dick— to think about anything but the woman downstairs.

the sweet spot

MEGAN BENT AT THE WAIST, reaching for her toes, groaning as her lower back protested. She'd spent the last few days training with Charley at the Silver Moon. And her body was reminding her that she wasn't twenty-five anymore.

The day after Charley told her about the job, she'd gone in and met Marcus, the owner, who hired her on the spot. After the doctor cleared her to do something other than lie around like a slug all day, she'd started work over the weekend and had the pleasure of being trained by the little ball of energy that was Charlotte Reynolds.

Just as Aidan had said, Charley had a daredevil streak about her, willing to try anything and to push boundaries. Nothing that would hurt anyone, including Charley herself—she wasn't totally reckless—but she did seem to have a habit of making Marcus shake his head with a frown more often than not. But Megan could see it was more like a father with his obstinate child.

Fortunately for Charley, she was also damn good at her job. As a Reynolds, she knew everyone in town, and they all loved her. Between her three brothers and half the local boys in love with her, Charley never had to worry about anything when an out-of-towner got a little too frisky.

Unfortunately for Megan, Charley being damn good at her job meant that the younger woman had put her through her paces over the last few days. Megan couldn't remember the last time she'd been so sore. But it was a welcome ache. Until she'd met her ex, she'd always been active, working and exploring new areas to photograph. She hated being bored, and her marriage had bored her to tears.

She dressed for the day and made coffee, pushing thoughts of her past away. What was done was done, and she had a future to look forward to in the Sunshine State.

The aching sadness in her chest when she thought about leaving Madison Ridge was another thing she chose to ignore. Everything here was just temporary, and she'd do well to remember that.

As they had more times than she cared to admit, her thoughts turned to her hot-as-sin roommate. She hadn't seen much of Aidan since their walk by the lake. They had opposite schedules, with her working more at night and Aidan working days. He'd offered to pick her up at night so she didn't have to walk home alone so late, but since she and Charley worked the same shift, she'd hitched a ride with his sister each night.

It was for the best anyway. She missed him. And that wasn't good.

She sat at the small table that faced the back of the house. The small cabin was quiet and still, which she expected but it didn't stop disappointment from clenching her stomach.

The sun shone through the windows that faced the lake, the light glinting off the water just beyond the colorful tree line. It made a beautiful picture.

She grabbed her phone and took a few pictures from different angles. It amazed her what the phones could do these days with editing and all. She'd almost forgotten how good that dopamine hit felt when she took pictures.

Photography was a passion she'd let go when she'd gotten married. It wasn't something she'd ever done professionally, only because she never had enough money to buy the equipment she wanted. And she never said anything to Nate because he'd have bought the best photography equipment known to man and sent it to her.

He already did so much, having his assistant send clothes, makeup, and other facial care products that she didn't ask for, so she wasn't taking anything else from him.

The man had more money than he knew what to do with, and she was his only family. Megan was never one for charity, and she only accepted the gifts because it would break Nate's heart if she didn't. But she wasn't asking him for anything else.

Now that she was back on her own without anyone telling her what to do, she was ready to find herself again. That girl she'd been missing over the last few years. The girl that had loved capturing moments in time forever.

When she finished her coffee, she dressed and gathered her things, excitement to capture the beauty around her on film—or her phone as it were—thrumming through her veins.

The day couldn't get more beautiful if it tried. The sun shone brightly, bringing the colors of fall to life. The mix of reds, oranges, and yellows made the trees look like a ball of flames sat atop them against an incredibly blue, cloudless sky. The temperature was just perfect for the ten-minute walk into the town that was quickly setting up a soft spot in her heart.

It didn't help that the blue skies reminded her of Aidan's eyes.

She didn't have a destination in mind but took pictures along the way of things that caught her eye. By the time she'd reached the square, she'd worked up an appetite and decided to check out The Sweet Spot. Plus, another cup of coffee never hurt her feelings.

Megan opened the door to The Sweet Spot and could barely squeeze in due to the long line. But it moved quickly as two women worked behind the counter, taking orders and filling them. A couple of young guys made coffees, calling out names, and another girl ran things out to the floor, delivering orders here and there.

It appeared Aidan's sister had quite the business. She looked around and found most of the patrons sitting with their caffeine and baked goods and their heads buried behind laptop screens or in girthy books. There were so many charming things to the town, at times she forgot there was a college a mile away.

As she moved closer to the front of the line, she watched the older of the two women and knew without a doubt that this was Aidan's sister Amelia. Her hair was dark where his was lighter, her blue eyes darker where his were brighter, but they had the same smile and the same tilt of the head when they were listening to someone talk.

Amelia and her crew were quick, and soon, the five-people-deep line she stood in disappeared, and she was at the head of the line.

"Hey," Amelia said, tapping on the screen in front of her, while moving out of the way of someone who walked behind her. She hadn't even been looking in that direction. When she did look up, her smile widened. "You must be Megan."

"How did you know?"

Amelia shrugged a slim shoulder. "I'm magic." She held the straight face for just a second before she chuckled. "Charley told me about you. Pointed you out the other night when I came into the Silver Moon. She was going to introduce us, but you guys were pretty busy."

"Oh, well, it's nice to finally meet you. I've heard a lot about you."

Amelia rolled her eyes and quirked her mouth. "I can only imagine what my brother must have told you."

Megan laughed. "It was all good, I promise."

"Now that I don't believe." Amelia smiled wryly and shook her head. "What can I get for you?"

"Well, I've also heard about these cinnamon rolls that are as big as my head. Got any?"

"Of course. Coffee?" she asked, tapping in Megan's order.

"Please. A large one, three creams." Megan handed her card over.

Amelia waved her card away. "First time here's on the house."

"Oh, well, thanks. I appreciate that. I don't think I've ever had anything on the house."

Amelia moved down the pastry case to where the cinnamon rolls—that honest to God did look as big as her head—sat behind the glass. "It's harder when you live in a city."

Megan tilted her head. "How did you know I was from the city?"

Amelia laughed and snapped a bag open. "Girl, this is a small town. Everyone finds out everything. Plus, Charley told me."

"Ah."

"Hey, I get it." Amelia moved away, tongs in hand, and reached inside the pastry case for the rolls. "I did the big city living thing for a while when I worked in restaurants. I made my way up to head chef in a place in New York before I came back home."

"Aidan mentioned that." She looked around the cozy bakery that smelled of sweet dreams and coffee. "How did you end up back here?"

Amelia chuckled as she slid the cinnamon roll into the bag. "It was by choice actually. After a while the stress and cutthroat world of that life quit appealing to me. Plus, I'm better at baking than I was at coming up with dishes that you'd pay a hundred dollars a plate for and still leave you hungry."

One of the baristas slid her coffee across the counter to her and moved back to the coffee machine to work on the next order. "Thanks," Megan murmured and lifted it to her lips, sipping the rich brew.

It was official. Amelia had the best coffee.

"That is so good. I'm ruined forever now."

Amelia's smile lit up her beautiful face. The genes that ran in the Reynolds family were crazy.

"Thank you. I try." Amelia brought over the food and set it on the counter, putting her hands on her hips. "You just missed Aidan. How's my brother treating you? Is he being all stoic and quiet like usual?"

"No." Megan shook her head, confusion coloring her voice. "Actually, he's been pretty great. I haven't seen him much since last week with our opposite schedules. But we've had some nice conversations. He was patient with me with my concussion. And the fact that I made a bit of a mess in his kitchen making a cherry pie." She shrugged. "Of course, he has that military and police training, so I'm sure he learned patience."

Amelia stopped, her brows meeting her hairline. "Hold on. I'm talking about Aidan. Aidan Reynolds. Are we talking about the same guy?"

Megan frowned. "Yeah, why?"

Amelia scoffed and crossed her arms over her chest. "Because that sounds more like my brother Del than it does Aidan." Her finger tapped along her bicep, a thoughtful look on her face.

Megan shrugged. "I haven't met any of your other brothers, though Aidan did tell me about them."

"Huh." She grinned and then moved to wrap up another cinnamon roll. "Here, can you take this over to Aidan?" she said, handing the bag to Megan.

"Sure. Did he forget it?" The pale pink bag crinkled when she took it from Amelia.

Amelia's grin grew as she leaned on the counter. "You could say that. He's riding the desk over at the sheriff's office. I'm sure he'd enjoy some…sugar to brighten his day."

Megan caught the mischievous gleam in Amelia's blue eyes. "It's not like that."

"Sure, okay." Amelia gave her a thumbs-up and an exaggerated wink.

Megan rolled her eyes and looked around. "It's not. I mean, he'd never go for a girl like me even if I were in the market. Or if he were in the market. But neither of us is."

"Did he tell you that?"

Did he? "Well, no." She sniffed. "But he didn't have to. I can tell. And I *know* I'm not looking for anyone. But I will take this to him since I've already taken it from you."

Amelia held up her hands in a hold-up type fashion. "No take backsies."

The bell on the door rang behind her, and Amelia glanced behind Megan. "Uh-oh," she muttered under her breath. "Megan, I'm going to apologize in advance."

"What are you talking about?"

"Good morning, ladies. How are y'all today?" Amelia smiled, addressing someone behind Megan.

She turned and found four women, all clearly in their seventies—all dressed in the same style track suit, but in different colors, with matching fanny packs—staring at her. The one in the front smiled and answered. "Right as rain. Just came from our aerobics class." Her smile still in place, she peered at Megan. "You must be the new girl in town. The one that got in that wreck. Megan, is it?"

It was eerie how this woman knew her name. But as Amelia said, small towns and all. "Yes, ma'am."

Amelia sighed and rescued Megan. "Ladies, this is Megan Gentry. Megan, this is the Poker Posse. The one in blue is Faye Casteel, the one in yellow is Clarice Martin, and the Goodwin twins,"—the one in pink waved her fingers with a grin—"AnnaMae in pink and EllaMae in purple."

Megan's head spun trying to keep the names straight, but she couldn't get past the words *poker posse*. "Nice to meet you, ladies. Can I ask? Why Poker Posse?"

Amelia chuckled, but Faye answered. "Well, my dear girl—and aren't you a pretty thing—we've been playing poker for decades. First with our husbands, may they rest in peace,"—all four women crossed themselves—"and now with each other. We hold tournaments for tourists and play to raise money."

"Don't buy the sweet act. They're hustlers that clean everyone out and raise a ton of cash," Amelia murmured near Megan's ear.

"Oh, okay." Megan bit her lip to keep from laughing. It struck her funny that these sweet looking little grandmas would hustle playing cards.

"Where are you from? Do you have family here?" Clarice wore a deep frown and looked at her like a bug to be crushed.

"Uh...I'm from Nashville."

"Are you here to visit family?"

Megan opened her mouth but before she could speak, the pink twin —AnnaMae?—piped up. "I heard you're staying with Deputy Reynolds. You gotta love a man in uniform. You lucky girl."

"I—"

The purple twin elbowed her sister aside. "Have you seen him without his shirt yet?" She patted her chest. "I bet he's just dreamy. If only I were fifty years younger."

"He'd still pick me over you," AnnaMae said, elbowing her twin back.

"Oh! You're just petty, you know that?" EllaMae said, swatting at AnnaMae's arm.

"Petty? I'll show you—"

"For God's sake, you two, knock it off. You're both old as the hills, and Aidan Reynolds will not be looking at the likes of you," Clarice snapped at the two bickering sisters. "Amelia, is our order ready? I'm sick of these two."

Amelia rolled her lips in to keep from smiling and nodded. "Yep, let me just grab your coffee."

As Amelia walked away and called to one of the workers to grab some bags, Megan stood there like a deer in the headlights, while the twins kept bickering, Clarice huffed, and Faye smiled serenely at her. "So, are you enjoying our town?" Faye asked.

"Um, yes. It's lovely. Everyone has been very welcoming."

"And how long do you plan to stay?"

"Okay, ladies. Here's your coffees and danishes." Amelia came around the counter and handed out the coffees and small pink boxes to each of the ladies. The twins took a time-out to take their items and slurp their coffee. "Y'all have a nice day. See you tomorrow."

"Let's go, ladies, we got poker to play." Clarice herded the twins out of the shop, but Faye stayed behind for a moment.

She laid a hand on Megan's arm. It was liver spotted, but surprisingly warm and soft. "I hope to see you around again, Megan. Our little town has a lot to offer. Take care of yourself." She winked and moved with the agility of a woman thirty years younger out the door, joining the rest of her posse on the sidewalk.

Megan turned to Amelia, who stood next to her looking out the front windows with a smile. "I feel…"

Amelia laughed and faced her. "Yep, I know. You've been properly broken in to our town now."

She crossed her arms over her chest and gestured to the bag Megan held with her chin. "You should probably get that to Deputy Reynolds. He does like his…sweets." Her grin and wink left no doubt as to what kind of sweet she was talking about.

Thinking about that implication made butterflies flap in her belly.

Megan rolled her eyes but laughed. "Bye, Amelia."

She started out the door, only to turn around and go back to the counter. "Um, where is the sheriff's office?"

With a laugh, Amelia gave her directions with a smirk on her pretty face and mischief dancing in her blue eyes.

Aidan was right. Amelia was a troublemaker.

A troublemaker with damn good coffee.

CHAPTER TEN
dangerous liaisons

WALKING the short block to the brick building in the near distance, butterflies took up all the real estate in her belly, leaving her feeling momentarily sick. She stopped at a bench and sat down to take a minute.

What the hell was wrong with her? She actually lived with this man. They were roommates. She slept in his freaking bed. Not *with* him, of course. But it was still pretty damn intimate to sleep on the sheets that he did before she crashed his bachelor pad.

She blew out a breath looking around the main square of the town where she'd stopped. People walked around, going about their business, hustling and bustling to the next place. Even small towns had hustle and bustle, just at a different cadence than a big city.

Even the big city hustle was nothing compared to the riot of feelings going on inside her.

It wasn't like she hadn't been near the man before, but that night on the deck, he'd been close in a different way. Before that night, things were decidedly platonic, even if she might have had some dirty little dreams about him. But that was before she got to know a little bit about him, broke through that more quiet side of him.

The problem was, now that she had, she wasn't sure what to do with it. She knew what she *wanted* to do with it, and while she'd seen the desire in his eyes before what she called the near-miss kiss, she didn't think Aidan would ever follow through. He was a good guy and respectful. He'd been the one to pull away that night, hadn't he?

Still, before he pulled away, she'd seen some signs. Signs that made her wish he wasn't such a good guy. Signs that told her if he ever broke free of that tightly coiled chain he kept himself on, he would ruin a woman for any other man.

Not for the first time, she thought the woman who made him break that chain would be a lucky bitch.

She leaned her head back and closed her eyes, letting her thoughts of him run wild for just a moment. Maybe if she thought about it now, before she saw him, she could act like a normal person.

The way his eyes had looked at her in the moonlit night, like he wanted to devour her in a couple of bites. The way his cologne subtly wrapped itself around her and drew her under his spell.

His lips? It was unfair for a man to have such beautiful lips. It did nothing but enhance his handsome face.

Then there was his voice. That deep, raspy timbre of his voice was panty-dropping. The slight hint of a Southern drawl. Kind of like a toned down Matthew McConaughey. All in all, she had it bad for Aidan Reynolds.

The only relief she found when it came to thinking of him was when she pulled out her little bullet friend and let it bring her the pleasure she craved. Unfortunately, her body wasn't fooled. Even though she had orgasms that left her panting, her body wasn't satisfied. It wanted the weight of a man, the touch of a man, the feel of his hard length inside her.

What was she saying? She didn't want just a man. She wanted Aidan. The star of her dirty fantasies.

But fantasies were all that they'd be. There could never be anything between them. She knew herself, knew that if she slept with him just once, she'd find herself falling in "love" and that was what she was trying to avoid. Sex didn't equate to love, but somewhere along the line, her heart never seemed to get that memo.

And that's how her heart always ended up making her look like a fool.

Not to mention it would just complicate their living situation, and so far there was no other place for her to go. She couldn't screw it up.

She blew out a breath and started to stand just as her phone rang. A smile curved her lips when she heard her brother's ring tone.

"I was going to call you today," she said by way of greeting.

Nate's chuckle was deep on the other end. "Yeah, sure."

"I was. I promise."

"How's my favorite sister?"

"You mean your only sister? I'm fine. Taking a walk in town before I have to head into work."

"Yeah, so tell me about that. You mentioned you were working in your last text. Why?"

"Well, Nate. I need money and—"

"Done. I can have Sharon send money to you."

"No!" She gripped the phone tightly. "Nate, do not send me more money. I mean it. Besides, I'm working at a local bar and grill type place. Serving and bartending. This is good practice for when I get down there."

"Yeah, but you were a damn good bartender. Come on, we've been through this. You didn't work in those high society places for nothing. You'll be fine."

"I know, but I've been out of the game for a while. Use it or lose it and all." She settled back against the bench and huddled up under her sweater when the breeze blew. "The girl who's training me is amazing. She's young, but I can see her running the place one day. Smart, energetic."

"Something you're not telling me, Meg-pie?" The use of the nickname he gave her a lifetime ago made her smile.

"Not at all."

"Okay, just making sure. Getting a job, telling me about your trainer that sounds like someone I should hire. I miss you and I'm looking forward to having you around."

Megan laughed. "Yeah, for about a week and then you'll be asking me when I'm moving out."

He joined in her laughter. "You're right," he said without shame. "But that's what I wanted to tell you. The guest house is done. So when you get here, we can just move you straight in there."

Megan sat up straighter. "Are you serious? I thought you were putting that off for another year."

"Well, I was. But then I decided that I would be exactly the way you said. I like my space, especially when I come off the road or during the off-season. I like to be able to rant like an animal without anyone seeing that when we have a shitty road trip or lose the playoffs prematurely."

"Well, okay. Thank you, Nate. That's amazing." She bounced in her seat. "I can't wait to get there. I miss you too. And I'm ready to move forward with my life."

Her gaze wandered over to the building where Aidan was probably doing official law enforcement things. In spite of her excitement, her chest tingled with dread at the thought of leaving when the time came.

But this wasn't her destination. It never had been. She just needed to enjoy the time while she was here.

"Nate, there is something I want to talk to you about."

"Sounds serious."

"Well, I don't know. Maybe. But I need some advice."

"Okay, well...shit. I can't right now. I've got a meeting with my agent. But I'll call you back later. Will that work? Or do I need to push my meeting? Because I can."

"No. No, of course not. It's not pressing. And I'm not even sure I know what I want to say just yet. So I'll call you later."

"Okay. Love you, Meg-pie."

"Love you too."

Taking a couple of deep breaths, she stood and walked the rest of the way to the station. Once inside, it didn't look anything like what she saw on TV.

There were no handcuffed criminals screaming about how they were innocent or the requisite hooker that was on some shows. There was no crazy, constant phone ringing. With the exception of the police scanner that sat on one of the desks behind the front counter that chattered away, it could have been any sort of office. Any sort of office that smelled like mildew, old coffee, and hadn't been updated since the eighties. Complete with wood paneling.

A woman who looked to be in her fifties with fiery-red hair pulled up in a bun looked up when the door shut behind Megan. She was dressed in tan khaki pants and a black polo shirt with the Madison Ridge Sheriff's Department embroidered on the front pocket. She smiled and walked over to the waist-height counter. "Can I help you?"

Megan returned her smile. "Hi, is Aidan available? I mean, Officer Reynolds? Or is it Deputy?"

"He's the Deputy Sheriff." The smile never wavered but the woman's eyes sharpened on her and she tilted her head, tapping a pen in her palm. "Is he expecting you?"

Megan shifted her feet and clasped her hands in front of her but also kept the smile on her lips. "Um, no. He isn't. I—"

"If you want to leave your name and contact info, I can leave a message for him. Or you can set up an appointment—"

"That won't be necessary, Rhonda. Hey, Megan. Come on back."

Aidan stood at the end of a short hallway in front of an open office door. He smiled, and she swore her heart skipped a beat.

"Hey, Aidan." Her heart beat a tapping rhythm against her ribs.

Damn, now she was a freaking cliché.

How many days had it been since she'd really seen him in the flesh? For more than a passing "hey, how are you?"

Over a week and that was too long in her mind. She ignored the little voice that told her that was a dangerous thought.

Army-green cargo pants covered those long legs, worn with work-battered boots that shouldn't be sexy as hell but were, and topped by the same type polo Rhonda wore that hugged his biceps and stretched across his broad shoulders. The backwards black cap just added to the sex appeal, showing off his stupidly handsome face.

God, it wasn't fair at all.

"Rhonda, this is Megan. My…roommate I told you about."

"Ohhhh…" The older lady's smile became friendly as opposed to feral. She swung the half door open. "Please come in."

"Thanks." Megan went through and as she passed, Aidan's co-worker didn't hide the fact that she was checking Megan out. If Amelia was to be believed, the whole town would soon know that Deputy Sheriff Reynolds's roommate brought him baked goods.

She walked down the short hall to where he stood. At the doorway, he stepped aside and held out an arm. "Welcome to my home away from home."

"Thanks." She walked past him into his bigger-than-expected one-window office.

He smelled so good, she nearly stumbled.

He closed the door behind him as she stood looking around his office. There were a few personal touches here and there, including a couple of glass awards on the shelves of a tall bookcase that lined one wall. He also had a scanner on a short filing cabinet next to his desk. A comfy looking sofa lined one wall and a low coffee table stood in front of it.

She raised a brow and turned to him. "It really is your home away from home, huh?"

He chuckled and turned down the scanner. "Yeah. Since the sheriff has been on leave, I've been here on call a lot. I was always here doing something." He gestured toward a chair, then leaned against the edge of his desk. "So what brings you in? I haven't seen you much over the last few days. Is everything okay?"

He crossed his arms over his chest, biceps straining against the shirt material. Her mouth watered at the long length of him in his tactical uniform. The dark shadow of stubble on his strong jaw, along with that backwards ballcap, gave him an edge of danger and power. Power that he kept on a tight leash.

There was something to be said about a man in uniform. She wanted to climb him like a freaking tree.

"Everything's fine. Just busy with work." Wow, she managed to get that sentence out and still sound normal. She held up the pastry bag. "Amelia said you forgot your cinnamon roll."

His brow furrowed and he reached for it, looking inside. "I didn't...Ah," he said, a smirk on his lips. "That girl is such a troublemaker."

More like wannabe matchmaker, but Megan kept that to herself.

"You got one too?" he asked.

"Oh yeah, I haven't been able to dig in yet though. Nate called me on my walk here."

He pushed off the desk to his full height. "Want to take these over to the sofa?"

"Yeah, sure." Though she wasn't sure sitting on a sofa next to him was the best thing to do. She might end up in his lap if she wasn't careful.

They laid out the food and dug in.

"How's your brother?"

"He's fine. Told me that the guest house is finished. A year earlier than he'd planned since I'm moving there now. So once I get there, I can move right in, and I won't have to live with him."

"Well, that'll be nice. To have your own space."

She flipped the fork over and licked icing off the tines. "Trust me, I'm reaping the benefits but so is he."

Megan turned her head to find Aidan staring at her mouth, the blue in his eyes darkened to an almost navy color. The air around them thickened, reminding her of the night by the lake and how he'd looked at her the same way. Her heart beat so loud in her ears, he had to hear it. She licked her lips but couldn't move anything else.

Aidan blinked then cleared his throat, looking down at his food. "I can't blame the guy. I love my sisters, but there's no way in hell I'd live with them *and* work with them."

"Right." She swallowed hard and tried to keep from fanning herself. When had it become so hot in his office? She set down her fork and wiped her fingers with a napkin, trying to think of anything other than wanting to rip off her clothes and beg him to bring her to release.

"Oh! I wanted to show you something." She leaned down to dig through her purse for her phone. Yep, show him pictures of pumpkins. There wasn't anything sexy about pumpkins.

Except that pumpkin pie normally had whipped cream on it, which she'd be happy to lick off Aidan's abs.

Get it together, Gentry.

She took a breath before sitting up. "I wanted to show you what I came across on my walk to work yesterday." She tapped the screen a couple of times and smiled when she found the pumpkin arrangement outside the general store. She held it up for him with a grin. "Is that not the cutest thing?"

Aidan leaned back, looking at the screen, and lifted his hand. When their fingers brushed, a jolt of electricity shot up her arm. If a mere touch like that lit her up, what would it be like to have those large hands on her body?

He grinned, looking at the picture, and she swore her panties spontaneously combusted in her jeans. "It appears superheroes are the theme this year." He narrowed his eyes and tilted his head. "That's a damn good rendition of the Hulk. For a pumpkin."

She nodded and shifted closer to him so she could see the screen as well, ignoring the cheers in her pants when she caught a whiff of the cologne that was quickly becoming her kryptonite. "Right? I thought the same thing.

His laugh was low and deep, dancing along her skin. "Looks like the Hanafords are starting early this year. They've set the tone for the competition."

She turned to look at him. Her chest fluttered as her gaze roamed over his handsome, strong-jawed profile. She was close enough to see his long eyelashes. "Competition?"

He nodded. "Every year, there's a pumpkin contest. The chamber of commerce sets a theme, and the shops in the square come up with a display and whoever has the best one wins."

"Really? That's so cute."

"Yeah, the fall festival is the culmination of the contest. They announce the winner on the Saturday night in the middle of the square. Then they open the old courthouse for a one night only haunted house."

"Oohh…that sounds like so much fun. When is this festival?"

"Well, today's the sixteenth? Next weekend."

"And it lasts all weekend?"

"Yep." He handed back her phone. "Friday night to Sunday afternoon."

She grinned. "I can't wait to see more displays and take pictures. It's going to be fun."

"Want to go with me?"

Her finger hovered over the screen, frozen, then she looked up at him. "Go with you where?"

"To the festival. I have to work the Friday, but I can get Saturday off. We can eat some bad carnival food and play some games. Find out whose pumpkin wins. If you'd be interested in something like that." His mouth pursed and he looked away. "That probably sounds kind of lame though. Compared to what you're used to, rubbing elbows with Nashville's elite."

Her eyes widened. Was that vulnerability in confident Aidan's eyes? "Are you asking me on a date, Aidan?"

He rubbed the back of his neck, his lips in a firm line. "I mean…we could go as friends. Since you're on a guy hiatus and all."

She looked down at her cinnamon roll and fought back the disappointment that settled in her gut. She had said that, hadn't she? *Well, shit.*

Lifting her gaze to his, she pasted a smile on her face and forced herself to find the good. "Of course. Absolutely, I'd love to go with you. As friends." She poked his shoulder and leaned close, a grin on her face. "Is it like a beauty pageant with pumpkinzilla-type behavior?"

"Pumpkinzilla?"

"Yeah, you know. Where the contestants get all shrilly when they run out of spray paint or wives screaming at their husbands that he cut that slashing jack o'lantern grin too much. Things like that."

His voice held laughter. "There has been known to be some antics that are talked about for decades at these things."

"Oh goodie!" She clapped her hands while at the same time her head went light. *It isn't a date, Megan. It isn't a date. Remember that.* "Yes, of course. I'd love to go with you. I'll see if I can get my shift covered that night."

Did he even know that his smile would be the death of her? He reached up and toyed with a lock of hair, wrapping it around his finger. "Okay, that's good."

His eyes were on hers, then focused on her lips. "You've, uh, got some glaze…" His thumb grazed across her bottom lip, the dichotomy of the roughness of his skin on the soft, tender skin of her lip sending a shiver through her.

He held her chin with his thumb and forefinger, and before she could figure out what was going on, Aidan was leaning closer and her eyes were sliding closed. Thoughts of how badly she wanted him swirled through her mind, crowding out all the questions of what was going on between them.

When his lips met hers, she sighed and fell into the kiss, her fingers curling into his shirt. His mouth was firm yet gentle and coaxing, making her open for him. When she did, his tongue slid against hers in a seductive dance that made her want to climb in his lap and have him kiss more than her mouth.

He tasted sweet, like icing and cinnamon and sex. Her skin flushed at the thought of his body on hers, this incredible mouth that was winding her up making its way all over her body.

Aidan groaned when she shifted closer, his hand moving to cup the back of her neck, taking the kiss deeper. His other hand moved high up her thigh and she moaned softly, wanting that hand to keep going until it reached her center.

"Hey, Aid, I think we need to go over—Oh shit. I'm sorry."

Megan jumped away from Aidan, who cursed under his breath. She wiped at her mouth as mortification set in. Aidan lifted his cap off his head and ran a hand through his hair before replacing it. "What's up, Landon?" His words belied the strained tone to his voice.

A tall, handsome deputy stood in the doorway, frozen in place, and his mouth snapped open and shut several times before he spoke. "I can come back."

What the hell was in the water around this town? So far all the law enforcement in this town looked like hot action heroes with their muscles and tactical gear.

Her cheeks burning, Megan gathered her things and stood. "No, you stay. I need to go. I've kept you long enough, Deputy Reynolds."

With a heavy sigh, Aidan stood as well. He frowned, and if looks could kill, Landon would be a corpse right about then. "I'll walk you out."

She edged her way to the door, closer to where the deputy stood. "No, please. I can see myself out."

When she turned, she nearly collided with Landon. "Oh, I'm sorry."

Landon stepped aside to let her by, a smile on his face, his beautiful amber eyes dancing. "You must be Megan. I'm Landon Grey. Aidan's cousin."

"I'm disowning you," Aidan said, his face foreboding and his arms crossed over his chest. "And then I'm firing you."

That look made flop sweat break out in Megan, but Landon just laughed it off and clapped Aidan on the shoulder. "Sure, buddy." He turned his attention back to Megan. "Are you feeling better after your accident?"

"Yes, thanks for asking. Listen, I've got to go run. Well, not really run. I kinda suck at running." She bit her lip and prayed that would keep her mouth from continuing its word vomit. "Anyway, I need to go."

She walked backward out of the door, knocking her elbow into the doorjamb. She rolled her lips inward to ward off the yelp of pain she wanted to release. As she started to turn away, Aidan's voice stopped her.

"Hey, Megan?"

She turned back to meet his eyes, rubbing her screaming elbow. "Yeah?"

There was that smile again. The one that seemed to be just for her. The one that made her swoon. The one that confused the hell out of her.

"To be continued."

t-r-o-u-b-l-e

"SHIT, man. I'm sorry about that." Landon closed the door behind him.

Aidan walked behind his desk and flopped down into his office chair. "Yeah, you look really sorry. Giving me that shit-eating grin right now."

Landon sat in the chair across from him and leaned back, smile still in place. "What can I say, Aid? I see how you look at her. And can I just say that it's about time?"

Aidan rolled his eyes, but a cold sweat broke out over him. "Whatever, dude. I'm not looking at her any way."

Landon threw up both his hands and said, "Okay, that's fine. You don't want to listen. I get it. But let me remind you that you're the one that pulled my head out of my ass when I almost lost Iris. Just trying to return the favor here."

"Well, I don't need you returning any favors, okay? There was never a doubt that you and Iris would get together. Hell, Megan doesn't even live here. As soon as her car is ready to go, she's out of here. She has a whole life waiting for her in Florida. So just leave it alone, got it?"

His tone was firm, no bullshitting. But why did saying all that out loud make his chest feel like he had a damn elephant sitting on top of it?

Landon crossed an ankle to his knee and laid his hands on his stomach. "Got it."

Aidan nodded and shuffled papers on his desk, trying to get his head together. "So, what is it you came in here for anyway, Grey?"

Landon leaned forward, one hand raised in a wait a minute gesture. "I have one last thing to say on Megan and then I'll leave it alone."

"Jesus…"

"Just listen. Look, maybe what you and Megan have—"

"Megan and I don't have anything."

"Fine, but I can tell you like her. And it appears for some reason, she likes your grumpy ass. Why not have some fun with her while she's here? Date, keep it casual."

Aidan's brow furrowed. "Date?" he asked, as though the word was foreign.

Yeah, you know that thing you asked her on with the festival?

No way, that's just a friends hanging together thing. She's on a guy hiatus.

Whatever, dude.

Landon nodded, confirming what the war in his head said. "Yeah, you know, see each other outside that cabin you're sharing. If you didn't want to do that, then maybe y'all just scratch an itch while she's here—if she's game for that kind of thing—and then you each move on. Like adults."

Aidan narrowed his eyes at his cousin. "She deserves better than that."

The fucker just smirked at him. "I'm sure she does. But you need to get laid, man. Get some of that tension out that has your shoulders permanently sewn to your ears. How long has it been anyway?"

"I'm not discussing my sex life with you," Aidan gritted out. It was more like he didn't want to admit the last time his cock had seen any action besides his hand.

Landon leaned his head back and laughed. "That long, huh?"

Aidan balled up a sticky note and threw it at Landon. "Fuck you.

We aren't all lucky enough to have a beautiful woman in our bed every night."

"Ah, but you could, Aidan. You could." Landon placed an elbow on the desk and leaned closer. "Trust me, there was a whole lot of eye-fucking going on in that doorway, and it wasn't all one-sided."

Aidan rubbed his forehead. "Can we please just stop talking about this? We have work to do. Law and order to uphold and all that."

He sighed in relief when Landon dropped it and started talking about festival weekend.

Aidan tried not to think about what would have happened if Landon hadn't interrupted. Would he have stopped at just kissing her? Would one taste have been enough right now? He'd been walking around with what felt like a permanent hard-on all week. The fact that he'd been working days and Megan nights had turned out in his favor. After that night on the deck, he wanted nothing more than to pick up where they had left off.

He didn't even want to think about what it meant that he still went home every night instead of sleeping on his office couch.

Landon wasn't wrong, and that was what stuck in his craw the worst. Given her reactions and the fact that she was on a guy hiatus, Megan was game for the casual thing. She'd given all indications she was interested, which surprised the hell out of him. He'd dated, fucked, Netflix and chilled—whatever the kids were calling it these days—with his fair share of beautiful women.

But Megan? She was on another level with all that dark hair, hazel eyes, and banging body. But he also liked her. She was funny, thoughtful, and smart. And while he didn't know the whole story about her divorce or why she was leaving Nashville, there was no doubt she was strong. Her ex was a fucking douche to let her go. Any man would be lucky to have such a woman at his side.

But it wouldn't be him. Not only was she leaving, but he also just wasn't a relationship kind of guy. All that entanglement could lead to love.

And love? Well, it just chewed you up and then spit you out. Everyone leaves at some point, and that pain for the one left behind?

Nope. Not for him.

He shoved all that aside and focused on what Landon was talking about. For the next forty-five minutes, they put together a plan for the festival weekend, figured out who would be on the schedule, and went over some incident reports.

Landon stopped in the doorway on his way out. "Been a while since we've had a round together. Want to meet up at Silver Moon tonight before the craziness starts next week?"

Aidan immediately thought of Megan, knowing she'd be working. He bet she was sexy as hell in action. He thought back to what Landon said earlier. Would a fling hurt?

It had been a while since he'd been out, just hanging out with his cousin in an unofficial capacity. And next week was going to be hell week with tourism picking up and vendors trickling in ahead of the festival.

"You know what? Yeah. Let's go have some beer, shoot some pool. I'll see if Noah and Del want to come out as well."

"Hell, yeah. Works for me. Eight o'clock?"

Aidan nodded, and they bumped fists. "Take it easy, Landon."

His cousin walked backward out of the office and tapped the bill of his ballcap. "Always."

* * *

Later that night, the Silver Moon Cafe was packed as usual, but they were able to secure a pool table when an arguing couple—she was accusing him of cheating, though given her attitude Aidan wasn't sure if she meant at pool or not—called it quits and walked away.

Stacks of quarters lined the edge of the table, indicating the guys planned to be there a while.

For the last hour, as he sipped his beer, he did his best to keep his eyes from wandering over to the bar where Megan was working. Her movements were quick, economical, and yet graceful as she took orders from patrons at the bar and filled orders from Charley and the other servers.

He had no idea how she kept all that straight, but one thing he could tell was that she was damn good at her job.

Not to mention that she looked fucking hot in the snug, black V-neck top. It stretched over her amazing tits, high and full. The sleeves had some sort of cutout, leaving only her shoulders bare before the sleeves ended halfway down her biceps.

"Aidan, you're up."

Noah's voice brought his attention back to the table, and he set his beer down before standing. He eyed the table, trying to remember if he and Del were solids or stripes.

"Stripes," Del said.

Aidan looked up and met his brother's stare. Del shrugged. "I figured you forgot since your attention seems elsewhere."

Aidan leaned over the table, setting up a shot, but flipped his brother off first. "I know. I don't need a reminder, Mom."

Del just chuckled and sipped his beer.

Aidan missed the shot, cursing under his breath. He walked back over to the high-top table and picked up his beer, glancing toward the bar, hoping to get a glimpse of Megan.

The sickly-sweet smell of cheap perfume assaulted his senses before he heard the voice. "So, this is where all the hot men are in this town tonight."

Del backed away and went around to the other side of the table with Noah.

Landon concentrated hard on lining up his shot.

Assholes.

Aidan glanced down as the town bad girl, Tara Moore, moved up beside him. She was dressed in her trademark tight top of some sort—tonight it was a sweater—and short denim skirt. Her face was caked with so much makeup that even though she was only a year older than he was, she looked like she had a decade on him. Her short red hair was styled in some sort of spiky mess that reminded him of porcupines.

Fitting because the woman was just as prickly.

"Evening, Tara." As much as Aidan didn't care for her, it was his job to keep the peace. Even if he was off the clock.

She licked her pink glossed lips and sipped on the drink in her hand. "I don't see you around here too often, deputy. Are you off duty tonight?"

Aidan's smile was tight. "I'm never off duty."

Batting her lashes, she chewed on the cocktail straw. Aidan wondered if she thought that was attractive.

She moved in closer, and the combination of too much bad perfume and vodka made him want to take a shower. "That's too bad," she purred, running her index finger down his bicep to his wrist. "I thought maybe you could show me your nightstick."

The guys were doing their best to hold back laughter. He was going to kick all their asses later. Instead, he shifted away from Tara and gave her a polite smile. "Sorry, we don't use nightsticks anymore. Nothing to see here."

"Yeah, nothing to see here, Moore. Move along." Charley walked up with a tray on her shoulder, her dark ponytail swinging behind her.

Tara narrowed her eyes, and her lips formed a sneer. "Why don't you just mind your own damn business, runt?"

Anger whipped through Aidan at Tara's words, but before he or his brothers and cousin could say something to send the nasty woman on her way, Charley dropped the tray on the table and charged toward Tara, fire in her eyes.

"Who are you calling runt—"

"All right, that's enough." Aidan grabbed Charley by the waist and hauled her back. He leveled a stare at Tara, while holding onto a squirming Charley. "I suggest you head out, Tara."

Her eyes were round, but she still straightened her back. "It's a free country. I don't have to go anywhere."

"Maybe so," Noah said, coming up beside Tara, "but that little runt knows how to fight."

Del stood next to him and gestured toward her short hair. "You don't have much to pull up there, but I guarantee you, she'll find enough to yank out of your head."

Tara slammed her glass on the side of the pool table and sent all of them venomous stares. "All you Reynoldses think you're so high and mighty. You think with all your money and your name it means something. But it don't mean shit."

She stormed off, shoving people on her way out the door.

"There may have been steam coming out of her ears," Landon said, leaning on his pool cue, a grin on his face.

Charley went slack in Aidan's arms and straightened her T-shirt and apron. "Bitch," she muttered. "How the hell Wyatt could be related to her is beyond me." Her face brightens. "Anyway, these are on the house, courtesy of our amazingly awesome new bartender."

They all gathered around the high-top table as she set out four beers and a Coke. She lifted one and turned to Del. "You going to drink yours?"

He shook his head. "Nope. The one beer is good. Thanks for the Coke."

"No problem. I figured you wouldn't, but Megan didn't know. I'll leave the extra beer for the winner of the game."

About a year ago, Del had found out that he had myasthenia gravis, a condition that caused weakened muscles, and in his line of work, it was too dangerous for him to work on set every day. He'd come home to film his final episode of his TV show, *Property Ace*, and ended up getting back together with the love of his life, Addison Davenport. These days, he ran the family business with Noah, filmed the occasional television special, and seemed to be happier than Aidan had seen him in years.

While so far, he seemed to be managing it fine with meds—though he couldn't drink much with them—a less stressful lifestyle, and regular workouts, you couldn't tell that Delaney Reynolds with the Hollywood smile had ever been anything but healthy a day in his life.

"Alright, see ya later, fellas." She gave each of them a punch in the arm as her farewell when she walked away.

Aidan looked toward the bar and found Megan's eyes. If he looked in a mirror, he knew he'd see the same expression in his eyes as he saw in hers. Her gaze traveled over his body before meeting his again. Across the crowded, noise-filled room, the hunger in her eyes was unmistakable. She wanted him as badly as he wanted her.

Rubbing a hand over his mouth, he stared at her through the crowd. It was as though time had slowed down, and the place had gone on mute. She licked crimson-red lips and sent him a saucy wink before turning her attention to the woman in front of her, breaking the spell he'd been lulled into.

He dropped down to the stool so he wouldn't basically announce to the whole place that he was hard as concrete and took a long pull of his beer. What he really needed to put the fire out in his gut would get him arrested.

But he feared there would be no putting out that fire until he fucked Megan Gentry's brains out.

"Seems like she's game to me."

Landon sidled up to him, holding a cue stick in one hand, his beer in the other.

Aidan cleared his throat and drank his beer again before he could speak. "Yeah."

"You going to go for it?"

Before Aidan could answer, Noah called him. "Aidan, you're up."

"Aidan needs a minute," Landon said around a laugh.

Noah and Del walked over, studying him.

"Stop staring," he snapped.

Noah tilted his head. "Are you okay? You look a little flushed."

"I'm fine."

"He likes a girl."

Landon really was looking to have his ass kicked.

"She's not a girl, you asshole."

Del narrowed his eyes, a smile on his lips. "Interesting that you didn't deny you liked her." He dropped down on the stool next to Aidan, hooking his boots around the bottom rung. "Who is she?"

Noah leaned against the pool table, arms crossed over his chest. "Is this the woman from the car accident that you took in?"

It appeared they were no longer playing pool. *Shit.*

Aidan rubbed a hand down his face. "Yes. I do like her, okay? But she's leaving town in a couple of weeks. And you know me. I don't do the relationship thing. Love's too much trouble." And pain. He didn't want to bear the pain.

Noah shrugged. "So what? If she's up for some casual fun, what's wrong with that?"

"Thank you," Landon said, making a sweeping gesture with his arm. "We had this exact conversation this morning."

"Seriously, man." Noah turned toward the bar and then back to Aidan. "She's fucking hot. What are you waiting for?"

Aidan scoffed. "That's rich coming from you, Noah. When was the last time you had a casual fuck?"

"Last week."

They all gawked at him, mouths open, eyes wide.

"What?" Landon asked.

"You sly dog." This from Del.

"Who the hell was it?" Aidan was glad to have the attention off him.

Noah rolled his eyes with a frown. "You can shut your mouths literally. And it's none of your damn business. She's not from here anyway."

"You never talk about her," Del said.

"It's called discretion, Del. We don't all have our lives splashed in the papers."

He nodded. "Fair enough. Thankfully, neither do I anymore. Much anyway." He sipped his Coke before focusing back on Aidan. "But let's get back to this one here. What's stopping you, Aid?"

Noah narrowed his eyes. "Yeah, it isn't like you've ever slept with a girl and then needed a relationship. Hell, I've known you to sleep with a few tourists and send them on their way. You like that about them. So, what's—"

"You like this girl," Del said.

Aidan looked down at the bottle in his hand and started peeling the label. "How can I like her like that? I hardly know her. She's been here a week."

"But what you do know, you like," Landon added.

Aidan rubbed the back of his neck. Fuck. He did like her. And he was afraid if he had her once, it wouldn't be enough. He'd be too attached. And he didn't do attached.

"It's just because we're in such close quarters. And she's hot as fuck. The fact that she's sleeping in my bed doesn't help either."

Noah lifted a hand. "Hold up. She's sleeping in your bed? How the hell have you not had sex with this girl yet?"

Aidan took the cue stick and reached over and stomped the end on top of Noah's foot. "Ouch, you asshole," Noah hissed out and lifted his foot up before Aidan could do it again.

"I'm sleeping in the loft. Have some respect. Honestly, I expected more from you, Noah."

He held up his hands in a shrugging gesture. "I apologize, but I'm flabbergasted by this situation."

So was Aidan if he were being honest. "Look, I'm just going through a dry spell right now. I'm bored with the local offerings. With the busy season coming up and the sheriff pretty much out of commission, I've had to step up and take over a lot of duties. Sex has actually been the furthest thing from my mind."

"But now it's the only thing, huh?" Landon nudged his shoulder.

Aidan downed the last of his beer and banged the cue stick on the floor. "Can we just finish the damn game? That's what we came here for."

"Yeah, you keep telling yourself that, cousin," Landon muttered low enough only Aidan could hear.

As he stood, Aidan's eyes found Megan's from across the bar. When she smiled and tilted her head in acknowledgment, he returned the smile.

He was in so much fucking trouble.

CHAPTER TWELVE

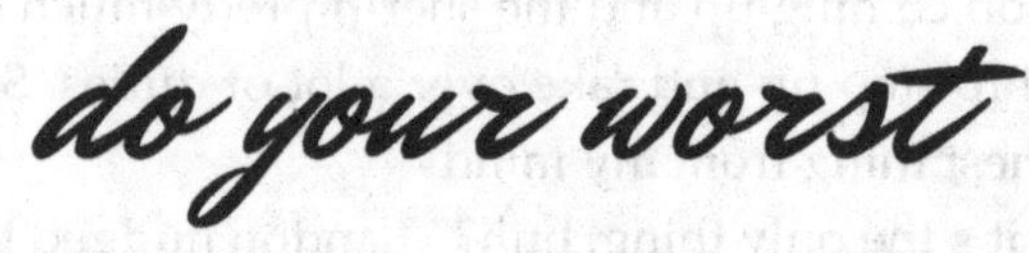

A COUPLE OF HOURS LATER, the Silver Moon Cafe had emptied out except for the workers and Aidan. The guys left at different times through the night, leaving him to camp out on a stool at the end of the bar, where he stayed out of the way but could watch Megan in action.

When it came time for her to leave, she walked over to where he sat, her hand running across the now clean and gleaming bar top. "You waited for me?"

He shrugged a shoulder. "Figured I was here. Save Charley the trip of driving you home."

Megan tilted her head. "It's my duty as a bartender to ask how many beers you had tonight."

He smiled at her. "One and a half. I didn't finish my second one. Then I switched to water. I'm good."

Somewhere during the evening, he'd decided if she was game, he would have her underneath him before the night was over. There was no way he was going to ruin it with alcohol.

She nodded, biting her lower lip, and looked away for a moment before looking back at him. "Give me a minute to get my things and I'll be ready."

"I'll be here."

She lifted the countertop and moved out from behind the bar, shooting him a smile as she walked by him, headed to the back. Above the smell of cleaning products from the bar and stale food from years of cooking, her perfume wafted up to him as she passed by him.

He adjusted his crotch and blew out a breath. He wasn't sure how much longer he'd be able to hold out being near her without touching her. His hands itched to touch every inch of her body. The time for helping himself with his hand was over.

"You're still here?" Charley came up beside him and leaned on the bar.

"Yeah, thought I'd take Megan home, save you the trip."

"Thanks, I appreciate that." Charley stacked her arms on the bar and laid her head on top of them. "I'm beat."

He brushed a stray hair out of her eyes and studied her. "You okay?"

She nodded her head, the movement against her arms making her hair fall back in her eyes. She brushed it away before sighing. "I'm just...physically and emotionally exhausted. I feel like I'm in a rut."

"Things not going well here? Or with Mom?"

Charley raised her head from the bar and turned around so she leaned her back against the bar. "Things here are fine. Marcus has started teaching me more of the business side. It's been eye-opening, and my degree is finally coming into play a bit." She sighed. "And Mom's fine. She's doing more travel, you know, so we don't get to butt heads as much."

"So what's the problem? Seems like things are going well enough."

She sighed and looked down at her feet. "Yeah, but...I guess I'm just bored. I've never really done anything. I mean, I've traveled some but not much. All I've ever done is work and college. I listen to all the things you and Del and Amelia have done and it sounds exciting. Megan has told me some stories of living in Nashville, and you wouldn't believe some of the people she met on the regular. Some of the biggest names in country music. They knew her on a first-name basis."

"Yeah, she told me. Though I didn't realize they knew her so well."

He probably should have realized that, but he had trouble reconciling the Megan he was coming to know with the Megan hanging with the high rollers. It made him want to know more about her. Where had she been other than Nashville? What had she done? How did that shape who she was now?

And this is why he hesitated. He wanted to know way more about her than was wise.

Charley's sigh brought his attention back to her. She looked back up at Aidan. "I guess I just want some adventures. I mean, except for Grace—who's perfectly content to stay in town and teach those rugrats —all of y'all have done something at some point. Noah went off to college before Dad died. Del, well he's been everywhere, you've been everywhere—"

"Because I was in the military, Charley."

"But still,"—she rose on her tiptoes, her voice rising in pitch and volume—"you did something. Amelia went off to France and New York." She sighed and stared out in front of her. "I wish I could be like Grace. Be content. But I'm not like her."

Aidan chuckled. "No, you're not and never have been."

She laid her head on his shoulder. "What do I do, Aid?"

It wasn't the first time she'd asked him that, typically with her head resting on his shoulder or his arm if he were standing since he had about a foot on her. She usually came to him first, instead of to their mother. That had been borne of them being the youngest two, and happened even more after their dad died and their mom was grieving.

Before he could answer her, Megan walked toward them, a smile on her face. "This is a sweet picture. Reminds me of Nate and me."

Charley lifted her head and painted a smile on her face. "Yeah, I like this one."

She tried to reach up and ruffle his hair, but he stood from the stool, and she couldn't reach his head. "But this one?" He jerked a thumb at Charley. "She's pesky like a gnat."

Charley gasped in mock indignance, making him laugh. He leaned down to hug her. She wrapped her arms around him, up on her tiptoes, and he murmured in her ear. "Follow your gut, Charley. Mine's never steered me wrong before."

When he pulled back, she looked up at him, a smirk on her lips. "Keep that in mind when you get home."

She winked and stepped away, before looking over at Megan. "You ready?"

"We're walking her to the car," Aidan supplied, when Megan looked between them.

"I'm ready."

A few minutes later, they'd tucked Charley into her car, with Aidan promising to catch up with her later. Then it was just the two of them in the night air, walking toward the SUV he'd driven from work.

It was a quiet ride home, but Aidan's senses were on high alert. It was as though his body was in tune to her every breath and every move. The air in the cabin of the SUV was so thick with sexual tension, it nearly stuck to his skin.

By the time he opened the front door to the cabin, he was so wound up he could barely see straight.

"I'm going to take a shower. Unless you need the bathroom first," Megan said, gripping her jacket in both hands.

Aidan closed the door behind him, closing off any escape hatch he may have and so that he didn't reach out and touch her. He shook his keys in his hand. "It's all yours."

She stared at him for what felt like an eternity before nodding and turning away without a word. He couldn't read her eyes, but the pull from her was almost more than he could bear.

He lay down on the couch and flung his forearm over his eyes. While he didn't date, he knew how to sweet-talk a woman into bed. What the fuck was he doing? She'd given him an opening and he'd blown it.

When the shower came on in the bathroom, he groaned and his cock grew painfully hard against the zipper of his jeans.

He'd imagined her in the shower before, but since the night by the lake, when he'd actually touched her skin, his thoughts were more erotic if that was possible. Her skin was soft and supple, and he imagined her moving that loofah thing all over her body, leaving behind that surprisingly intoxicating mix of lavender and vanilla scent. When she came out of the bathroom, the hot, damp air from the shower would smell just like her. And so would his bedroom.

He unbuttoned and unzipped his jeans and pulled his aching dick from his boxer briefs, squeezing it to relieve some of the pressure. He arched his back off the couch while working his hand down his length, wishing he was that loofah she used. Or the river of water that sluiced down her body, going in places that he wanted his hands and tongue to be.

Lost in the thought of her curves, the dips, and that one particular valley he wanted to become familiar with, Aidan almost missed the fact that the water was no longer running.

Shit.

"Aidan? You still out there?"

Double shit. "Yeah, what's up?" he called back, but didn't rise from the couch.

"I, um. This is embarrassing. I don't have a towel. Can you bring me one?"

Triple shit. He'd forgotten to bring the towels out of the laundry area and back into the bathroom.

The universe was really testing his resistance with this woman.

Or the universe is telling you to give in and go for it, dumbass!

Yeah, that too.

"Sure. One second."

After tucking it all back in and zipping up, Aidan retrieved a towel and went to the bathroom door, where Megan had it opened slightly and was hiding her body behind the door.

She smiled and reached out. "Thanks."

When their hands brushed, they both stilled and stared at each other. The steam from her shower rose between them, looking like a vision coming from the mist.

Megan closed her eyes for a moment, and when she opened them, desire burned bright, causing her normal hazel eyes to turn a mossy green. "Aidan, please."

Lust burned him from the inside out and yet his heart dropped to his knees hearing her plea. Had he been wrong? Had he read all her signs wrong?

"Please what?"

"I want you. Please put me out of my misery and fuck me."

Somewhere in the back of his mind, he heard the chains snap. And without thinking, he moved forward, pushing open the door. Megan didn't step back or step away—she just stood there, all of those glorious curves, wet and on display, lifting her chin.

Aidan wrapped a hand behind her neck, the wet tendrils of her hair cooling his heated skin along the back of his hand. "Are you sure this is what you want, Megan? Once I start, I won't be able to stop."

"Yes. If you stop, I might kill you."

He wrapped his other arm around her waist and yanked her damp body up against him, crushing his mouth to hers. Her arms came up around his neck and she rose up on her toes, pressing herself against him.

Just as he knew it would, the enchanting scent that was Megan wrapped around him and weakened him in the knees.

Her lips…those pillowy lips he'd been fantasizing about were soft against his. But he wanted more. He coaxed her lips apart with his tongue, and she opened for him without hesitation. Her hand went into his hair and he tilted his head to deepen the kiss. The hand on her neck fisted into all that hair he'd wanted covering his chest. The only sound around them was their heavy breathing and his heart pounding in his ears.

When he thought that he would come in his jeans simply with a kiss that rocked him to his soul, he pulled gently on her hair to break them apart. "Bedroom."

She nodded, her eyes hazy with lust. "Now."

Megan jumped up and wrapped her legs around his waist. He caught her tight little ass in his large hands. He nearly lost his balance when he realized that the inferno that brushed his fingertips was her wet and ready pussy. He tightened his grip so he didn't drop his still-slick-from-the-shower girl and practically ran into the bedroom.

Her giggle in his ear made him feel like a million bucks. When was the last time that had happened?

"Are you giggling at me, you tempting wench?" he asked, teasing her.

"I am." She nipped at his jaw, her hazel eyes dancing in mischief.

"Oh, you're going to pay for that," he growled.

She giggled again as he laid her down on the bed, covering her body with his. He leaned up on his elbows and looked down at her. "I hope you're ready for it."

The teasing look in her eyes disappeared, replaced with a fiery desire. Under him, she spread her legs wider until he was cradled in between her hips. The heat from her core pressed against the fly of his jeans. A small gasp escaped her lips, and she moved her hips in little movements against him, as though trying to find the right pressure. In response, he rubbed his hard-as-stone, jean-covered cock against her, causing her to gasp again.

"Do your worst" was her breathy reply.

It was all he needed to hear.

"Where are you going?" she asked, panic lacing her voice, when he got to his feet.

"I want to look at you."

A smile touched her lips and she ducked her head, a pretty pink blush staining her cheeks. It matched the rest of her glorious body. She lifted a knee up as though trying to cover herself up.

"Now, don't go all shy on me now, babe." He reached out and moved her knee to the side so that his stare had full access to the landscape of her rosy skin and glistening core.

A second ticked by before she raised her head and looked him in the eye. One side of her mouth curved. "Look your fill, then."

And he did.

What he wanted to do in that moment was devour her, fuck her into oblivion. But if this was a one and done type of thing, he was going to imprint her on his brain. He was going to need this memory for his personal spank bank after she said adios to Madison Ridge.

He rubbed a hand over his mouth as he gazed down at all the slopes and planes and curves that all came together to make the most beautiful body he'd ever laid his eyes on. It was as though God had spent some extra time making this woman.

His gaze started at the top of her head, where dark hair fell in a curtain behind her in damp ropes, then continued to the slope of her neck and shoulders. Full breasts that he couldn't wait to get his hands and mouth on sat high and proud, the nipples hard and a gorgeous dusky-pink color.

Her stomach was flat, and Aidan was happy to see that he couldn't count her ribs. In his mind, there was nothing worse than a woman thinking she needed to be a bag of bones to turn on a man. Her hips flared, and Aidan had no doubt they'd be perfect to hold onto when he took her from behind.

Because he would before this was all over. He'd mark that tight ass as his own.

His perusal continued over her pussy that gleamed with her desire. His stare stayed on that area for a few extra seconds, enough to make her squirm and fist the covers beneath her.

"Aidan, just you looking at me like that makes me want to come."

He grinned and she moaned, but kept his gaze on the promised land before letting it slide down the curves of her shapely legs. Legs that, even though she was of average height for a woman, were a mile long.

"Jesus, Megan. You're stunning."

His desire increasing, he lifted a hand to the back of his neck, pulling the white T-shirt he wore over his head in one fluid motion. Megan lifted up on her elbows, her gaze on his chest, licking her lips as though she were ready to devour him the way he wanted to devour her.

Apparently, it was her turn for an appraisal, and he was going to give the lady what she wanted.

Her eyes followed his hands as he reached for the button of his jeans and released it with a flick. He grinned when she bit her lip and sat up a little straighter when he unzipped his fly. It was a painful process given how hard he was, but he managed. His cock was an insistent motherfucker, poking its head out from the waistband of his boxer briefs.

Megan continued to lie there, her hungry gaze an almost tangible feeling on his skin, while he shucked the rest of his clothes and stood before her naked. Her eyes were wide as she stared at his cock, and she licked her lips again when he took it in his hand and stroked it.

He needed to do something to keep his impending orgasm at bay.

She took her time bringing her gaze back to his and when she did, it told him everything he needed to know without her saying a word.

He moved over her, bracing his arms on either side of her ribcage, and lowered his head to her gorgeous breasts. He lapped at one nipple, his tongue drawing circles around it before pulling it into his mouth and sucking hard. She arched against him, her hands locked around his head, pulling him close.

When he'd given each nipple proper attention, he moved farther down her torso, dropping hot, open-mouthed kisses along the expanse of soft skin. He closed his eyes and rubbed his nose against it, reveling in the desire that surrounded him like a cloak.

He kneeled at the edge of the bed, running his hands up her thighs, spreading her legs farther apart. His lips followed the path his hands took, trailing hot kisses up and down the inside of her thighs, getting closer and closer to her center but never quite touching her there.

Aidan stared at her center, running the tip of his finger between her warm folds and up her seam. She quivered under his touch, and a low moan came from her.

"You like my touch, baby?"

Her hands gripped for the sheets underneath her. "Yes. More. Please."

Satisfied he'd reduced her to one-word sentences, he leaned forward and ran his tongue up her seam before sucking on her clit, causing her back to arch up off the bed.

"Easy, baby. Hold still." He laid a hand over her lower belly, his large hand spanning from each side of her pelvic bones.

"I just…oh God. That feels so…"

He smiled and continued his ministrations with his tongue, burying himself in all of her essence.

After a few more flicks of her clit and inserting two fingers into her tight channel, he heard her breathing change and felt the way her pussy clamped down on his fingers, and he knew she was close.

"That's it, dirty girl. Come for me. Let go."

Her hands fisted and his name burst from her throat. "Yes! Oh Aidan!"

When the convulsions stopped, he stood and looked down at her, rubbing his mouth with the back of his hand. Megan threw an arm over her eyes, her chest heaving as though she'd run from a fire.

He fisted his cock in his hand and let her come back down a little bit before he took all that she'd be willing to give. She dropped her arm onto the bed and lifted her head to meet his stare. "I think you may have fried a few circuits."

"Well, bring them back online, baby. I haven't done my worst with you yet."

what have you done to me?

MEGAN IMAGINED what Aidan would look like under all those clothes. His snug T-shirts and jeans had hinted at the glory beneath.

But now that he was standing at the end of the bed, looking down at her, she realized she'd been woefully unprepared for the majesty that was Aidan Reynolds.

He was the whole package—the thick dark hair, bright blue eyes that held her captive like a tractor beam, the dark stubble that shadowed his strong jaw. His shoulders and chest were broad and strong with perfectly chiseled pecs. It was obvious the man stayed in excellent shape as the six-pack abs could attest to.

And he'd been hiding those tattoos under his shirts. She'd have to examine those later because, damn, they were hot on his tanned skin.

She licked her lips as her gaze traveled down to his narrow hips with—dear God—that sexy-ass V that seemed to point to exactly what she wanted. His thighs were long and lean but muscular. And what was between those thighs?

Holy mother of God.

Aidan easily had the biggest cock of any man she'd been with. But it wasn't just size—which she had to admit intimidated her just a bit—

it was the curve and veined skin. Penises weren't usually the hottest part of the man even if they felt good, but Aidan had a beautiful cock.

Not to mention he was a silver-tongued devil that knew exactly how to push all her buttons. Evil man.

He was without doubt out of her league in every way, shape, and form. And yet, somehow, here he was naked in front of her.

He reached over and opened the nightstand drawer, pulling out a condom. Ripping it open with his teeth, he started to roll it over his cock, when she sat up, stopping him.

"Wait."

He froze, the condom covering the tip, looking at her from under hooded eyes. "Is something wrong?"

She shifted, bringing herself to the edge of the bed, and looked up at him with a smile. "Let me help you."

He smiled back and raised his hands. "I'm all yours."

She positioned the condom on his tip and then covered it with her mouth.

"Holy fuck, Megan." With both hands, he gathered her hair on top of her head, the tips of the long locks tickling her back.

She held back a smile and moved her mouth down his length, unrolling the condom as she went with her tongue and lips. When he hit the back of her throat, she swallowed and breathed out her nose, while he muttered a string of curses. She reached around and grabbed his ass, fingernails digging into the tight skin. She pulled back before diving back down over his cock, the taste of the rubber filling her mouth, but she didn't care. She relished the warmth of his length and the way the tables had turned.

She wanted to give him everything he asked for, willing to give him as much as he wanted to take.

When she pulled off him with a pop, he pulled her to her feet and turned her around. "Get on your knees and bend over."

Her pulse thrummed with excitement as she did what he asked. Her legs were spread wide, and his hand was flat against her back. He gently pushed her down until her boobs and cheek were pressed against the warm, rumpled sheets. An involuntary shiver shot through her body when he ran his hand down her spine and rubbed the globe of her behind, the tip of his hard length rubbing against her opening.

Was it bad that she was slick and needy with desire so close on the heels of the mind-blowing orgasm he'd already given her?

She writhed under his hand and moaned, willing him to do something, anything. But mostly, she really wanted him inside her. "Aidan, please."

"Please what?"

Megan pushed back against him when he rubbed against her sensitive center again. "Fuck me."

"You've got a dirty mouth. You think a bad girl like you should get what she wants?"

"Yes. I promise I'll be a good girl." God, he was driving her crazy.

"We'll see about that. Tell me again what you want, Megan."

Talk? She could barely breathe. "I want you to fuck me, Aidan. Please."

The words barely left her mouth before Aidan pushed into her, opening her wide. Her loud gasp mixed with his growly "fuck." It was a thin line between pleasure and pain, and all she knew was that she wanted more.

"Holy shit, you're tight. Relax, baby. I'm not all the way in." Aidan's words were strained. "Breathe for me."

She relaxed her muscles that had a stranglehold on him, and he pulled out before slamming in again. This time he was fully inside her, in territory no man had ever been.

His fingers flexed on her hips, and he stayed still for several seconds. "Jesus, you feel amazing."

"So do you." She could barely form coherent sentences. All she could do was feel. He filled her up to the point she almost couldn't breathe.

But she needed friction, she needed him to move. His hands held her hips tight so she couldn't move, but God, she needed him to hit all those nerves again. She squeezed her inner muscles causing him to curse.

"Fuck, baby. You keep doing that it's going to be over before we really get started."

"Aidan, I want to feel more of you. Move inside me. Please."

"I just need a second," he rasped out.

She squeezed again, and his cock filled her more if that was possible, making them both moan. "You ready for me, Megan?"

"Yes, please. You're driving me crazy."

"I won't be gentle."

"I don't want gentle. Make me pay for being a tempting wench."

He ran a hand down her spine again, his touch soft, stroking. "You have been a bad girl."

"Yes, make me pay."

He leaned over her back and his voice was deep and hoarse against her ear. "Do you realize what you're asking of me? I just want to know what you can handle. And that you're okay with it."

She lifted a hand and ran it over the back of his neck, trying to soothe and let him know she was game for whatever he threw her way. "I can handle it, Aidan. I want you to ruin me for all other men."

She didn't have to let him know he'd already done that before they crossed this line. Megan wanted to take everything he was willing to give. If this was her only shot with Aidan, she was going to steal it like a thief.

"Shit, you're too good to be true." His voice sounded like he'd swallowed sand.

He lifted up off her and pulled almost all the way out before slamming back into her. She cried out with pleasure, and when he did it the next time, she pushed back as he pushed forward. He picked up the pace and wrapped a handful of hair in his fist. He pulled until she felt the beginnings of the pinprick of her scalp. It's like he inherently knew where that line was between pleasurable pain and flat-out savagery.

All she knew was that it was too much and not enough.

At one point, his hand lightly smacked her ass and it went straight to her core, making her clit vibrate. "More," she groaned out.

"You like that, bad girl?" His next slap stung and pushed her closer to the pinnacle.

"Yes."

Her skin was covered in a sheen of sweat, and oxygen was a premium commodity as Aidan continued to pound into her, anchoring her to him with his grip on her hips. The bed slammed against the wall with every thrust he made. Thrusts that pushed them closer and closer to that peak.

"You feel me growing inside you, baby? That's what you do to me. You make me crazy too." Still moving his hips against hers, he leaned forward and rubbed that bundle of nerves between her legs, making her see stars.

Megan could no longer form words. All she could do was feel as she reached the summit and watched the world explode around her before the descent.

Somehow she could manage to scream out one word against the bed, "Aidan!"

With a triumphant roar, he shouted her name and stilled against her. Deep inside her, his dick twitched as his release spilled into the latex.

He collapsed on her back and rolled them over in one motion so that he was behind her. They both panted as the smell of sex mixed with fabric softener from the sheets filled the air. It was erotic and made her smile.

When they'd caught their breath, Aidan moved away. "I'll be right back."

She lay there, still unable to really move, trying to bring her brain and body back online so she could tell him how he'd just rocked her whole fucking world.

Within a few moments, he was back, condom disposed of, and slid in behind her. He wrapped an arm around her waist and yanked her up against his chest. She snuggled her back against his front and closed her eyes.

Yeah, she could sleep for a hundred years, just like this.

"I'm sorry if I was rough." Aidan's voice was low and laced with something that sounded like regret.

Megan twisted around and faced him. His eyes were closed, and a worried crease formed between his eyes. He had the longest eyelashes she'd ever seen on a man. Her heart swooned thinking about how he worried so much about her. And how much he'd come to mean to her in such a short period of time.

She ran a finger between his brows, trying to soothe out the lines, and swallowed to catch her breath before speaking. "Aidan, look at me."

When he did, those blue eyes were an interesting combination of sated lust and concern. God, this man may be the death of her. "Don't apologize. I liked it rough. No, actually, I loved it rough."

His thumb traced the line of her bottom lip. "You sure I didn't hurt you?"

"Positive. You didn't hurt me." Her tongue darted out and swiped at his thumb on her lip.

The worry line faded away, and those eyes she found she wanted to just stare into anytime he was around darkened with desire, causing a slow simmer to start in her belly.

Good God. What was happening to her? Since when was having one—actually make that two—orgasms not enough?

And yet, her body was beginning that low, steady burn of desire building. She shifted closer to him, and to her delight, he cupped her cheek and tilted her face up to meet his eyes. For several seconds, all he did was look at her, his eyes roaming over her face. A slow smile curved those talented lips. "Megan, what have you done to me?"

She was just about to ask him the same question, but before she could answer, his mouth covered hers.

It was a kiss that made her toes curl.

━━━

"So what's the tattoo symbolize?"

They were lying face to face, tangled in the sheets. She didn't have a clue of the time and didn't care. All she knew was that she didn't want the night to end. She'd lost count of how many orgasms she'd had so far, and the longer she lay in the bed with him, touching him freely like he was hers, the harder it was to stay on her side of the bed.

It was made worse by the fact that his hand hadn't left her ass for the last several minutes.

Megan ran a fingertip over the black ink on his shoulder, studying the lines and letters of the dog tags he'd had permanently penned into his skin.

"The dog tags are for the guys I lost in my unit."

Her eyes flicked up to his. They were closed, but his breath was even, almost as though he were asleep. She rolled her teeth over her bottom lip, wanting to ask more but unsure if she should.

As she mulled it over, he opened his eyes and looked down at her. "I know you have a million questions, Gentry. You wouldn't be you if you didn't."

"Well, yeah. But I don't want to be insensitive."

"Ask away."

She raised a brow. "Seriously?"

"Yeah." He paused as something like resignation passed in his eyes. "I'm serious."

She snuggled closer to him but continued to trace the lines of the tattoo. She didn't want to break the connection of their touching. "Will you tell me what happened?"

He blinked and rolled his lips inward, not speaking for several moments. The silence stretched for so long that Megan started to tell him not to worry about it. Then he started to talk.

"It was during my last tour. I'd been pretty lucky up to that point. We'd had some men get injured, but we hadn't seen much action that time around. We only had a couple of weeks left to go and then we were headed home."

He stopped, and his eyes glazed over, as though reliving whatever it was he went through.

"We had some intel that told us there were some guys holed up in an abandoned building making bombs. It was dark and quiet. We could hear a couple of guys talking. I knew enough of the language to know that they were talking about the bombs."

His nostrils flared as he exhaled. "They started to laugh, which I thought was odd, given the circumstances and what they'd been talking about. I realized they were laughing because they'd rigged parts of the building. And we had no idea where."

Megan had an idea of where this was going and her heart broke for him. She wanted to soothe him, say something to ease the pain, but for once in her life, she had no words. So she kept her mouth shut and continued to stroke his skin.

"One of the guys tripped a wire. Took out him and the two guys around him. After that it was chaos. The building was old, made of crumbling stone, so it started to fall apart." He stopped and sighed, his gaze meeting hers. "We went in with seven and came out with three. It was my last tour. I figured if I couldn't protect my unit, I didn't belong there."

Aidan Reynolds was without a doubt a protector in every facet of his life.

"Four tags—one for each guy lost."

He nodded.

"And this is why you don't sleep well."

He nodded again. "I'm better than I used to be. I don't have nightmares anymore. It's been a while now."

But being who he was, Megan would bet her next breath that the guilt weighed on him like a cinder block. She leaned forward to read the words on his skin. "What are these numbers under their names?"

"The service number and military ID. The dates are…"

"Their birth and death dates." Her heart broke in two for this man who seemed so confident in his ability, so sure of himself and keeping all of those he loved safe.

She swallowed against the knot forming in her throat. Again, Megan had no words that would comfort him. But she did have other ways.

Leaning forward, she dropped kisses on each of the tags. A small sigh escaped his lips, and she moved her way across his collar bone and up his throat, where his Adam's apple bobbed and his pulse bumped. "Megan…" her name came out on a low, guttural breath.

It was all the encouragement she needed.

She pulled the sheet away from them and pushed him onto his back, straddling his lap. Her hands roamed the expanse of his chest, and she moved her hips over his hard length. He groaned and gripped her hips. "Hmmmm…Megan. You're teasing me."

"Shhhh…I'll take care of you." She leaned down and pressed her breasts against his hard chest. She placed a kiss under the lobe of his ear. "I want to feel you. All of you. I'm clean and on the pill."

His hands ran up her spine, fisting in her hair. He gently tugged and she pulled back until their eyes met. "I just had a physical. I'm good."

Her lips curved and she raised up on her knees. With her eyes on his, she lined his cock up with her entrance and sank down on him. Their gasps and groans filled the room.

He filled her to nearly bursting and when she moved, taking him in and out, he hit every single one of her nerves. Even though she'd had more orgasms with him than she'd had in the last year, she was close again. And wouldn't last long if she went any faster.

With her hands flat on his chest and his hands in a vise grip on her hips, she moved slowly. She wanted to feel every inch of him, every vein, every groove before they both exploded into bliss.

He bared his teeth but never said a word as their gazes held. She'd learned Aidan was a dirty talker in the bedroom, but it was as though they'd made a silent agreement to just let their bodies do the talking this time around.

It didn't take long for their desire to ignite further. She dropped her head back and her breaths came out in small pants as she moved her hips faster over his, taking him deeper. Her hands curled into his chest, her fingernails scraping his skin.

He grunted and thrust his hips up into her every time she came down. Her mouth dropped open as his thrusts went deep and hit that spot that would soon detonate.

Soon, their motions were more erratic and frenzied.

"Fuck, I'm going to come." He ground out the words as she encouraged him on with a hip tilt when their hips met. That growl from him when she did that only spurred her on as well.

All she could do was whimper as the world around her narrowed down to a pinpoint before exploding in an inferno that burned hotter when he came deep inside her.

Megan fell onto his chest, both of them panting and slick with a sheen of sweat.

"You're going to be the death of me, woman," Aidan said between heavy breaths.

"Same, man."

She turned her head and kissed his chest before sliding off him. He got up and came back a few moments later with a warm washcloth and dry towel. With tender movements, he cleaned her up and kissed her belly. The action caused a warm flutter there that had nothing to do with desire and everything to do with an emotion she wouldn't allow herself to feel.

He threw the towels into the hamper and curled up behind her. "Night, baby."

"Night." The words came out as a whisper because her throat was clogged with emotion.

She reminded herself this was just fun and to go with it. His breaths became slower, his chest rising and falling against her back in a steady rhythm.

If this was all she had, then so be it. She was going to enjoy the ride while it lasted.

CHAPTER FOURTEEN

pancakes &
polaroids

THE SOUNDS of pans clanging woke Megan. Face down on the bed, she lifted her head, sniffing the air and smiling when the smells of bacon, pancakes, and coffee hit her nose.

She rolled over and stretched her arms over her head and pointed her toes. Her body was more relaxed that she'd been in…well, had she ever been this relaxed? Raising up on her elbows, she looked over at her phone to see it was early. Six a.m. early.

After wrapping the sheet around her body, Megan followed the sound of music into the kitchen and stopped at the sight that greeted her.

Aidan stood at the stove, in nothing but a pair of black sweatpants that hung low on his hips, flipping a pancake in one pan and eggs in the other. He sang along to "Feels Like the First Time," which couldn't be more appropriate. She leaned against the wall and just watched, her blood starting to hum.

The muscles in his back danced when he moved. Just the simple act of moving the pan set off a ripple that made her lady parts sit up and take notice. And the man actually moved quite well to the music. No wonder he was amazing in bed. He knew how to use that body in a number of ways.

When he started singing along to the chorus, she smiled and rubbed at the base of her neck, swallowing hard. Sweat broke out on the back of her neck. She wanted to fan her face, but she wanted to continue her unobserved appraisal.

How fair was it that this man looked like *that*, could cook, had that hot protector thing going on, and could sing? It didn't seem fair. It was a wonder he had any friends.

But that was the other thing about him. He could be grumpy, but for some reason, that just endeared the townspeople to him. Then again, after seeing him with his brothers and cousin the night before, she had to wonder what the rest of the clan looked like. There was a lot of beauty in that gene pool.

He turned from the stove to the island where two plates sat ready to do their duty. He glanced up and did a double take when he saw her. If she'd been wearing any panties, they would have melted on the spot at the smoldering look he gave her. "Good morning."

Damn, that sexy rasp danced along her skin just as it had before. She had really hoped she'd be more immune to his charms after she'd been properly fucked by him. Judging by her body's reactions though, it appeared she was at his mercy.

Not that she was going to show him that little tidbit.

She returned his smile. "Good morning."

He plated the pancakes and eggs. "Hungry?"

She walked closer to the other side of the island. "Famished. I had a long night of physical activity."

He chuckled and bit into a piece of bacon. Her nipples hardened as though remembering the feel of those teeth scraping against them. "You and me both. Take a seat and I'll bring the plates over. Syrup?"

"Yes." The one syllable was all she could manage around the desire that had grabbed her by the throat.

When he set the plate in front of her a few moments later, he put a finger under her chin to tilt her head back. "Hello, beautiful." He lowered his mouth to hers in a sweet kiss that made her heart swoon right out of her chest.

"Hello, handsome," she said when they came up for air.

She looked down at the plate in front of her and her mouth dropped. "How did you know what kind of eggs I liked?"

He set the coffee down before taking the seat next to hers at the small square table. "Lucky guess. You just strike me as someone who'd like her eggs sunny side up. They're a little messy, but delicious, just like you." He leaned over and kissed the side of her neck, his stubble tickling her sensitive skin. Then he looked at her plate as though making sure that's what he'd cooked. "Are they okay?"

She nodded as tears inexplicably filled her eyes. He was too much. How did he notice all those little details? She covered up her mini emotional meltdown by taking a gulp of the piping hot coffee, which promptly sent her into a coughing fit.

Just perfect. At least now she could explain her teary eyes.

"Jesus, Megan, are you okay?" Aidan's face was pinched with concern, and he reached over to pat her on the back.

She lifted a hand to stop him from touching her. If he touched her bare skin right now, she might do something super mortifying like melt into a puddle on the floor. "I'm good." When his eyes narrowed, she said, "I promise."

A couple of minutes ticked by in silence while they both shoveled in some food. To Megan's surprise, though, it was a comfortable silence, even after her little awkward coughing fit. Not what usually happened the morning after for her.

But she still needed to talk. Needed to know what happened from here.

Megan chewed and swallowed before she spoke. "This is delicious, Aidan. Thank you."

"You're welcome. You work tonight?"

"Yeah. How about you?"

"I'm second shift today." He sipped his coffee—like a normal human would with hot beverages—and looked her in the eye. "Want me to stop by the bar? Pick you up later?"

Her lips tilted up. "I'd like that. But only if the end result of tonight is a replay of last night."

There. She'd laid down the gauntlet. Let's see what he did with it.

He took her small hand in his warm, larger one and brought it to his lips. His blue eyes were like twin flames as he looked at her over their joined hands. "That's a guarantee."

The butterflies in her belly that had started to flap took flight. And her heart did a slow flip in her chest, making it hard for her to breathe for a moment. "Really?"

"Yeah. Unless, that is, you don't want to."

She swirled her fork through the syrup pooling on her plate, unable to meet his eyes. "I just thought you might be one and done."

He stared at her for a moment before dropping her hand. As quickly as her happiness set in, it fell away. Was it something she'd said? But then he pushed out his chair and motioned her over. "Come here."

When she stood and started around the table, he snagged her waist and pulled her into his lap, wrapping his arms around her waist. She fell onto that warm chest, and when her bare shoulders touched his skin, sparks set off like little fireworks.

Aidan pinched her chin to bring her gaze to his. "Listen to me. Are you listening?"

She nodded, her heart racing in anticipation of what he was about to say. Would it destroy her?

"Good. While you're here, there will be no one else but you. I don't want anyone else but you. Hell, I haven't wanted anyone else since you showed up in town. And I haven't been with anyone in a while now."

She smiled, but shifted her gaze to where his pulse bumped in his neck before looking back up at him. "I want you too. It's been a while for me as well." She sighed. "But I am leaving in a few weeks."

"I know." His tone was solid and strong, sure. But for a split second, there had been a shadow that crossed his eyes before that confidence settled back in. He paused for a moment as though mulling something over. Finally, he tapped her leg. "I have something for you."

"For me?" she asked as she stood.

He didn't answer, just crossed the living space and headed up to the loft. A few minutes later, he returned with a medium sized rectangular cardboard box in his hand. He dropped into his chair and pulled her back in his lap before setting the box in hers.

"What's this?" she asked.

"Just a little something I found the other day."

She smiled and lifted the edge of one flap so that all of them opened. When she pushed aside the white tissue paper, she gasped. "Oh my God, Aidan. Where did you find this?"

"In one of the antique shops in town."

With both hands, Megan lifted the vintage Polaroid camera and turned it from side to side. "It looks just like the one we had when I was a kid." She pulled on the top and when it popped out, she laughed in surprise. Aidan's bare chest rumbled against her back when he chuckled.

"I don't know a lot about cameras but this one was in the display window at the Old Towne Antique Shop. When I saw it, I thought of you."

She swallowed back tears that wanted to clog her throat, and for a moment she couldn't speak. Memories of her parents and Nate flashed through her mind. It was bittersweet to think about that time, and the grief rushed back in, overwhelming her.

Aidan rustled around in the box and produced a blue and white box of film. "Art, the owner, actually had two boxes of film for it that weren't expired. He put one in the camera and said you could actually buy it online." He chuckled. "I didn't even know they still made film for cameras like this."

She continued to stare at the camera as the memories faded and Aidan's deep voice brought her back to the present. A tear rolled down her cheek, and she brushed it away but not before he saw it.

"Megan? Why are you crying?" His body tensed under her and his eyes widened.

She nearly laughed at the panicked look on his face. "Don't worry, Aid." She patted his chest—his warm, smooth, bare chest. Between that and his thoughtful gift her insides were beginning to warm again. "These are happy tears, I promise."

The knitted brow and crease that formed between his eyes when he was worried eased away. "Okay, good. It's never good for a guy's ego when he gives a girl a gift and she starts crying."

She hugged the camera to her chest and leaned forward, kissing his cheek. "It's the best, most thoughtful gift anyone has ever given me."

A growling sound came from his throat, and his hands began exploring, setting off those fireworks along her skin. "I've got some other places I'd rather have you kiss me..."

She wiggled against his growing erection. "I know you do, but first let's take a picture."

"Megan...No." His tone was a warning. One she ignored.

"Please?" She leaned forward and rubbed her nose against the side of his neck, his Adam's apple bobbing when she let her tongue take a swipe against his skin. "I'll make it worth your while."

"Fine," he growled out. "Take a picture."

She let out a little squeal and positioned herself in his lap, leaning back against his chest, and stretched her arms out. He dipped his chin to her shoulder. "Smile!" she said.

She pushed the button, and the camera whirled for a couple of seconds before spitting out the picture. Megan pulled it out and said before he could shift, "Another one!"

He rolled his eyes but didn't protest. Especially when she moved in close, snuggling up to him. "Hmmm...I like that."

Aidan ended up letting her take two more—one of her kissing his cheek and one of him nibbling on her neck—before he took it from her hands. "Okay, enough for now. We've got other plans."

She moved off his lap, but her feet barely touched the floor before she found herself upside down over his shoulder. "Aidan! What are you doing?"

"I need to show you all those places that I need kissed. And we've got a couple of hours before I need to be at work." He smacked her sheet-covered ass, and all she could do was laugh when she barely felt it.

"Well, I guess we'd better get to work then."

He laid her down on the bed, tearing the sheet away from her body and shucking his sweatpants. When he covered her body with his, her body hummed, and she closed her eyes giving herself over to his kisses.

CHAPTER FIFTEEN

one way ticket

THE FOLLOWING Saturday dawned cool and sunny, and the waning day promised a crisp, clear fall night, perfect for the festivities that had taken over the town square.

The week leading up to the fall festival in town had made Megan's head spin. The Silver Moon and the sheriff's department were both geared up for the tourists that descended on the normally quiet, small town by the end of the week. Even though Megan had grown up in cities, she expected the chaos there. It was unexpected for a mountain town.

Marcus had hired on a few college students to help serve for the season, which Charley told her started with the fall festival and didn't let up until New Year's. He'd already hired another bartender in anticipation of her impending departure, which was the only reason she was able to work the day shift that Saturday and meet Aidan for the festival.

Megan did her best not to think about the fact that her time in Madison Ridge was coming to a close. She'd heard from Jake at the beginning of the week letting her know that all but one of the parts he needed had come in and the repairs were moving along nicely.

And while she and Aidan hadn't seen each other all that much over the past week, when they did, they had a hard time keeping their hands to themselves. The man's appetite was voracious, and it seemed he could exist on a couple of hours of sleep. Megan caught herself yawning in the middle of her shift a couple of times but managed to cover it up.The truth was she felt amazing. Sure, she'd traded beauty rest for phenomenal sex, but she'd once read orgasms made the skin glow and she was all for that.

Her skin must be positively radiant right about now.

Megan wasn't sure she'd ever had so many orgasms in her life, certainly not in one week, and definitely not more than two in one night. Aidan had shattered that record a couple of nights before. Just thinking about it made her skin tingle and her panties damp.

What the hell was she going to do when she left?

"Okay, chickadee. What's going on with you?" Charley sidled up next to the bar where Megan was arranging bottles. Or was supposed to be arranging bottles for the next shift.

"Nothing's going on. Why?"

"Because you've been staring at that wall of liquor like you've never seen it before, and I've watched you try to cover up yawning for the last hour. I give a solid A for effort, though."

Maybe she wasn't hiding the no sleep thing as well as she thought.

"I just didn't get a lot of sleep last night."

"Really?" Charley drew out the two syllable word into four.

"Yep. Just a case of insomnia is all."

Charley nodded. "Must be something about that cabin. I saw Aidan earlier today at the bakery, and he said the same thing when I asked why he was dragging ass."

Just hearing the man's name made her pulse bump harder. And then snatches of their nightly antics would play in her head like a montage in a movie. Heat grew in her face.

"Hello, Megan?" Charley snapped her fingers in front of Megan's face.

Megan jerked her head back and looked over at Charley. "What?" She sighed and shook off the daydreams, facing her friend squarely. "Charley, I'm fine. I promise."

The younger woman crossed her arms over the black T-shirt she had on for work, a frown on her lips. "You finally did the deed with Aidan, didn't you?"

Megan couldn't tell if Charley thought that was a good thing or bad thing, so she hedged. "What makes you think that?"

Charley rolled her eyes. "Please. The two of you were eye-fucking each other all night long last weekend. And every time I've seen either of you this week, you've had this combination of tired and yet glowing look about you. That can only mean one thing—amazing sex."

Megan bit her lip. "Would it bother you if we were?"

"Well, you just answered my question. But honestly? Hell, no." She scrunched up her nose and held up both hands. "But please. No details. I love my brother to death and I know that women find him attractive. But he's still my brother."

"Charley, your brother is fucking hot."

Charley shook her head and stuck her fingers in her ears. "La la la la, I can't hear you."

Megan laughed, and Charley dropped her hands. "Seriously though, I get all that but I just can't hear details. I want to know nothing about my brothers' sex lives. But I do think it's about time he actually found someone for more than a quick fuck."

"Charley, we've only known each other for a couple of weeks."

Charley grabbed a water out of the small fridge under the bar and hoisted herself up on it. She shrugged and opened the plastic bottle. "So what? Aidan's liked you ever since the car accident."

"What? No, he hasn't."

Charley took a long sip and swallowed before nodding. "Yeah, he has. I know my brother. He's protective by nature."

"Well, see? That's all he was doing. His civic duty."

"His civic duty doesn't extend to giving up his bed to a complete stranger. Trust me. He knows enough people that he could have found you a place to stay. Aidan likes being alone. He likes his space and freedom. You're staying with him still because he wants you there." She paused, looking Megan over. "Not to mention he looks at you a certain way."

"What kind of way?"

"The way Reynolds men do when they find their person. I saw it with my dad and I've seen it with Del and Addison and Landon with Iris."

"I thought Landon's last name was Grey."

"It is, but his mother is a Reynolds. It's in the blood."

Megan reached over and straightened a bottle of whiskey, ruminating over what Charley said. She didn't really believe that. Things were different now, but there's no way a guy like Aidan would have offered up his space unless he saw no other way out.

"Well, your mom had actually offered up her second bedroom. But she called me this week and said that with all the work she's had to do with the festival, she hasn't had time to get the room cleaned up."

Charley's smile widened until she busted out laughing.

"What?" Megan asked, bewildered.

"Oh gosh." Charley wiped out her eyes, still chuckling. She sighed before looking at Megan, smile still in place. "My mother never said a word to me about cleaning out that room for you, or I would have helped her get a move on it."

"She didn't…? Hold on." Megan's brow knitted in confusion. "Why would she say that then? Your mother doesn't strike me as a woman to make empty promises."

Charley swung her legs in front of the bar, playing with the cap on her water bottle. "She's not. But after she gave it some thought, she let it fall by the wayside." She held up a hand when Megan opened her mouth to protest. "My guess is that Stella is trying to get another one of her kids to find their soulmate. She worries about Aidan."

"Why does she worry?"

Charley looked down at the smart watch on her wrist and jumped down off the bar. "She has her reasons. I gotta go get ready, shift starts soon. That new guy on bar tonight?"

"Yep. What time is it?"

"Quarter to six."

"Oh shit! I'm supposed to meet Aidan at the station at six." She signed off on the closing checklist and shoved it in the drawer.

"Really, now?" Charley was hot on her heels as Megan ducked under the service bar and headed toward the hallway that led back to the employees only area. "Got a date?"

Megan pushed open the door to the employee lounge that held lockers and an area for the employees to take a quick breather. It was an area Megan appreciated and while small, was nicer than other bars she'd worked in.

She went to her locker and pulled out the blouse she'd brought to change into. "I guess you'd call it that. I don't know. He told me about the pumpkin challenge and offered to take me to the festival tonight to see the reveal."

Charley sat on the bench, straddling it. "See? I'm telling you. He likes you." She clapped her hands. "This makes me so happy. We could be sisters!"

Megan pulled her T-shirt off and pulled the snug, scoop-neck blouse over her head. "Charley, you have sisters," she said with a wry smile, sticking her arms through the sleeves.

"Yeah, but you know what I mean."

"Also, I'm leaving in a couple of weeks. Once my car is done."

"Yeah, but what about long distance?"

"I don't know. We haven't talked about that. We're just having fun right now. Enjoying each other's company."

Charley sighed and looked down, rubbing her hands over her knees. Her voice was quiet when she spoke. "Aidan took care of me after our father died. He shielded me from a lot of things, and with my other brothers being so much older, he was like my brother-slash-father figure."

She looked up at Megan, the same blue eyes as the brother she loved so much shining with unshed tears. "I just want to see Aid happy. And he's happy with you, Megan."

Megan's heart broke for the young woman in front of her and her family that lost a man that meant so much to them way too soon. It was a feeling she knew well having been so young when her parents had died. And she understood Charley's bond with Aidan because she had the same bond with Nate. Though they'd never really gone into great detail about their stories, it was as though she and Charley recognized kindred spirits.

She pulled her purse and jacket out, shutting the locker with a metal clang before going over to Charley. Megan pulled Charley to her feet and hugged her.

Neither spoke for a few minutes while Charley clung to her. When Megan pulled back, she smiled at Charley and brushed a wayward hair out of her eyes. At that moment, Megan's heart swelled with something like love and longing for her own sibling. "Thanks for saying that. Aidan makes me happy too. We'll just see what happens, you know? My life is in such disarray right now, I'm just trying to take things one day at a time. But for now, I gotta go."

They said their goodbyes and Megan waved at the incoming crew as she hustled out the door.

But she couldn't help but think about what Charley had said as she walked along the square on her way to the station. What *were* they going to do once her time in town was over? There was an ache in the back of her throat when she thought about leaving. Leaving the town, Charley, and most of all, Aidan. The thought of not seeing him every day left a hollow feeling in her gut that she didn't care for at all.

But she'd lived her life long enough for a man. For the first time in her life, she was unattached, untethered to a plus one, and she wanted to give that life a chance before she hitched her wagon to someone else. She needed to figure out who she was without a man.

Didn't mean she couldn't have some scorching hot sex with a hot-as-sin small town deputy sheriff in the meantime though.

The thought of said man made her smile, and she picked up the pace, the station just a block away. The outside lights burned bright in the fading daylight, acting like a beacon for her.

The door was open as always—since there were no "closed" hours for law enforcement—but the tiny lobby and front office area were empty.

"Hello?" she called out, walking toward the front desk. She craned her neck and found the door to Aidan's office at the end of the hall was closed.

She called out again a little louder this time, and his door opened. The man who had dominated her thoughts for nearly three weeks—ever since she'd met him—filled the doorway. He had his cell phone at his ear and a frown marred his lips.

God, even with a frown, the man made her heart rate accelerate.

But when he realized it was her, his lips curved into a glacier-melting smile and he gestured for her to come on back.

Megan walked toward him, her eyes never leaving him.

There really was something about a man in uniform. From the Madison Ridge Sheriff's department black polo that stretched across his chest, down to the khaki cargo pants that made him look impossibly tall and rugged, to the ass-kicker combat boots he wore on the job, Aidan Reynolds made her blood run like molten lava.

He interjected a "yeah" or "no" here and there, but his gaze blazed a trail over her from head to toe, causing her belly to jump at the heat in his eyes that lured her in. When she walked past him at the doorway, she made sure to brush close to him, give him a little taste of his own medicine.

The man made her feel like she had a one-way ticket to Lustville. Hell, at this point she was the mayor and permanent resident.

The door shut with a quiet click that ricocheted in the small office. She turned to face him as he stood behind the desk, his eyes never leaving hers, but he lifted a finger signaling for her to give him a minute. With a smirk, she nodded but turned on her heels and walked over to the one window in his office. With a glance over her shoulder and a yank of the cord, the slats of the blinds folded, closing off the view of the town.

He tilted his head in question and said something into the phone. The primal thump of her heartbeat in her ears drowned out everything. She wanted him in her mouth, wanted to be in command of the man who was in command of the office they stood in and the town beyond the walls. She wanted to break his control that he held on to so tightly in a place other than the four walls of the cabin.

She wanted to be a bad girl and have him punish her for it in the way only Aidan could.

Her body on fire and her mind set on giving him something to remember long after she left, Megan crossed the room to stand in front of him. When she lowered to her knees, his jaw tightened, and the words he spoke into the phone faltered slightly.

With her eyes on his, she unbuttoned his jeans and lowered the zipper. The rasp of the metal was magnified in the quiet of the room since whoever was on the other end of the phone was speaking. Megan's eyes dropped to his erection as she rubbed her hand up and down the length through the cotton boxer briefs. It jerked at her touch and became impossibly harder and longer, the crown poking up at the waistband. Aidan cleared his throat and tried to speak into the phone.

She released his cock from its confines and wrapped it in her hand, giving it a couple of long tugs from root to tip. Just like everything about this man, even his penis was a work of art. It was swollen and waiting for her mouth. Her mouth that watered.

He coughed, and she glanced up to find his gaze hot on her. When she ran her hand up and down the hard length again, he canted his hips forward. When he tried to put his hand on her head, she moved out of his reach and wagged a finger at him with a cheeky grin. He rolled his eyes with a heavy sigh but put his hand back on his hip, letting her take the lead.

She laid her hands on his hips and licked the head like it was the best lollipop she'd ever had, swirling her tongue around the engorged end before dipping into the slit where it weeped with precum. She groaned and looked up at him when she flattened her tongue against him and took him deep into her mouth. God, he tasted amazing. It was an erotic combination of soap and salty man.

He covered up his groan with a cough. "Yeah. I get it. Look, sheriff, I've uh…I've had an emergency come up…no, it's fine. Nothing serious, but I…uh…"

His voice faltered and he squeezed his eyes shut for a moment before he could continue. "I've got to take care of an issue."

Their eyes met as her mouth closed around him again and moved up and down his shaft. Each time she took him in, she left him slick, making it easier for her to take in his full length. When he hit the back of her throat, he ground out into the phone. "Talk later."

He threw the phone on the desk and grabbed her ponytail in one hand and lifted his shirt with the other. His eyes blazed blue fire. "Fuck…"

His hand fisted in his shirt holding it out of the way, his abs contracting and releasing with each thrust. He panted every time he pushed into her mouth.

"You want me to fuck your amazing mouth? That what you want? You dirty girl." With her mouth full of him, all she could do was nod and hum her agreement. His eyes nearly rolled into the back of his head.

Megan wasn't sure she'd ever been so turned on in her life. Watching Aidan be vulnerable with her when he was one of the strongest men she knew was the sexiest thing she'd ever seen.

She wasn't sure why she bothered with underwear when he was around. It either ended up off her or so wet she had to take them off.

Aidan guided her up and down his long length, his breathing changed to a pant, and, if it were possible, he grew bigger in her mouth. "I'm close, baby. So close."

Megan wanted to help him chase down that release, give him all that she could and take all that he wanted to give. She picked up the pace and his hips bucked into her mouth.

"Shit, Megan. I'm gonna come. Fuuucckkkk..."

His groan was low and guttural as rope after rope of his release hit the back of her throat. His grip on her hair loosened and he slumped against his desk, his eyes closed as he tried to regain his breath.

She sat back on her haunches, wiping the corners of her mouth with her index finger and licking her lips. She couldn't stop the grin forming on her lips if she tried. "You okay?" she asked.

He opened his eyes and held out his hand, helping her to her feet before tucking himself in and zipping up. "I'm fucking fantastic." Pinching her chin, he lifted it up and lowered his mouth to hers. It was a slow, sweet kiss, a nibble of her lips before he pulled back then leaned his forehead on hers. "Hi. I missed you today."

When he said things like that, causing her heart to go into free fall, showing her a side that he showed only a select few people, she wondered what the hell they were doing. And how the hell she was going to continue life post Aidan.

"I missed you too."

It was the truth and that was the shitty part of the deal. But she pushed the nagging thoughts away. One day at a time, isn't that what she'd told Charley? She needed to heed her own advice.

He lifted his head and looked down at her through narrowed eyes and a crooked smile. "You're a bad girl, Megan."

She bobbed her head side to side. "I don't know. Maybe?"

"You know what happens to bad girls?"

"Are you going to show me?" God, she really hoped he'd show her.

His eyes darkened and he licked his lips. "I am. But you'll have to wait until we get home. We're running late."

She dropped her jaw. "You're going to make me wait?"

He chuckled and dropped a quick hard kiss to her lips. "Consider this phase one of the punishment."

CHAPTER SIXTEEN
friendly competition

PUNISHMENT INDEED.

Walking around the town square with a crowd of people, being stopped here and there by various townsfolk, should have put the kibosh on his caveman need to haul Megan over his shoulder and take her home. He couldn't wait to get between those creamy thighs with his tongue and his dick, make her scream his name in a way that both soothed and aroused him.

But being near her, walking side by side in the crisp night air did nothing to abate that need.

It didn't help that she looked hot as fuck. Again. With the snug scoop neck, fire engine-red shirt that matched her fire engine-red lips, tight black jeans, topped with a black leather jacket and matching heeled boots, she was mouthwatering in a bad girl, rocker chick way. It drove him wild.

When she'd walked toward him in his office, all thought left the head on his shoulders and traveled south so fast he'd been lightheaded and simultaneously granite hard. He'd hardly been able to speak to the sheriff regarding the upcoming holidays, much less come up with a coherent thought. And then when she'd dropped to her knees and pulled his dick out, sucking him off and blowing his mind?

It'd taken all he had to get the guy off the phone.

Yeah, he was going to enjoy paying her back in kind when they got home.

Home. When had he started thinking of his cabin becoming their home? Sure, that's where they'd both end up tonight, but he could have thought *his house* or *the cabin.* But no, he'd used *home,* which for him had always equated to family and love. Yet, it had rolled through his mind with zero thought. As though it were normal.

What the fuck?

"Ooohhhh, I love this game." Megan stopped in front of the Skee-Ball booth and turned to him, a huge grin on her face. "Let's play."

She picked up one of the wooden balls and tossed it up, catching it in her hand. With a shapely hip jutted out, she smirked. "I'm pretty good at this game. I bet I can kick your ass."

Aidan pushed away the thoughts that had started to form in his mind. He was making too big of a deal of it. It was a normal thing to say. His cop brain was reading way too much into it.

He had a hot date and a competitive streak a mile wide. *That* was what he needed to focus on.

He walked closer and caught the ball in midair. "Are you now? Well, I'll have you know that I'm better than pretty good. I'm a master."

She rolled those beautiful hazel eyes. "A master? Says who?"

"If you went to Mountain Arcade, you'd find my name is still at the top of the leaderboard from when I was fourteen."

Megan stared at him for several long beats before bursting into giggles. "Okay, there's a lot to unpack there. First,"—she ticked off on a finger—"you guys still have a bona fide arcade here? Not a Dave & Buster's kind of thing but an old-fashioned, honest-to-God arcade?"

"Complete with the smell of mildew, seizure-inducing noise, frozen pizza, watered-down sodas, and hand-dipped ice cream."

"Wow. Okay. And second, I'm still going to kick your ass."

Aidan laughed a real laugh—something that he seemed to do more in the last two weeks with her than he had in the last several years—and pulled her close, dropping a kiss to her forehead. "It's cute you think so."

Megan nodded. "Okay, you asked for it, man."

"I'll even let you go first." He tossed the wood ball back to her, which she caught against her chest, while he paid the booth attendant, a local high schooler, for two games. "Thanks, Ricky."

"Sure thing."

She shook her arms out before shoving the sleeves of her jacket up to her elbows and leaning over at the waist, getting into a throwing stance. Then she stood up straight. "Loser buys me a hot dog and a funnel cake."

"Are you saying I'm going to lose?"

She spared him a glance. "I like mustard on my dog and cinnamon sugar on my funnel cake, Reynolds."

"Just shoot the ball, Gentry."

Ten balls later, Aidan's jaw hung open and the booth attendant watched in growing fascination. She'd hit a bullseye on nearly every single shot. Not a single one rolled into the dreaded ten point hole at the bottom.

She turned to him, hands on her hips and a smug smile on her lips. "You're up, lawman."

They traded places and she dropped a ball into his hand. He blew out a breath. *Calm down, man. It's just a friendly game of Skee-Ball. You got this.*

After the first four balls hit the bullseyes, satisfaction began to hum on his skin and a small smile lifted one side of his mouth. Out of the corner of his eye, he noticed movement. He made the grave mistake of looking over to find Megan shedding her jacket, that snug red shirt a beacon to his horny soul.

He was leaned over, his head turned to look at her. When she noticed, she smiled and wiggled her fingers in a wave. "Don't mind me, I'm just getting hot."

With her jacket folded over one arm, she tossed her head back, her long ponytail—that had fallen like a dark waterfall over his fist in his office—swinging down her back. Her head came back down and she fanned her face. "Warm, don't you think?"

Her eyes danced in mischief, and his gaze traveled down to her breasts where her nipples stood like hard points, a siren song to that caveman inside him lurking to spring free. His crotch grew tight in his cargo pants and he glanced over at the young man. "Ricky," he barked.

The young pimply-faced kid turned the color of Megan's shirt at being caught ogling her. He snapped his mouth closed. "Sorry, sir," he mumbled.

When Megan only smiled innocently, Aidan blew out a breath. "Son of a bitch," he muttered.

The next two balls bounced off the back wall and ended up in the large circle with the least amount of points. He had four more chances to bring his score up but even if he hit the bullseye, he wasn't sure he could do it.

He shot four more times and ended up thirty points shy. Megan clapped her hands and bounced on her toes when she turned to Ricky. To Aidan's dismay, her jacket had magically ended up back on her body. "What do I win?"

Ricky showed her the wall of huge stuffed animals, and she chose a large yellow-and-black striped tiger. When she hugged it to her face, Aidan couldn't help but laugh and kiss her smiling lips.

"You didn't play fair, beautiful. You really are a bad girl."

Her eyes gleamed, and her full lips curved in a smile that nearly stopped his heart. The lust she was giving off in waves to him was in complete contrast to the stuffed animal against her cheek. "Are you going to show me just how bad I've been?" Her voice dropped to where only he could hear.

"You bet your ass I am."

"Good." She slipped her hand in his and tucked the animal under her arm. "I'm ready for food now."

"Let's go. Let me take that." The damn tiger was nearly as big as she was.

They walked toward the row of food trucks and trailers showing their wares at a slow leisurely pace, bantering back and forth about the Skee-Ball game.

"Aidan!"

He turned to find a couple he went to school with walking toward them.

"Margot, Rob. How are you guys?"

"Good, how about you?" Margot asked, her gaze wandering over Megan with curiosity.

"Good. This is Megan Gentry. Megan, this is Margot and Rob Davidson and their daughter, Abby."

Margot extended her hand. "Megan, it's nice to meet you. I've heard a lot about you."

Megan's smile stayed in place while her gaze slid to Aidan's for a second before focusing back on his old high school friend. *How does she know about me?* her gaze asked.

"Well, it's nice to meet friends of Aidan's." She looked down at the little girl. "Especially pretty girls like you. I love that pumpkin shirt. So pretty with all the glitter."

Abby looked up at Megan, her big blue eyes wide. "Do you like glitter?"

Megan nodded. "I love glitter."

Abby nodded. "Me too, but mama says it makes a big mess. But I just love it so much she lets me wear it anyway."

The adults chuckled before Abby pointed at the tiger tucked under Aidan's arm. "Is that yours?" she asked around a finger in her mouth.

"It's actually Megan's. I won it for her playing Skee-Ball."

To her credit, Megan didn't correct him, just narrowed her eyes and pursed her lips trying to hold back a smile.

"Is that true?" the little girl asked. "Is he your prince or something?"

Margot dropped her forehead into a hand. "Oh no. I'm sorry. She's obsessed with everything Disney princess."

"Do you like Disney princesses, Miss Megan?"

"I do. Hey," Megan's hand slid out of his when she crouched down to get eye level with the girl. "Do you like that tiger?"

Abby glanced up at the tiger and back to her, nodding.

"Okay, well if it's okay with your mom and dad, I'd love for you to take it and give it a good home."

Abby spun around, her dark hair swinging around with the motion. "Daddy, please? I know you tried so hard earlier to get me a stuffed alligator but I'd be happy with a tiger. Please? Please?"

Rob smiled down at her and sighed. "Yes, you can have it."

The little girl jumped up and down as Aidan handed it over to Megan to give to Abby.

"Now, you have to promise to take great care of him, or her, whatever you decide, okay?"

The end of the tiger's tail dragged the ground as Abby swung back and forth, her arms wrapped around its neck, her cheek resting against the head of the stuffed animal.

Aidan was struck by a vision that nearly brought him to his knees. The vision of a little girl with Megan's dark hair and his blue eyes. He could see it in technicolor and it caused his vision to blur.

"...Aidan."

He tuned back in when he heard his name. "I'm sorry, what?"

Rob looked at him funny for a second before saying, "I was just thanking you. You okay, man? You zoned out for a minute."

"Uh, yeah. Fine. Sorry about that."

Rob clapped him on the back. "No worries, man. Y'all let me know if you need any volunteers for the parades again this year. I'd be more than happy to help with crowd control."

"Will do, buddy. You know I'll take you up on that."

They shook hands, and everyone said their goodbyes before they parted ways.

Megan sighed and slid her hand back into his before snuggling up to his arm. "What a sweet little family. Abby is so stinking cute."

"She is. They tried a while with no luck. It took an anniversary trip to Vegas to get Margot pregnant."

Megan laughed, her smile huge. "I love stories like that." They walked a few more moments and closed in on food row as it was dubbed. The smells of sweet funnel cake, hot dogs, pizza, peppers, and turkey legs all mingled together to form an intoxicating scent that would always remind Aidan of the festival.

"You ever thought of having kids?" she asked.

He looked away and swallowed before answering. "Once upon a time I did. But things change."

"Things like what?"

He shrugged. "Just life. Things don't always end up how you expect them to."

All he had to do was look at his parents as an example and at how devastated his mother had been at the sudden loss of her soulmate. And she'd never remarried.

Or his brothers. Sure, Del and Addison were back together now, but they'd lost a decade of time together and both had gone through hell while apart.

And Noah? His wife had grown bored of small town life just a year into their marriage, and they had divorced.

Marcus lost his wife to cancer five years ago and the man was just now beginning to come out of the hold grief had on him.

His sisters had yet to find true love, and he thought they were better for it. His cousin Emma and her fiancé, Shane, and Landon and his wife, Iris, had managed to defy the odds so far. But he thought of them as special cases. It just didn't work that way for him.

Life was full of curveballs especially when it came to love. And love always had an expiration date.

Megan was quiet, but continued to stay snuggled up against his arm. In spite of his stance on love, he enjoyed her company, both in and out of bed. He wanted to be near her, and he thought about her constantly when they weren't together. She made a mess of his kitchen, took pictures of everything, generally left disarray everywhere, but she was kind, giving, compassionate, and a damn sex goddess in bed. She drove him crazy in all ways possible.

It should have made him want to find her another place to stay for the duration of her time in town. But for the life of him, he couldn't bring himself to push the issue. Maybe it was because he was enjoying life for the first time in a long time. Maybe it was because he was going into this with his eyes wide open, knowing there was an expiration date to this and therefore his heart was safe.

Whatever it was, he wanted her near and was going to keep it that way as long as he could.

Megan pulled him to the hot dog stand where they loaded up on hot dogs, chips, and cold Cokes. They followed that up by funnel cakes —cinnamon sugar for her and powdered sugar for him—and they sat on a bench, people watching and him telling her the life stories of the people he knew. Some of them he embellished just to hear her laugh. It was a contagious laugh that made him join in. It also never failed to make his hands itch to touch her in some way—a brush of a hand or rubbing the ends of her ponytail with his fingers.

Fortunately for him, she appeared to feel the same way. She leaned into him whenever she found an opportunity and sat close to him, her scent mingling with the fragrant night air to wind him up a little more. Much to his surprise, he found he loved every minute of it.

When it was time to walk to the center of the square for the pumpkin contest winner reveal, he took her hand and lifted it to his lips, kissing each knuckle on her soft, delicate but competent hands.

Her lips curved into a smile. "Hmmmm…what's that for? I like it."

He grinned against her hand. "I'm having a great time tonight. It's been a long time since I've enjoyed the festival. I'm usually working it."

She leaned into him and kissed his cheek. "I'm having a great time too. Thank you for asking me to come."

His grin turned wicked as he turned his head, bringing their lips within a hair's breadth apart. "Nice choice of words, beautiful. But I'll never ask you to come, I'll demand it." His voice was low and husky, her breath coming in small pants from between those lips where the red lipstick had faded.

Her gaze, blazing with want, went from his lips to his eyes. "Don't make promises you can't keep, Reynolds."

He half growled, half chuckled, leaning even closer so that their lips brushed. "You and that fucking mouth, Gentry."

"Isn't it illegal for a deputy to be making out on a public bench?"

"Now, Ame, why would you cockblock the poor guy? He hasn't gotten laid in years."

Aidan froze and sighed heavily before leaning back on the bench, away from Megan and her bewitching heat. He glared at Amelia and Del—the two biggest antagonizers of the group—who stood about ten feet away with all of his siblings and his cousin Emma.

Fuck. This wasn't exactly how he wanted to introduce Megan to the rest of his family.

Wait. Did he want to introduce her to them? That meant things, didn't it?

No. Hell, she'd met most of them already just by being in this small town where his family had been entwined since they'd founded it centuries ago.

See? No introductions to be made, except for Grace, who stood next to Amelia, trying to hide a grin.

"Leave him alone, Ames," Grace said, coming to his rescue. "Can't you see he's trying to woo the poor girl?"

Jesus, her too?

So much for a rescue. With another sigh, he stood, Megan's hand still in his own. She followed suit, biting her lip as though trying not to laugh, as they joined the group.

"Megan, you know Amelia since you're in her place every day, but her lookalike pain in the ass is Grace. And the other one standing next to Amelia who wisely never said a word is my cousin Emma. Where's Shane?"

She jerked a thumb over her shoulder. "He's in line getting me a hot chocolate." Emma held out a hand. "It's so nice to finally meet you, Megan."

Megan returned the handshake and waved at the others with a huge smile. "Hi, it's so nice to meet you guys. I've heard so much about you. All of you." She looked up at him, mischief in her eyes, dropping her voice to a stage whisper. "Now, which one did you say was trolling for a date at this thing?"

Noah and Del burst out laughing like the juveniles they were, and something he couldn't identify swelled in his chest. His girl fit right in. He grinned back at her and wrapped an arm around her shoulder.

"Oh, that would be Amelia. Definitely."

Amelia's jaw dropped and her eyes narrowed on her brother. "You're going to pay for that," she said, pointing at him, which only served to make him laugh, causing the whole group to gawk at him.

When Amelia recovered, she turned a mock accusing glare to Megan. "And you. What happened to chicks before dicks and all that?"

Megan's eyes widened. "I know, but he's got this huge—"

Aidan covered her mouth with his hand before she could finish. "That's enough for now," he said, the rest of the group laughing.

"You got a live one there, Aidan," Noah said.

Didn't he know it. And he wouldn't change it for anything.

<hr>

They joined his siblings and walked over to the center of town to watch the pumpkin reveal. With the roads around the historic courthouse closed for the festival, people filled the road, walking around to look at the small tent displays of various sponsors for the festival or artsy and crafty people selling their wares. Others were setting out their camping chairs to settle in to watch the reveal.

It was more than revealing the winner of the pumpkin displays. It was also the official kickoff of the holiday season in town. It was where they reminded everyone about the Halloween parade and all of the upcoming Thanksgiving—another parade, because this little town loved their parades—and Christmas festivities that turned the town into a Hallmark movie.

Most of the stores made their annual revenue in just these few months, and with the crowd made up of locals as well as tourists, it was information that everyone wanted to know.

The Reynolds clan had found a stretch of curb to sit on where they could see matriarch Stella on the small, makeshift stage.

Shane, Emma's fiancé, joined them a few minutes later, and Aidan made the introduction to Megan.

As most women were when they met Shane, Megan was slightly tongue-tied. The man looked like he stepped straight out of the pages of a magazine and was a certified billionaire as the CEO of his family's vineyard and winery company, with the local Gold Mountain Winery being part of his company's portfolio.

If Shane wasn't such a great guy, Aidan might be a little jealous. As it was, Shane was like a brother to him now and took care of his cousin, who was like another pesky sister to Aidan. And for that, after all Emma had been through, Aidan would forever be grateful to the man.

"Who's the blonde with Stella? She looks familiar." Megan pursed her lips, and Aidan could see the wheels turning in her brain.

"That's Addison Davenport, Del's fiancée."

"No wonder she looked familiar." She paused a minute. "Good Lord. They are a stunning couple. It must be like looking into the sun when they stand together."

"Eh," he shrugged, "to me it's just Del and Addie." He wrapped his arm around her shoulders and leaned in closer to her ear. "Addie's beautiful, but she doesn't hold a candle to you, Megan. I've never met a sexier woman in my entire life."

She blushed to the roots of that rich, chocolate-brown hair, and before she could respond, the mayor tapped on the microphone. A whine went through the speakers, and a collective groan rose from the crowd.

"Sorry about that, folks. Let's get started so y'all can get back to enjoying the festival." He cleared his throat. "First up…"

Thirty minutes later, Stella and Addison were headed toward them, and as much as he was ready to get his girl back home so he could do all the things he longed to do, he wasn't getting away without talking to his mom. She talked with his brothers and sisters for a moment before making her way to him and Megan.

Stella's eyes lit up when she saw him. "Baby,"—she cupped his face and kissed his cheeks—"you made it tonight. Are you on call?"

"Nope, off for the whole night." He wrapped his arms around her shoulders and inhaled Chanel N° 5 and the same perfumed shampoo that was his mom's trademark. Whenever the world went sideways, he could always get set back to true north after a hug from her.

"That's great. And never happens."

Aidan chuckled. "Yeah, I'm going to owe Landon big time."

Her smile grew when she turned her head and her gaze landed on Megan, who was standing behind him chatting with Addison and Del. "I'm sure it'll be worth it," she said. She studied him with her sharp gaze that saw everything. "She makes you happy."

He looked down and shifted his feet, and even though he stood head and shoulders taller than her, Aidan felt like a kid again under her steady gaze. "Yeah, I mean we're having a good time while she's here. But it's just temporary."

Stella tilted her head. "She doesn't act like someone who's here temporarily." She looked back at her son. "You make her happy too."

Aidan watched her interact with his siblings and cousin, a funny feeling in his chest that he couldn't explain. For the second time that night, he thought how well she fit into the most important circle in his life. His family. The people who knew him best and loved him anyway.

Somehow or another, Megan had wormed her way into that circle as well.

"Maybe." He cleared his throat, trying to get the sudden strangling feeling out of it.

Stella laughed. "Oh baby, you do. It's in the way she sneaks glances over here when you aren't looking and the look in your eyes right now because you're thinking about her. You don't even have to be looking at her."

"I don't look at her any special way, Mom. I can't." Could he? No, he couldn't. "It doesn't matter, she's leaving soon, making her way down to Florida. She's got a whole new life lined up for herself down there. A brother waiting for her to run his business. She's not staying."

"Do you want her to?" Stella asked with a raised brow.

"I..." Did he? What would it be like for her to stay here? See her longer? "I guess. Yeah, I do." He shook his head. "But I'm not asking her. Besides, I like my life here. It's fine. We're just having fun. I can't do serious."

Stella let out a heavy sigh, but put an arm around his waist and her head on his shoulder. "I can't say I understand why, Aidan. But I guess you have your reasons. Maybe one day you'll tell me."

She pulled away and kissed his cheek. "You've got a rare night off. The festival's about over. Why don't you take your girl home, Aidan?"

"She's not my girl," he protested on a huff.

But how many times that night had he thought that same thing?

Fuck.

Megan started toward him, and his mother walked away, stopping Megan halfway. They chatted for a minute then exchanged a hug before Megan continued his way. She stopped in front of him with a grin and her cheeks pink from the brisk air that was starting to get chillier.

"Ready to head home, gorgeous?"

Her eyes lit up. "Are you still going to punish me?"

Aidan looked around to see if anyone was looking at them and moved forward, slipping a hand around the back of her neck and tilting her face up to his and gripping her hip with the other hand. "Baby," he whispered against her lips, "you have no idea how much trouble you're in. My dick has been hard for you the whole night watching your ass in those jeans."

Her eyes fluttered and a gasp slipped past her lips, her breath fanning across his face and sending a bolt of electricity to his crotch.

"And don't think for one second I've forgotten how you used those amazing tits to distract me at Skee-Ball."

"Sore loser, I won that fair and square." Her words held a teasing lilt to them, but she was as turned on as he was since the words came out breathy.

He grinned and a moan slipped out of her. "Oh, Megan. Gorgeous Megan. I'm going to have fun with you tonight."

Her eyes rose to meet his and she nipped at his lower lip. "Challenge accepted."

time for dessert

BY THE TIME they walked to the station, picked up his vehicle, and made the short drive to the cabin, they were both so turned on they barely cleared the front door before Aidan grabbed her by the waist and pulled her to him.

Megan gripped the lapels of his polo shirt to pull him even closer, and he shoved them against the front door, their body weight slamming it shut behind them.

Jackets were shoved to the floor, and they were a tangle of lips, tongues, and hands. Aidan couldn't touch her in enough places.

"Too…many…clothes…" Megan muttered against his lips.

Aidan reached behind his neck and pulled his shirt over his head, only leaving her lips long enough for the shirt to clear their faces. She put a hand on his chest before he could move back.

"I don't know why, but when you take your shirt off that way it is so sexy."

He grinned and moved in closer, pinning her to the sturdy wooden door with his hips. "If I didn't want to fuck you so bad right now, I'd put it back on and take it off for you all night."

"I'd rather you fuck me."

"Good girl."

He took her wrists and placed them on either side of her head and held them there. With his tongue, he drew tight circles on her neck before sucking the soft skin into his mouth. Her gasps went straight to his dick, and he wanted nothing more than to be inside her, fuck her against the wall, relieve the pressure that had built all night long. Watching her for the last few hours was extended foreplay.

But he had plans for her.

With one hand, he shackled her wrists above her head, his thumb stroking the inside of her wrist. Her pulse bumped under the thin skin there, giving him an indication of how turned on she was.

His other hand cruised down her chest and yanked down the scoop neck of her shirt beneath her breast, exposing a lacy red bra that didn't cover much of anything. Her breasts swelled over the edge of the fabric as though begging for him to touch them. Her nipples were already diamond hard beneath the fabric. He looked up at her from under his lashes. "Did you wear this just for me?"

She glanced down at him and nodded. "I thought you might like it."

"You thought right."

She rolled her teeth over her bottom lip, but didn't say anything, just kept her eyes steady on his as he pulled the shirt over her head and flung it away. Her eyes fluttered closed when he flattened his tongue against her lace-covered nipple. She dropped her head back against the door and arched her back trying to get closer. He tightened his hand around her wrists slightly just to let her know he wasn't letting go.

He licked and nibbled until the fabric was soaking wet before moving to the other peak, repeating the process. Her nipples were so hard they protruded from the flimsy fabric, making him harder still. "Beautiful," he murmured.

She bucked against the grip he had on her wrists. "Tsk, tsk, Megan," he murmured against the slope of her breast, tightening his fingers slightly. "You continue to be a bad girl and I'll have to restrain you."

Her breathing quickened. "Aidan, please."

He moved up her body, dropping hot, open-mouthed kisses all along her skin. "You've been a bad girl, haven't you?"

Her head nodded against his as he drug his tongue across the soft skin of her neck. "Say it."

"I've been a bad girl." The words were a strangled whisper.

"That's right. And bad girls have to know their actions have consequences."

Aidan stepped back and spun her around so that her chest was flush against the door and snapped his handcuffs on her wrists. "You have the right to scream my name. You have the right to come if you're a good girl."

Her surprised gasp turned into a moan, her cheek against the cool wood. Small pants came out of her parted lips.

Aidan moved up into her, running his hands down the side of her body, then squeezing her hips. "Are you okay?" he whispered in her ear.

"Yes."

"If you want me to stop, say pumpkin, okay?"

A smile curved her lips. "Okay."

"Do you want me to stop?"

"No."

"Okay, then don't move and don't turn around."

He hurried into his bedroom and into the closet where he found what he was looking for. With a grin, he got everything in place, then went back to the living room to find she'd followed instructions and hadn't moved.

God, even with her bottom half fully clothed, seeing her wrists cuffed just above that supple ass made him steel hard.

"You've been a good girl, Megan. You'll be rewarded for that."

He walked up behind her and put his mouth at her ear. "Last time. Do you trust me?"

She nodded.

"And if you want me to stop, what do you say?"

Her lips curved as she glanced over her shoulder. "Pumpkin."

He rewarded her with a hot, open-mouthed kiss just below her earlobe, causing her to arch her neck to the side, giving him better access. He kissed down her neck and across her shoulder blades from one side to the other.

When she closed her eyes and dropped her head back slightly, he took the scarf he'd found in her suitcase and covered her eyes, tying it at the back of her head.

"What's that?"

Aidan was relieved that her voice was more curious than nervous. "One of your scarves. This is part of your punishment for teasing me in that second-skin shirt and throwing me off my game."

"So now I can't touch or see you?"

"Nope. Part of the punishment, babe. Now, come with me." He took her by the shoulders and guided her to the bedroom.

At the doorway, he fished the key out of his pocket and uncuffed one of her wrists, then lifted her arms over her head, looping the cuffs over the pull-up bar he'd installed in the doorway, before snapping it back in place.

Megan moaned softly, a sound that went straight to his crotch.

He stepped back, taking in the long lines of her body as she stood there with her arms over her head, her back arched. "I'll be right back."

"Wait, where are you going?"

He chuckled and went to the kitchen, grabbing caramel sauce from the fridge. He had no clue how it ended up in there, but it was a practically brand-new bottle that he was going to put to good use.

But before he did that, he needed to rid them of the rest of their clothes. He watched her face as he flicked the button on her jeans and lowered the zipper. She bit her lip, and her red lace-covered chest rose and fell with every laborious breath she took. He removed her sexy-as-fuck boots and peeled the jeans down her legs, tossing them to the side.

"Turn around." He barely recognized the husky voice that was his.

When she did, he nearly blew his load when he saw that the panties not only matched, but they were a thong that left her beautiful ass bare and on display for his eyes only.

"Holy shit, Megan."

"You like them?"

"Fuck, yeah."

From the curves of her arms and shoulders down to the arc of her back and flare of hips that begged for him to hold onto them, the woman was like a sexy siren sent to destroy him. He wanted her so bad he ached.

"Turn back around."

She did as he asked and let her head fall back, arching her back, offering her body to him. "So, now that you have me like this, what ever will you do with me?"

The first hint of nerves colored her voice, and Aidan's pulse spiked, his cock becoming impossibly hard and increasingly uncomfortable in his pants.

"Well, I think it's time for a little bit of dessert."

"Dessert?"

"Yeah." He popped the top of the bottle and she bit her lip. "Want a taste?"

"Sure."

Aidan squeezed a dollop of the caramel on the tip of his finger and rubbed it along her bottom lip. She ran her tongue along it and hummed. "Hmmm…sweet."

"My turn." He leaned forward and kissed her, stroking her lips and tongue with his own, tasting the sweet, creamy syrup on them. With a flick of his wrist, he unsnapped the front clasp of her bra and moved the cups away, freeing her breasts from their confinement. He lifted the bottle and squeezed, letting a large puddle of caramel form on her chest. With two fingers, he painted her body with the sticky concoction. Her dark rose-colored nipples were diamond-hard peaks as he slathered them with the honey-colored syrup.

She moaned loudly, biting her lip. "Oh, my God." Her breath came in pants as he continued his way down the curve of her belly and finished at her pubic bone. Dropping to one knee, Aidan flattened his tongue just above her clit and licked the stickiness from her skin. The muskiness of her skin and the sweetness of the caramel made for an erotic combination that made him desperate for her.

But he wasn't near done with her yet.

He worked his way up her body until he reached her breasts,

where he licked and sucked them clean. Her breaths came faster and she whispered, "More, please."

Who was he to say no?

He kneeled and lifted one of her legs over his shoulder, opening her up for him to see her lace-covered center. Sliding his hands around and gripping her ass, he brought her forward, inhaling her scent before tugging on the thong. With one pull, the lace tore and fell to the floor, making her gasp and drop her head back between her shoulders. She canted her hips forward, and his mouth clasped onto her clit, licking and sucking her pussy until her moans and gasps filled the room. She hissed out a "yes" while he fucked her with his tongue.

"God, Megan. You taste so fucking good."

"Please don't stop." She rocked her hips forward, murmuring incoherent words, her breaths coming in pants, before her body went rigid with release, then slowly relaxed as she rode out the waves of pleasure. If she hadn't been handcuffed to the bar, he had no doubt she'd have slumped to the floor.

"Aidan, oh my God. That was amazing." Her voice was faint, almost a whisper. "But I still need you inside me."

"I'm here, baby."

Aidan stood and shucked his jeans, his hard-on bursting free from his boxer briefs as though breaking out of cotton jail. He stroked himself as his gaze raked over her from head to toe.

"You're so beautiful it hurts to look at you." He swallowed against the emotion in his throat.

Her sigh came out ragged. "Aidan…"

"Turn around."

She did, the cuffs clinking against the metal bar above her head. He stepped up behind her and she was so wet, he had no issue sliding inside. He gripped her hips and buried himself deep. Their groans mingled together as he hit that spot inside her. The muscles in her back danced under her skin. Her ass was a fucking masterpiece, and he watched as he moved in and out of her, deep and slow. He couldn't tear his eyes away if he tried. She gasped every time he moved back into her, making him want to push her a little more.

He thrusted inside her then stopped, buried deep. With one hand, he gathered a handful of her hair and leaned forward, kissing her long, beautiful neck. Megan's breath came in pants when the hand on her hip moved to the front and cupped her mound.

"Oh, God," she said, her words coming out in a breathless whisper.

"Megan, you're so fucking beautiful like this." His balls ached seeing her so open for him.

He brought his hands back to her hips, her long hair falling over her shoulder, leaving her back bare for him to watch. His fingers tightened on her hips, and he picked up the speed of his thrusts. Her gasps turned to moans as he slammed into her hard and so deep there were times he didn't know where she began and he ended.

He looked down at her as he moved inside her, with her arms bound above her head, blindfolded and vulnerable but willing to give him everything he wanted and take what she needed.

His release bore down on him like a freight train, and when she pushed back against him and begged for him to fuck her harder, there wasn't anything he could do to stop it.

"Holy fuck!" His balls tightened up, and two more hard thrusts later, he stilled, his come filling her up.

He swore he blacked out for a moment.

There was ringing in his ears.

When their breathing returned to normal and his vision restored, he untied the blindfold and unlocked the cuffs. She turned around, a huge smile on her face. He lifted her wrists to his mouth, where he showered the dark pink skin with kisses.

Without another word, he picked her up and carried her into the shower, where he washed her off from head to toe, getting all of the sticky caramel off her body. He washed her pussy with gentle strokes of a washcloth, causing her to shiver. Their mouths kept meeting in sweet, soft kisses that made the shower take twice as long.

When they were done, they dried each other off and made their way into the bedroom, where they curled up together and passed out.

A few hours later, Megan woke him up, straddling him and worshiping his body with her hands, lips, and tongue. When he couldn't stand it any longer, he rolled her over and slid inside her again, just as easily as before. But this time, his strokes were slow, their touches more like caresses, and no words were spoken.

At one point, as she writhed underneath him, Megan opened her eyes and met his. In that moment, he was hit hard by a realization he'd been hoping to avoid since he met her. It was a realization he knew he'd have even if he wasn't balls deep in her.

He was completely and utterly in love with Megan Gentry.

CHAPTER EIGHTEEN
love lies

THE SMELL of coffee was better than any alarm clock.

When the aroma of the rich brew hit her nose, she rolled over and reached out blindly, her hand hitting empty and slightly cold sheets.

She shoved up and looked around the dark room. What the hell time was it? A glance at the clock on his nightstand showed it was early, barely seven a.m.

How did the man always wake up before her? No matter what time she woke up, he beat her to it.

She found one of his T-shirts lying across the end of the bed and pulled it on. It hit her knees and hung on her like a dress. She had no idea where her clothes from last night ended up. The thought of last night and how he'd pushed her boundaries made her body tingle all over again.

It was official. No other man would ever surpass Aidan in the bedroom. At least she'd have the memories of the way he'd made her feel.

Barefoot, she padded out into the kitchen, the room dark except for the under-cabinet light he always left on. "Aidan?"

She walked over and glanced into the living area, coming up empty. "Aidan? Are you up there?"

When there was no answer, she climbed the ladder to the loft and peeked over the edge.

Empty.

Where the hell was he? The cabin was only a thousand square feet. It wasn't like there were all that many places for a man his size to hide.

The back door opened and Aidan stepped inside, shutting the door behind him. He brought his head up and stopped when he saw her standing there. There was a hesitation, but he smiled. "Hey. I didn't mean to wake you."

"You didn't."

They stood there a moment, just staring at each other. And in that moment, Megan knew without a doubt she was in love with him. She'd thought it before, but now she knew.

The thought nearly brought her to her knees.

And it wasn't because he stood there, shirtless, in nothing but a pair of sweatpants that hung low on his narrow hips. Hips that had spent most of the night against hers, while he was buried inside her.

No, it was because he was strong, yet gentle. Dirty, but sweet. Protective, but not suffocating. He always made sure she was okay, from the very first moment she'd laid eyes on him in the middle of the road. He'd taken care of her every step of the way. She didn't want to leave that. Where would she ever find a man like him again?

She wouldn't. There was no other man like Aidan Reynolds.

And yet that was the whole problem.

She was becoming attached to a man again. A man she barely knew, in the grand scheme of things. All she knew was that in her heart of hearts, she could honestly say she'd never felt this way about any man before.

But she didn't want to fall in love with him. She didn't want to fall in love with anyone. She needed to know she could take care of herself again.

He set his coffee mug on the table and walked toward her. "Come sit with me?" he asked, reaching his hand out for her to take.

She slid her hand into his warm palm and sat next to him on the couch. They sat side by side, knees touching, not saying anything. Megan swallowed, confused. They were never awkward around each other and yet they were acting like they hadn't already seen every inch of each other's bodies.

"Ah, fuck it," Aidan muttered, before pulling her into his lap, her thighs straddling his hips. He wrapped his arms around her back and pulled her close, nuzzling his face into the crook of her neck. She wrapped her arms around his neck and held on.

He breathed her in deep, his breath tickling her skin. It was a move he'd done a dozen times during their short time together and it always made her smile.

But she didn't feel like laughing. In fact, sorrow built in her chest. "Aidan, is everything okay?"

He didn't say anything, just placed a soft kiss on the side of her neck before pulling back and looking at her. She searched his eyes as he stared at her. "What is it?"

The way he kept staring at her but not saying anything made her stomach flip like she was on a roller coaster and about to be sick.

"I want to apologize," he finally said, his voice low and edged with regret.

Her brow knitted. "For what?"

"For last night." He looked down at his hands that were rubbing up and down her bare legs. The roughness of his palms on her smooth thighs normally made her crazy. But right at that moment, there was nothing but an icy fear in her gut.

He took her wrists in both of his hands and kissed the faded pink marks the cuffs had left behind. "I'm sorry if I was too rough. I—"

She laid her fingertips over his lips. "Shhh…don't apologize. Please. Last night was nothing short of amazing. I've never felt closer to anyone in my life."

"Me too. I've never done that type of thing with anyone before." His eyes implored hers as though trying to make her understand.

There'd been a shift between them last night, and it was like they'd connected on another level. And even though he touched her gently and she straddled his lap in little more than a thin layer of cotton between their skin, there had been another shift at some point from last night to this morning. But it was one that made her nervous as though she was hanging on the edge of a cliff by her fingernails.

And for the first time since she'd met him, she wasn't sure he'd be there if she lost her grip.

"I believe you. But why are you telling me all this? Why the apology? I thought we talked all through this last night." She ran her fingers through the hair that stood on end like he'd shoved his hands through it all night.

He cupped her face with one hand and moved his hand to the back of her neck. When he tried to pull her down to him for a kiss, she laid a hand on his chest. "Talk to me, please. What's going on?"

His eyes searched between hers for a few moments before he shook his head with a soft smile that didn't quite reach his eyes. "You're right. I just want to make sure I didn't hurt you."

"No, I'm fine. I promise."

This time when he pulled her down for a kiss, she didn't stop him. His lips were insistent but soft, coaxing her lips apart. When she opened for him, his tongue swept inside and he tilted his head to deepen the kiss. It was a kiss that shot lightning all the way to the tip of her toes.

His other hand skated up over her breasts, grazing her nipples into hard points. She moaned against his mouth, her body on high alert, her heart pounding against her ribs. He canted his hips against her core, his hard length rubbing against her clit.

"Oh, yes," she whispered and dropped her head back, and Aidan made quick work of feasting on her neck. Even after the hours they'd spent devouring each other last night, it was like the desire between them couldn't be slaked.

But there was a nagging feeling in her gut that told her to take notice of the way he touched her this time. Inherently, her body knew it was different than any other time between them.

Aidan stood with her in his lap and swung around to lay her down on the couch. He pushed down his sweats, and having gone commando, his erection sprang free and seemed to stretch for her. He ran a finger down her wet seam before inserting it inside and curling to find that spot. Her back arched off the couch and all she could do was groan.

Then he was inside her, moving in and out of her in a steady rhythm until his thrusts became harder, more insistent. It was almost as though he was trying to imprint her on his brain.

When he lifted up and looked down at her, joining their hands beside her head, the emotions that built in her chest brought tears to her eyes.

She loved this man. More than anyone she'd ever known.

He continued to hammer into her, reaching higher and higher inside her with every thrust, their gazes locked until they both hit the edge, and she cried out when the world around them shattered and his desire poured into her.

"Megan..." Aidan whispered into her hair, his hips still lazily pushing against her until he was totally spent.

They lay there a few moments catching their breath. All too soon, he lifted up on his elbows and laid a soft kiss on her lips. "I..." he swallowed, his Adam's apple bobbing. "I have to go take a shower."

Before she could formulate a response, he was up, pants pulled on, and walking away. It wasn't until she heard the thump of the bathroom door and the snick of the lock turning that it occurred to her what was different between them.

With his saying nothing at all, he'd said everything she didn't want to hear.

▭

"I've got to go. There's an accident out on Highway 11 that needs assistance." Aidan's voice came from behind her.

She sat at the small table looking out at the lake where the day was cloudy and the fog was rising over the water in a fine mist. While he was in the shower, she'd gotten dressed so she wouldn't feel so vulnerable. She sipped her coffee and nodded. "Okay. Well, be careful."

He came around into her line of sight, fully dressed, including his boots. His hands were in the pockets of his work jacket. "I don't know how long I'll be."

"I'll be here." She couldn't look at him, knowing he was pulling away from her and she had no idea why.

"Are you mad at me about something?"

Megan turned her head toward him. He held the back of the chair with one hand, his fingers tight on the wood. His hat was pulled low so she couldn't see his eyes, but his lips were in a flat line and his shoulders were hunched at his ears. He looked ready to pounce and not in a good way.

She tilted her head. "Why would I be mad? You're only acting like you hardly know me this morning."

"I wouldn't exactly say that, since we fucked on the couch not twenty minutes ago." He closed his eyes and grimaced as soon as the words left his mouth. "I'm sorry, I didn't mean it like that."

In spite of the crack that appeared in her heart, she waved him off. "Don't think twice about it, Reynolds."

"Shit." He ran a hand through his hair. "I can't talk about this right now, Megan."

"Don't worry about it, Aidan. You have to go."

He stared at her for a beat longer until his phone on his waist rang. With a curse, he jerked it off his waist and barked a hello into it, then left without a word.

She didn't even jump when the front door slammed behind him. Even though she was in love with him and wanted nothing more than to plead with him to tell her what was going on, he would have to come to her. There would be no more games when it came to her heart.

Even if she'd finally found the man she knew without a doubt she'd love forever, she was done begging a man to love her.

CHAPTER NINETEEN
life, interrupted

THE RED AND blue lights cut through the gray fog, tinting the air an eerie purple color.

Shit. This wasn't good. A cold, ominous feeling whipped through him. Accidents were always bad, but some were worse than others. And that dark, clawing in his throat wouldn't let up. Fire trucks, an ambulance, and a state patrol were already on scene.

The fog that had rolled in had already wreaked all sorts of havoc on Madison Ridge, and it was only a little after eight in the morning. This was the fourth accident called in this morning alone but the worst one yet. And the scanner kept going off.

It was going to be a long day.

Aidan pulled his SUV off to the side of the road, cutting the sirens but leaving the lights on. Flares lit up the road to guide any traffic that came through. Fortunately, that time of the morning, there wasn't much.

His gut clenched as he looked around and didn't see anyone but first responders running around back and forth. Where were the passengers?

He walked up to the officer on scene, who gave him a rundown of what they'd been able to piece together so far. Single car accident, driver appeared to leave the road, ending up in the woods, wrapped around a tree, and from what they could tell there was only a driver. No passengers, but the driver was DOA.

Aidan nodded grimly, his chest tight, then thanked the officer. He zipped up his jacket against the misty, chilly air and began walking the area, taking notes and pictures with his tablet for the accident report. Trying to piece the puzzle together.

A few minutes later, there was some shouting from the EMTs and they started to pull the gurney out of the woods. When they cleared the wood line, the look on their faces and the sheet over the body confirmed what Aidan already knew but had hoped was bad info.

Shit. That feeling of foreboding he'd had since he got up this morning intensified. He met them at the back of the ambulance.

"Hey, Aidan." John, one of the EMTs and his former classmate, greeted him, his shoulders slumped. "It's Rob Davidson."

Aidan froze, that yawning hole in his gut intensifying. "What?"

John shook his head and pulled back the sheet. Rob's lifeless body lay still on the gurney, and Aidan dropped his chin to his chest.

Shit shit shit. He'd just seen the man last night. With his wife. And young daughter.

The daughter Megan had given her stuffed tiger to.

The pressure in Aidan's chest was almost too much to bear. He wanted to throw something. Anything. But emotions had no place right then. He nodded curtly at John to cover him back up.

"We need—" John started.

"I'll handle it." Aidan stalked off and called Landon.

"Hello?"

"Hey, man, I know you were on last night but I need your assistance." Aidan gave him a rundown, his voice emotionless. If there was one thing he knew how to do, it was compartmentalize. He called upon that skill he'd mastered and shut out anything that looked like emotion. Find the cold, the numb. He could think about all the repercussions later.

Because he knew what he had to do next, and it was the worst part of the job.

But why did it feel like he was walking to the edge of a cliff? With nothing but blackness below? Having grown up in the area and being a deputy in town for the last three years, this wasn't the first time he'd known the victim. What made this one so different?

He shoved the thoughts away and focused on what had to be done. Facts. The tire tracks on the road, all the other little details that would tell them the story of what ended Rob's life. He wanted to make sure he had as much info as possible when he went to see Margot.

He made more notes of the scene in his tablet, informed the tow truck driver of what was going on when they arrived, and updated Landon when he showed up.

Landon shook his head when Aidan told him who the victim was. "Aw, damn. I didn't know him well, but he was a nice guy."

"Yeah." His voice was clipped, and Landon raised a brow.

"You okay, man?"

Aidan nodded once and handed him the tablet. "Fine. I need to go talk to next of kin."

"You mean Margot? She has a name, Aid."

Aidan got in his cousin's face. "I know she has a fucking name, okay? But you know as well as I do that emotion has no fucking place right now. None." He stepped back, his jaw bunched. "Now, go do your damn job."

Landon, being Landon, didn't back down from Aidan. They both knew tragedy was part of life, but it didn't make it any easier. "Aidan, I can handle this if you want me to."

"No, I got this."

He didn't have it at all. His heart fucking ached as he drove to the Davidson home. He knew one universal truth in that moment. Margot's whole world was about to change course. He'd known her since first grade and yet he was now going to be a part of the worst day of her life. And Abby's.

Life was about to knock them down, and he was the messenger of it.

His mind flashed back to the day that had changed his family's life. He remembered when the sheriff had walked into the house and told his mother that their life as they knew it was over. That the man who

Aidan had looked to, had wanted to be just like, was gone. In an instant. Here one second, gone the next.

The shadowy memories dissipated as he pulled up into the driveway and shifted the SUV into park before sitting there a moment, trying to pull it together.

He wished Megan were with him. To comfort him. To let him bury his face in her hair and inhale her scent. Calm his soul.

And yet this whole situation he was dealing with was why he didn't want her around. Because he knew why this particular case bothered him, and she was at the root of it. She'd gone and opened his heart, and now he didn't know if he could close it back.

But he needed to if he was going to survive.

With a heavy sigh, he pushed out of the vehicle and went to the door. He blew out a breath to steady his heaving stomach before he rang the doorbell. The cheery ringtone irritated the shit out of him.

Margot opened the door, her brow crinkled in confusion but a smile on her lips. She ran a hand over hair that hadn't yet seen a brush and pulled the belt on her robe a bit tighter.

"Aidan. Hey. What's up? If you're looking for Rob, he isn't here." She peered around him. "He should be back any minute now though. Want to come in and wait?"

Aidan dug deep into his well of military and law enforcement training to keep his face as impassive as possible. He squared his shoulders and clenched his fists at his sides before releasing them. "I'm actually here to see you."

"Me? Oh, okay. Come in."

When he cleared the door, he took his hat off and ran a hand through his hair before placing it back on his head. "It's about Rob."

Her chin came up, and she swallowed. Her chest rose and fell quicker than it had before. She knew. She touched her fingertips to her mouth and wrapped her other arm around her own waist. Turning, she went into the living room off the foyer.

Aidan followed her, glancing around the room. It was a space that looked lived in. A comfortable couch, large TV hanging on the wall, pictures of the family on the mantel. A fleece throw was rumpled in a pile on the wide side chair by the window. A cup of coffee sat on the table next to it. He imagined that's where she had been sitting when he rang the bell.

Her life before.

She sat on the edge of the couch, her hands between her knees, her legs bouncing. She whisked a stray hair out of her face and waved to the sofa next to her. "Please, sit. And tell me what happened."

Normally, Aidan would have stood to deliver the news. But he did as she asked and went to sit next to her. He took off his cap again and held it in his hands. "There was an accident. It looks like he lost control of the vehicle somehow and left the road. Ended up in the trees."

He swallowed, wishing like hell he was anywhere else.

"Tell me everything. He was my husband. I want to know." Her voice wavered on the last word, and her eyes filled with tears.

He blew out a breath and told her everything he knew at that point in the investigation and that she'd need to come to the hospital to identify him.

And that was when she lost the fight to be brave. Her body folded over and was racked with sobs. A box of tissues sat on the coffee table, and Aidan set them in front of her before running a hand down her spine, trying to comfort her.

He was tossed back to when he was thirteen years old and doing the same thing for his own mother. He'd been the one to answer the door when the cops came to tell them his father was dead. Charley had been in her room playing and too young to answer the door.

But at thirteen and with his older brothers gone off to school or whatever it was they did at the time, his dad, Paul, had always told Aidan he was the man of the house while Paul was gone. He'd need to protect his mother and sisters. Protect the home.

It was a job that Aidan had always taken to heart.

He'd done his best to help his mother, but there were just some things he couldn't do. But when they told his mother her life would never be the same, he'd done all he could. But he'd still felt helpless. Much like he did right now.

He listened to the mournful sounds of a woman who'd lost her husband, knowing he'd never hold her again, kiss her, make love to her, take out the trash, protect her when she's scared, and be a united front against the world.

It was when he promised himself to never feel that kind of pain. Certain pains were inevitable because he loved his family. He'd be devastated to lose any of them in a tragic accident like his father or Rob.

But to love someone with your heart and soul so that once they come into your life, you can't imagine them not being there? It was a different type of love than sibling or parental love. One he'd never experienced. One he never wanted to be vulnerable to.

Megan's face came to his mind. The breath in his lungs backed up, and it was hard to breathe.

"Mommy, are you okay?"

Margot's head came up and she wiped away her tears. "Um, yes. I'm fine, baby."

Aidan took Margot's hand. "Look at me."

She brought her watery stare to him.

"Don't lie to her, Margot. Trust me when I tell you this. I've been in her shoes. She needs to know the truth so you both can grieve. Don't push her away."

Margot stared at him for a moment before tears filled her eyes again and streamed down her face. She nodded. "I forgot about that. You're right."

Abby stood at the bottom of the steps in her footed pajamas with puppies dressed as ghosts on them. A little hand came up and rubbed one of her eyes but she was watchful.

Margot held out an arm. "Come here, baby. I have to tell you something."

"Where's Daddy?" she asked, padding over to her mother. "He said he was going to get donuts. Said since I was such a good girl last night, I could have a frosted one."

At her words, Margot bit her lip and looked at the ceiling, tears falling into the edges of her hair. Abby stood next to her mother, those greenish brown eyes confused. "Why are you crying, Mommy?"

Aidan cleared his throat. "Hey, Abby. Remember me? We met last night at the festival?"

Her eyes lit up and she smiled. Aidan's heart broke. Abby had her father's smile. "You and that nice lady gave me the tiger."

He forced a smile on his face, though he didn't have to try too hard. Like her father, her smile was infectious. "That's right. And you were very brave to take that tiger. Miss Megan was having a terrible time making it behave."

Abby giggled. "He's the best tiger ever. He's a good boy for me." She tapped a little finger on her chin. "Maybe Miss Megan didn't give him enough treats."

Aidan chuckled softly. "Maybe not. But see how brave you are? And you know what? Your mommy has something to tell you. And when she does, I want you to remember how brave you were taming that tiger, okay?"

Abby squinted her eyes and pursed her little lips but nodded, looking at her mother. She climbed into Margot's lap, who instantly pulled her daughter close and held on like it was her last lifeline.

In that moment, it was.

He cleared his throat and stood. "I'm going to give you some privacy, okay? When you're ready, I'll take you to the hospital."

Margot wiped her nose and sniffed. She looked over her daughter's shoulder, nodding. "Thank you, Aidan."

He walked outside and got back in his SUV, not wanting to hear the cries from a little girl who'd lost the first man she'd ever loved. Who didn't have near enough time with him.

Again, he thought of Megan. His heart turned over in his chest thinking of her now and as a little girl like Abby, learning her parents were gone. It just dawned on him that Charley and Megan were near the same age when they'd lost a parent. Or in Megan's case, parents.

His fingers tightened around the steering wheel, trying to ignore what he knew in his heart. Because the one thing he did know was that the pain he just witnessed in Margot's eyes, that he'd seen in his mother's years before, and Marcus' face when he lost his wife, he wanted no part of at all.

Megan had thrown him off course a bit, but what he'd just had to do reminded him of the promise he made himself twenty years ago. The only people that could have a place in his heart were his family. It would be bad enough to lose them. But if his heart and soul were involved? If he loved someone like Megan and life decided to take her away?

He'd never survive.

better as a memory

MEGAN LET herself into the house shortly after six o'clock. When she hadn't heard from Aidan all day and with no shift to work, she ended up calling Charley, who rounded up the girls and they had dinner and drinks.

The small cabin was dark, save for one small lamp on the side table in the living space, which was empty. A scraping noise from beyond the double doors leading to the deck caught her attention.

She found Aidan kicked back in one of the wrought iron chairs. She bit her lip when she saw a highball glass in his hand that was propped on the arm rest. A half-empty bottle of Jack sat on the side table.

Her heart rate sped up. It seemed odd for him to be sitting in the dark drinking whiskey neat.

She crossed her arms and sighed. He'd never called her during the day. Knowing he was working, she hadn't tried to call him either. And she had to hold on to her resolve that she wasn't going to lay down everything for a man again.

She crossed the deck and leaned against the rail in front of him. His long legs were propped up on the deck rail, his eyes unreadable in the dark. "Hey."

He took a swallow of his drink before responding. "Hey." His voice was rough as though he'd swallowed a bag of sand.

"Bad day?"

"Yep."

"Want to talk about it?"

"Nope."

She looked away, past the tree line and down to the dock where they'd first gotten to know each other. "Aidan, I can't help you if you won't tell me what's going on."

"Maybe I don't want your help. Ever think of that?"

"I'm sorry if you had a bad day, but you don't need to be an asshole."

He rubbed his eyes with his thumb and forefinger. "I know. I'm sorry."

Megan lowered herself to the unoccupied chair and waited him out. A blind man could see that he was in massive pain and doing his best to forget it, even if just for the night.

But they both knew that never went well.

Finally, he dropped his hand and looked at her with a bleary stare. "The accident this morning. The one I left for?" He blew out a breath. "It was Rob Davidson."

She gasped, her heart dropping to her knees. "The man I met last night at the festival? Abby's dad?"

He nodded and tossed back what was left in his glass, hissing through his teeth. "Yep. Don't have all the details yet, but what we do know is that it appears he lost control, left the road. Wrapped his truck around a tree. The only saving grace is that he was killed on impact. He didn't suffer."

"Oh my God, Aidan."

"Yeah." The neck of the bottle hit the side of his glass as he poured another two fingers of whiskey.

Tears fell down Megan's face as she thought about Abby. She was so little and too young to lose a parent. It was a pain no child should have to face, especially so young. There were all sorts of memories that would never be made now that her father was gone. The father daughter dances, the threats of cleaning his gun when the first boyfriend came around, the walking her down the aisle when she found the man she'd given her heart to.

And Margot…her heart broke again thinking about what it must be like to have the love of her life snatched away from her. A man by all accounts she'd known her whole life and planned to spend the rest of her life with.

But it was a life interrupted.

Megan reached out and put a hand on his arm. "Aidan…"

He shoved up from the chair, causing her to pull back, her eyes wide. His long legs ate up the space on the deck as he paced it.

"I had to go tell Margot and Abby that the man they loved was gone. I changed their lives forever today." He shoved a hand through his hair, causing the short strands to stand up. "It's not like it was the first time I've had to give this news to people I knew. But today was different…"

"Well, I-I'm sure it—"

"It made me think of when they came to the house and told my mother my father was dead. I was thirteen when I answered the door to find them standing there, changing our lives. I knew right then and there I never wanted to feel the pain I saw my mom go through. I never wanted to be close enough to a human to be hurt that way."

He sighed and continued pacing. Megan's heart raced in her chest, wondering where he was going with all this. Her gut told her that something had shifted today, and she was going to be on the losing end of the deal.

He continued. "It's part of why I was a good soldier and why I'm a good sheriff. I can compartmentalize that. Besides my family, I don't let myself get close ever. I have rules to keep that from happening." He stopped, his chest heaving, and looked over at her. "And then you showed up and everything went right out the window." His words were laced with a bitterness that sliced right through her.

"Who are you trying to protect? Yourself?"

"Me, everyone around me. In my line of work, I can't make mistakes. I can't be emotional. I vowed that day when my father died that I would protect my family. The only ones I let in. I would protect them from what I could, however I could, and for me that means keeping emotion out of it."

Megan shook her head, confused and her heart aching. "I don't understand. What are you trying to say?"

"I'm saying that I can't think or do my job when you're in my head, Megan. I broke my own rules and now I'm paying for it by letting emotions in. I can't do that."

He blew out a breath and looked away. "Today reminded me of what I need to do. Who I need to be. And that means that this thing," —he waved a hand between them—"whatever it is, has to end."

Her breath caught in her throat. "What about last night?"

"What about it, Megan? We fucked. We had a good time. Let's leave it at that."

Anger and mortification mixed together to form a potent concoction that was liable to kill her. "That's all this was to you? Fucking?"

He held out his arms to the side. "What else did you think this was? Huh? We've always had an expiration date. You were here until your car was fixed and you could leave town. Hell, you have a job waiting for you in Florida. Your brother is expecting you to run his bar."

He advanced on her. "So you tell me, Megan, what the hell did you think this was other than a good time?"

She shook her head and looked away, her jaw set. The worst part was he wasn't wrong. The trees beyond the deck blurred from the tears. "I-I thought that maybe we could try to work something out."

"No, that's never going to happen."

"But why?"

Aidan sighed and closed the distance between them, taking her hands in his. He wouldn't look her in the eye. "Megan, listen to me. I can't be who you want me to be. I'm not built to be anyone's someone. I will only hurt you."

"You don't think you're hurting me now?"

He was silent for a long moment before speaking again. "I think the hurt you feel now will fade." He brought his gaze up to hers. "One day you're going to find the man you're supposed to be with. And when you do, I'll just be a memory to you. A guy you spent a couple of weeks with having great sex. I'm just a blip in your life, Megan."

"No, you're wrong, Aidan. I love you."

"No!" He pushed away, running both hands through his hair as he paced away and then back to her. "You don't love *me*. You love love. You told me that yourself. And I don't want to be another mistake for you."

She shook her head. "This is different, Aidan. I've never felt this way about a man, the way I feel about you." She scoffed. "And I've been in 'love'"—she made air quotes—"enough to know that what we have is different. What I feel for you is different than anything I've felt for anyone else. I know this is real. Why won't you let me in?"

"I don't believe you. I don't think you really know what's real and what isn't. Can't you see this for what it is? The sex is amazing. You literally blow my mind. But I don't do love and you can't help but love. It's just who we are. And outside of sex, we just don't work. We never will."

Her body was numb. If her heart was beating, she had no idea. And her brain waded through molasses, unable to process what had happened between them.

"I just…" She raised a hand to her forehead. "Last night we were in complete sync. I *felt* you let me in. Lower your walls. Now you're shutting me out again. It's enough to give a girl whiplash."

He looked away toward the placid lake beyond the trees. When he looked back at her, his eyes were calm, cold pools of blue. It made her shiver as the breeze blew.

All of the walls were firmly back in place.

And she was on the outside of them.

"We never promised each other anything." He shrugged his broad shoulders but kept his gaze averted. "We had a good time. Let's leave it at that."

Realization hit her like lightning. "You're scared."

He shoved his hands in the pockets of his jeans and looked down for a moment before meeting her stare. "Maybe I am. But it's still over."

She rolled her teeth over her bottom lip and swiped at her tears, anger beginning to take over. Anger at herself for being so stupid to truly fall in love, only for it to be with a man who couldn't love her back. For failing at her own goal of figuring out who she was. And angry at Aidan for refusing to see what they had and reducing their time together to nothing more than sex.

She couldn't make him love her, no matter how much she tried. She blew out a breath and crossed her arms over her chest, hoping it would keep what was left of her heart intact.

Aidan turned and started to go inside, pausing at the door. "I'm going to Noah's for the week. Stay here as long as you need. I'll be back for some things tomorrow, but I won't bother you."

"You shouldn't drive. You've been drinking." What the hell was wrong with her? What did she care if he was reckless?

But that was the whole crux of her problem, wasn't it? Why her heart was in million pieces at her feet.

"I'm gonna walk." He paused and cleared his throat. "For what it's worth, if I could love anyone, Megan, it would be you." And then he was gone.

It was the king of parting shots, landing in the center of her chest, in the space her heart used to occupy before she met Aidan Reynolds.

Numb, she sat down in one of the chairs, pulling her knees up to her chest.

Well, she hadn't begged for him to love her. Hadn't begged him to choose her. At least she had that going for her. She was free to figure out who she was in life.

But all she knew was she'd never felt more alone.

but more than a memory

AIDAN STARED at the ceiling of his brother's spare bedroom. Rain fell steadily outside the window, the gloomy, gray day fitting his mood nicely. He hadn't slept at all the night before, and between the late night with Megan and the long ass day yesterday, Aidan was running on empty. But he couldn't turn his brain off long enough to let sleep take over.

The night with Megan when he realized he was in love with her felt like a million years ago. Had it really been less than forty-eight hours ago? When he closed his eyes, he could still see her beautiful body stretched out for him, his hands free to explore. His fingers and lips still felt the soft silkiness of her skin.

Fuck. He sat up and swung his legs to the side of the bed, leaning his elbows on his knees, his head in his hands.

He needed to move. To do something other than lie in this bed and think about *her.* He'd ended it and he had good reasons, damn it. So why did he feel like total shit?

Aidan grabbed his T-shirt from the floor and pulled it on as he made his way out to the kitchen. Noah, who looked up as Aidan walked in, sat at the table scrolling through his tablet.

"Mornin'. You look like hell."

Aidan scratched the back of his head. "Thanks. I feel like hell."

"There's coffee and pastries. Amelia brought over some blueberry muffins earlier."

"Thanks. What time is it?" he asked, padding over to the coffee pot.

Wallowing in his misery, he hadn't bothered to check the time. Since he'd worked Saturday and all day yesterday, he was off for the day. It was both a blessing and a curse.

"A little after seven." Noah raised a brow. "You sleep at all last night?"

Aidan poured his coffee and snagged a muffin from the bakery box before sitting at the table with his brother.

"Not really." He took a bite of the muffin and frowned while he chewed. "Did Amelia change her recipe?"

"They taste the same to me."

"It tastes different." Aidan shoved it away and sipped his coffee.

Noah set down the tablet and clicked it off. With a snick, the screen went dark. He folded his arms over his chest and eyed Aidan. "So what happened?"

"What do you mean?"

Noah pursed his lips and exhaled quietly as though praying for patience. That was one thing he had to give his oldest brother. The man had the patience of a saint. While Noah may look just like their father —honest to God, some days it was like looking at a ghost—he had all the patience of their mother.

"I mean, while I don't mind you camping out in my spare room for a while, I'd like to know why you're not staying at your own home."

Aidan's thumb rimmed the coffee mug. "I told Megan she could stay there until she left."

"That's great. Still doesn't answer my question though, bro." Noah leaned forward. "Why aren't you with Megan?"

"Our little fling or whatever the hell it was ran its course."

"Uh-huh. And you parted ways amicably? If it just ran its course and all. No harm, no foul, right?"

Aidan looked over at his brother, who didn't smirk, just watched him patiently, waiting for him to explain why the hell he'd let Megan go.

He blew out a breath and leaned back in the farmhouse chair. "Look, you know me. I don't do relationships. I have no desire to get attached to someone so that I can get hurt."

"So you think you can just have fuck buddies your whole life and nothing more than that?"

Well, hell. When Noah put it like that, it seemed ridiculous. And fucking lonely.

"I don't know. All I know is that I never want to feel that pain that love brings. I saw what it did to Mom when Dad died. And Marcus when Naomi died. I've never wanted to let anyone in." Until Megan.

She was right. He *had* let her in that night. His world had shifted on its axis, and he didn't know what to do about it.

"Except you did let her in, didn't you?" Noah sighed. "Look, I don't know what that's like either. Losing someone you love that much."

"Didn't you love Sara?" Aidan hadn't really known Noah's ex-wife very well since they'd managed to get married and divorced while Aidan was in the army.

"Sure. At least, I thought I did. And it hurt when she left, but it was more because I'd felt like a fool for rushing into it. We're both better off apart. But the kind of love and loss you're talking about is different. It's the soul changing kind."

He'd never been the type of guy to show emotion, especially for anyone outside his family. But Megan made him feel everything and not in a small way.

He'd felt all the emotions he'd never wanted to feel.

"Yeah." Aidan looked down into his black coffee. "I just don't think I'm built for the soul changing kind. Too much trouble. I got enough trouble keeping law and order in this town."

"I suppose." Noah stood and gathered his tablet and mug. "I have to head to the office. Going to be a slow day with the rain, but the paperwork never ends." He paused, tapping his finger on the mug handle. "I have to apologize to you."

Aidan's brow furrowed. "For what?"

"For not stepping up and being a better brother to you when Dad died. You were just a kid, and you took on so much."

"I don't need your apologies. You didn't do anything wrong. You and Del were off at school. It wasn't your fault you weren't there. It's just the way it happened."

"I appreciate you trying to let me off the hook, but I still carry a lot of guilt about it."

"Well, don't. After you and Del left home, Dad said I was the man of the house if he wasn't around. To protect the family." Aidan shrugged. "So that's what I did."

Noah stared at him. "Yeah. It makes sense now."

"What makes sense?"

Noah shook his head. "Nothing. I gotta go. Make yourself at home. Stay as long as you need. Mi casa, su casa and all that. I don't think I have to tell you this, but try to keep from getting your shit everywhere though."

"Have we met? You've seen my cabin."

"Yeah, but it bears repeating."

Aidan stood from the table. "God, you really are an old man now."

"Hey, you might be as tall as me now, and I may be pushing forty, but I can still kick your ass. Right now I have a pricey piece of electronics that holds my whole life in one hand and coffee in the other, but if I didn't, you'd be in a headlock, my friend."

Aidan laughed—an honest to God laugh—and for just a moment he forgot about the woman who'd brought laughter back into his life. "Right. Hey, can you drop me off by the cabin on your way in? I can be ready in a few."

"Yep."

Aidan cleaned up after himself—he'd never tell his sister he'd thrown out the muffin—and Noah dropped him off at the cabin minutes later.

"Thanks for the ride. I'll grab dinner for tonight."

"And beer. Don't forget beer."

"Got it, beer."

With a wave, Noah pulled away and Aidan slowly made his way up the walkway, unsure of what he'd find once he was inside. His stomach flipped like he was on a twisty roller coaster. It was a ride he wanted off of, but couldn't find the stop button.

One foot in front of the other, man.

Why the hell was he thinking about the time he'd half carried her up the walkway? The first day he'd met her? Even that day, he'd been fighting how enchanted he was by her. As he walked up the concrete path to the door, those feelings hadn't changed in the three weeks since that day.

When he opened the front door, his heart sank. He didn't have to look around the small house to know that she was gone.

He didn't have to see that all the small feminine touches she'd put on the place in her short stay had been swept away.

The scarf he'd used to blindfold her and that she'd worn to work last week that laid over the back of one of the chairs in the small dining space.

The lip balm she'd said she needed because she wanted to make sure she didn't have dry lips when he kissed her. He could still taste the strawberry flavor of it on his tongue.

The bench at the end of the bed where her suitcase had sat, clothes poking out the side, was gone, the brown leather top visible again.

The bathroom vanity was neat, everything in its place again, her giant makeup bag no longer taking up half of the already small space.

The brass key he'd given her to his house sat in the middle of the island in the kitchen.

Everything was tidy and back to the way he liked it.

There was a stillness in the air that hadn't been there since Megan came into his life.

It had once brought him peace.

Now it brought him nothing but pain.

He flopped down on the couch and pressed the heels of his hands to his eyes. She couldn't have gone far but she may as well be a million miles away. She'd left a message loud and clear by leaving.

He knew she still had to be in town, but he wasn't going to go after her. He loved her, but he couldn't give her what she wanted. That wasn't fair to her.

Besides, it was what he'd wanted anyway. He had called it off. She said she loved him, but she herself said she couldn't be trusted to know what love was. And he didn't want to be vulnerable to the pain another could cause.

And the two of them? When it ended—not *if* but *when* because it always ended—it would be messy. Messy was another thing he didn't do.

So if he'd done the right thing, why did it hurt so fucking bad?

◼︎

Over the next couple of days, he managed to take grumpy asshole to a new level. He was spoiling for a fight, and if Landon hadn't intervened, he would have found one with a tourist from the city with a big-ass mouth. He wanted to punch something so bad that Landon had to push him off the smartass that he'd pulled over for speeding through the square. The motherfucker had given Aidan attitude and he'd seen red.

He was thankful Landon had been nearby and seen the whole thing go down.

After that he'd gone to the gym that Landon's wife, Iris, ran, but after an hour of punching the shit out of a bag and running on the treadmill until his lungs begged for mercy, he only felt slightly better.

Thursday morning, Aidan watched the sun come up—again since sleep seemed to have left with Megan—and he had the entire day with nothing to do stretched out in front of him. The week had been shit. He never saw her, but Charley assured him she was safe. But that's all she would tell him.

His sister did tell him he was an idiot and no, she wouldn't tell him where Megan was. It was just as well. He had to keep telling himself that he was the one who pushed her away, told her he had rules, and he didn't do relationships.

Maybe if he said it enough times, he would convince himself that he wasn't a dumbass.

Or maybe he'd just drink some more. He'd never been much of a hard liquor drinker, but whiskey was turning out to be a great friend when he needed one. It was about the only thing that was kind to him, at least for a little while.

Midmorning, he was hurtling toward a nice whiskey buzz when the doorbell rang. And whoever was on the other side was insistent.

He stood from the couch and only stumbled once in his haste to get to the door. His heart soared, hoping it would be Megan on the other side of the door.

That hope sunk like a rock when he found his front porch crowded with people he loved but had no desire to see.

Because they weren't Megan.

"What the hell are y'all doing here?" he asked, his words sharp.

Charley barged her way in, catching him off guard—his reflexes were whiskey delayed after all—and forcing him to step back out of the way. His mother, Marcus, and Landon took advantage of his surprise and followed in Charley's wake.

"Well, just come on in then." He slammed the door hard enough to rattle the panes of the windows in the door.

His mother turned to him, her hands on her hips. "You may be a grown man, but I'm still your mother and I deserve more respect than that."

Ah, shit. He rubbed the back of his neck, another razor sharp edge of guilt slicing through him. "I'm sorry, Mom. I didn't mean to be an asshole."

Charley scoffed from where she was pacing in the living room. "Please, everyone knows how much of an asshole you've been the last few days."

"What do you mean everyone? What are they saying? And who is *they* anyway?" So many emotions rioted around his head at that moment, his head spun. But he latched onto anger because it was one emotion he could handle. The others—some he didn't want to name— he didn't know what to do with.

Landon stood next to the couch, arms crossed over his chest, and leveled Aidan with a stare. "It doesn't matter, but you haven't made any friends this week, Aid."

"And this isn't like you at all," Marcus added, his deep voice booming in the room, as he sat on the sofa.

Stella watched him for a moment before she turned and glanced around the living room. Her eyes narrowed on the bottle of whiskey and the empty glass next to it. "Doing some day drinking, are we?"

He wanted to lie, but he just couldn't. He'd never been able to lie to his mom. And even though pain ate at his soul, he wasn't going to start now. "Yeah, you could say that."

With a sigh, she sat next to Marcus and gestured to the chair next to the sofa. "Take a seat."

"Mom, I—"

"Aidan Samuel Reynolds, sit your ass down."

The room went quiet at his mother cursing. She rarely did it and when she did, everyone sat up and listened. He bit back a sigh and took a seat. He leaned forward, elbows on his knees, and looked at her. "You have my attention, now what?"

"I want—" Stella started.

"You're an—" Charley interrupted.

Stella glared at her youngest. "Shut it, Charlotte."

"Well, hell, y'all are making your mama use everyone's full names today," Marcus muttered. He ran a hand through his silver hair and frowned.

Charley snapped her mouth closed, but Aidan swore steam poured from her ears.

Stella turned her attention back to Aidan. "I want to know why you broke it off with Megan."

"I want to know why this is anyone's business," Aidan shot back.

"Because this"—Stella gestured to him and the messy room in general—"isn't you. Losing your cool on the job isn't you. Day drinking? Come on."

"You're a mess, man," Marcus added.

Aidan dropped his head and ran a hand through his hair. He let out a long and heavy sigh before lifting his head again. "It had run its course. That's all."

Charley scoffed again from her perch on the arm of the sofa. Stella glared at her but didn't say anything. "Ran its course?" Stella asked. "So you look like a broken man who's had his heart stomped on because it ran its course?"

"I don't…it doesn't matter. Okay? I don't do relationships. This isn't a surprise to anyone here."

"No, but the way you're reacting to it is a surprise." His mom leaned forward mimicking his stance. "Why don't you do relationships, Aidan? And don't lie to me because I hate that. Besides, I think I already know the answer."

He bounced his leg and bunched his jaw. Why couldn't they understand? Why didn't she understand of all people? If she knew, why did she want him to say it out loud?

He shoved off the chair and paced. "I've never been the guy to let my feelings show. If I kept them to myself, I could control things, keep from being hurt."

Stopping in front of his mom, he jammed his hands on his hips. "When Dad died, I watched you lose yourself to the pain for so long. You functioned for us kids, and I've always admired you for that. But you were so sad for so long." He shifted his gaze to the man he considered one of his uncles. "Same with you, Marcus, when Naomi died. It nearly killed you guys. And I…"

He stopped and looked at the ground and took a couple of breaths before he could continue. "And then I saw it firsthand again the other day when I had to tell Margot Davidson that her husband was dead. It was like reliving Dad dying all over again. And I never want to deal with that pain."

Stella and Marcus glanced at each other before looking back at him. His mom's eyes were shiny with tears, and he hated that he put that look on her face. "Aw, Mom. I'm sorry. Please don't cry."

"Aidan,"—Marcus shifted to the edge of the sofa, folding his hands together and pausing for a moment—"losing Naomi was the worst thing to ever happen to me. That much is true. But she was also the best thing to ever happen to me. I wouldn't trade a single moment that I ever had with her to feel less pain. And you know what else?"

His dark, chocolate-colored eyes pinned Aidan to the floor. "Your dad was like a brother to me. He was one of the few people that would give this weird, nerdy kid a chance when my family moved to town. Your family, back to your grandparents, was nothing but kind to me and mine, even when many in town weren't so welcoming. I'll never forget that. And I would never trade a moment I had with him for less pain. You know what I'm saying?"

"I hear you, but—"

"No." Stella's voice was strong and sure, in spite of the unshed tears in her eyes. "There are no buts, son. You're right. I did lose myself for a while after your dad died. And I'm sorry you had to see that."

The smile she gave him was bittersweet. "I loved your father with all my heart and soul. That man drove me crazy in every way possible. But Marcus is right. I wouldn't trade a thing in this world to not know the pain. You know what pains me the most? The thought of never giving him a chance, never having loved him. Not only do I have six beautiful children that each have a piece of him to carry on, but I also have all the memories to keep him alive."

She rose and came to stand in front of him. She wrapped her hands around his. "I saw how the two of you were with each other. How you looked at her like she was the most precious thing in your world. It made me so happy to see you happy. You can push people away all you want, baby. And while it may make life easier for you, less messy, it's also incredibly lonely." She ran a hand over a lock of hair that fell over his forehead. "Don't you see you're just trading one kind of pain for another? With no memories to sustain you?"

"So what you're saying is it's better to have loved and lost than to lose love or whatever that saying is?"

Stella smiled and squeezed his hands. "It's a cliché for a reason, love."

Aidan sighed and looked down at their joined hands. "I never thought about it like that. All I know is that you were devastated when Dad died. And I always thought that if you never loved someone so much, you'd never feel that pain."

"You love her, don't you?" Stella asked gently.

He rubbed a hand over his heart and grimaced. "Yeah. I'm so in love with her it hurts. And I didn't think that was possible. It's only been a few weeks. How is that even possible?"

"Oh, baby. When you know, you know." Stella drew him in for a hug. "You're an amazing man, and I'm so sorry that we didn't talk sooner." She pulled away and cradled his face in her hands. "Don't be miserable. You know as well as anyone how short life is. We only get one shot. Make it count."

He nodded and wrapped his arms around her. God, he loved her. Even in her darkest hours she'd been an amazing mom and shown his brothers and sisters love. It was the way his father would have wanted it. And in her infinite wisdom, despite her pain and suffering, she'd figured it out a long time ago.

He closed his eyes as something shifted in his heart. In his mom's arms, he swore he could feel another pair of arms surrounding them. A peace that Aidan hadn't felt in too many years to count settled over him.

But on the heels of the peace, panic set in. He pulled back and looked over at his sister. "Charley, please tell me. Is Megan still in town? Where is she?"

Charley crossed her arms over her chest, but her face softened. "Yeah, she's still here. But she's getting her car back today. I talked her into sticking around tomorrow so we can give her a going away party at the Silver Moon."

"Shit." He ran his hands through his hair. Panic clawed at the back of Aidan's throat. He'd been an epic jackass to Megan—*If I could love anyone, it would be you.*" Who says that kind of shit?—and he had a lot of ground to make up.

"What can we do to help?" Marcus asked, coming to stand by his mom.

With his hands on his hips, his gaze wandered over the cabin, trying to think of how he was going to come back from this colossal fuck-up. Just when he figured something out, was he going to lose her?

A picture on the fridge caught his eye. Crossing into the kitchen, he snatched it from the stainless steel. It was one of the selfies they'd taken when he'd given her the camera, the morning after their first time together.

In this particular shot, Megan's eyes were closed, but the smile on her face radiated happiness. Her shoulders were bare, and her dark hair fell around them. He nuzzled her neck with a hint of a smile on his lips, and her free hand cradled one stubbled cheek.

He'd loved her even then.

It clicked what he needed to do. And he prayed that he could convince her that she was the best thing that had ever happened to him. The only one that could bring down his defenses and make him a better man.

She was messy to his neat. Whimsical to his grounded. Risk-taking to his risk-averse. Warm to his cool.

She made him want to be all those things he wished he was. She made him whole.

She was his.

He turned to Marcus. "Can you hold her up somehow tomorrow?"

"I can come up with something."

Charley launched off the arm of the sofa and rushed into the kitchen, bouncing on her toes. "You got a big gesture planned? You know you're going to need one, right? Can I help?"

He looked over at his younger sister. She was a royal pain in his ass, always had been. But he loved the hell out of her. She had one of the biggest hearts and wanted him happy. Hell, she'd known before he did how he felt about Megan. Not that he'd ever tell her that.

He looped an arm around her neck and brought her in close to rub a noogie on her head. She yelped and tried to push him away. But when he dropped a smacking kiss on the top of her head and said, "Absolutely," she slid her arms around his waist and squeezed.

She looked up at him, hope in her eyes. "You can do this, Aidan."

He'd seen it before when they were kids, whenever she asked him a question about things. For just a moment, they were thirteen and seven again. He took that faith she had in him and hung on to it.

He had a feeling he was going to need it.

wreck me

"I REALLY WISH you'd stay tonight and leave in the morning. What's the rush?" Charley asked, her lips curved down into a frown. "I mean, don't you think you should start your trip refreshed in the morning?"

Megan chuckled as she stuffed the little gifts that she'd received in her handbag. "You're the one who told me a few days ago that leaving now in the middle of the day would be good for traffic in Atlanta."

Charley crossed her arms over her chest and leaned back in the chair, then glanced at the smartwatch on her wrist. "Yeah, well, I'm rethinking that logic now that the time is here."

Megan smiled and laid a hand on Charley's arm. "I'm going to miss you too." It was just her and Charley left. Everyone else had gone on their way, and Marcus said he had some paperwork to do before they opened for the night shift.

She sighed and looked around the empty Silver Moon Cafe. "I wasn't here long, I know, but I'm going to miss this place too."

"It's not too late to stay…"

"You know I can't stay. For a lot of reasons." One of them being trouble wrapped up in a gorgeous six-foot-four package that had broken her heart.

"You could always stay with Mom and me tonight. It's just a night, Megan."

She shook her head. "No, thanks. I'm pretty sure I've worn out my welcome. It's time for me to head out."

Megan bit her lip to keep the tears from forming in her eyes. Again. She was physically leaving Madison Ridge, but her heart would always be there as long as Aidan had it. And she had a sneaking suspicion that he'd always have it, even if he didn't want it.

"I'm sure Emma could find you another room for the night."

"Are you kidding? I can't ask that of her. She was generous as it was."

Emma and Shane had been more than generous, giving her one of their vacant suites over the last few days. It had been a beautiful room. At least what she'd seen of it since she'd spent most of the time in bed, sleeping away her heartache. Henderson had called Wednesday and said she could pick up her car the next day. She'd had all intentions of heading out that afternoon. Even though she wanted to stay, she was also more than ready to put distance between her and the small town that had changed her life.

But then Charley came by and told her Marcus wanted to have a going away party for her on Friday, begging her to stay. She'd reluctantly said yes. Aidan wasn't the only Reynolds she'd grown fond of, and it was the least she could do for Charley. She was really going to miss the little firecracker too.

Charley glanced at her watch again and stood quickly, gathering her purse. "Um, okay, that's cool. But since you're leaving me can you do a favor for me before you leave?"

Standing as well, Megan raised a brow at Charley's sudden change in demeanor. She'd never seen the woman fidget before, and she kept glancing at her watch, then tapped it a couple of times. "Sure. Is everything okay?"

Charley looked up and brushed a wisp of hair from her face. Her face lit up in a smile. "Yep. Just peachy." She took Megan by the elbow and started for the door.

"Shouldn't we tell Marcus we're leaving so that he can lock up behind us?"

Charley waved her free hand. "Nah, we're good."

"Okay, so what's the favor?"

"Oh, yeah. Can you drop me off over at the bookstore on your way out of town? I could walk, but I have to be back for my shift in a little while. And my feet are already sore."

"The bookstore? Yeah, I guess. Where is it?"

"On your way out of town. I'll show you."

Charley tugged her toward Beatrix, who looked good as new, parked in a place in front of the Silver Moon. "Ready now. Right now."

Megan shook her head with a chuckle as she unlocked the doors and they slid in. "You got a date with a hot book or something?"

Charley pulled the seatbelt across her chest. "Something like that."

She practically vibrated in her seat and peered out the side window like she was looking for someone.

Megan eased out of the space and started down the short street leading out to Center Street and the main square area. "Charley, seriously. Are you okay?"

Charley turned her head and finally looked Megan in the eye. Her lips were curved in a mysterious smile. "I'm great."

Megan shook her head again. "Alright then."

At the end of the road, Landon stood blocking traffic from driving down Center Street and around the square. "What's going on? It looks like the road's closed."

She glanced in the rearview mirror and started to put it in reverse when Charley said, "He's waving you on, Megan."

Sure enough, Landon had the side street traffic stopped but waved her forward and directed her to the right. They waved at him, and he gave a thumbs-up.

She turned onto Center Street, and when she noticed people lined up along the edges of the road, she slowed down. "Are they about to have a parade or something?"

For once, Charley didn't say a word, but when Megan glanced over at her, she found her friend with a mile-wide grin.

"What—"

At that moment, she recognized several of the people standing along the side of the road, some of them holding something in front of them. Curious, she slowed the car to a crawl, trying to see what they were holding.

Her jaw dropped when she saw a picture she had taken of the cat that hung out at the inn, blown up and put on a large sign board someone was holding. It had been one of the first pictures she'd sent Aidan as a silly thing to do.

The car jerked when she slammed on the brake to see the rest of the signs people held up. Her gaze slid over several more pictures she'd taken, silly ones she'd sent to Aidan from her phone and others she'd taken with the Polaroid he'd given her. It was like a progression of her time there in Madison Ridge.

"What is all this?"

Charley leaned over and pulled up the emergency brake. "Why don't you go find out?"

In a daze, she nodded and got out of the car. She walked down the middle of the one-way road, looking to her right and left at all of the pictures. The people holding them smiled and waved. It dawned on her that her car was the only one on the street, and she turned back to Charley, who'd gotten out and leaned against the hood. "Go on, Megan," she called out with a grin.

Megan turned back around and kept walking, her mind whirling. What was going on?

The pictures of the town stopped at the slight curve where the main drag and the side road met. The spot where she'd had her wreck. She gasped when she saw Aidan's family standing in front of her. Each held a sign with an arrow on it, directing her where to go.

Her heart pounded, and hope ran through her body followed by a healthy dose of fear that she was dreaming. And then when she turned the curve, finding Aidan standing in the middle of the road, in the exact spot she'd first laid eyes on him, she realized that it wasn't a dream after all.

He lifted his head and their eyes met, her breath catching in her throat. Even yards away, the pull he had on her was intense. Everything around her fell away. The fact the whole town was an audience flew from her mind.

God, he was gorgeous. On the outside of course, with those

muscular arms, granite cut abs, blue eyes that held her captive, and the grin that always incinerated her underwear.

And in spite of the fact that he'd broken her heart, Aidan had a good heart and soul. He loved hard when he did love people—it was just a small circle that rarely opened to let anyone in. It hadn't opened for her and that's what hurt the most.

She wanted to run to him and jump in his arms. Forget that he couldn't love her.

She wanted to turn and run all the way to Florida. Forget she ever knew him.

Instead, as he held her gaze and walked toward her, those hands her body craved shoved into his pockets, her boots were glued to the pavement, unable to go either way. He stopped in front of her, close enough that she could reach out and touch him, smell his cologne and the scent that was just Aidan, but not so close that he invaded her personal space.

Megan both loved and hated it.

"Hey." His voice was low, husky, and danced along her skin like a live wire. It just about did her in. But she had to remember he'd hurt her. He didn't love her, didn't want her.

He'd been clear.

"Hey." She squared her shoulders and lifted her chin. "What's this all about?"

"Me and you. Us."

"There is no us, Aidan. You made no bones about that. Remember? I said I loved you and you said I couldn't be trusted to know what the hell I was talking about."

He nodded, his eyes shadowed with regret. "You're right. I did. And I'm sorry for what I said. It was cruel. You trusted me with something about yourself and then I used it against you. I'll always regret that."

She bit her lips to keep them from trembling and looked away, blinking hard. He was apologizing, but he wasn't asking her to stay. There was no way she was going to let him see her cry. When she was pretty certain the tears wouldn't fall, she looked back at him, keeping her back straight.

"Apology accepted." She glanced around at the town, all eyes on them. It made her think of those Hollywood rom-coms where the whole town stops what they're doing to see if there's a happily ever after. "Is that why you closed off roads and have the whole town out here? So you could apologize?"

"No." He stepped forward, and when she didn't move, he continued to move forward until they were toe to toe and sharing the same air. "I did all this because I want the whole world to know I'm in love with you."

Her head snapped back. "What?"

"I said I'm in love with you."

He took her hands in his and turned them over before dropping a kiss on the inside of each wrist. Aidan raised his head and pinned her with his laser blue eyes. "My life before you was black and white and damn lonely. I convinced myself I just wanted to be alone—wanted privacy."

He paused and looked down at their joined hands. When he looked back up, he lifted a hand to cradle her face, and God help her, she leaned into it instinctively. "Truth time. I want what my parents had. But I'm scared to death to have it. After my dad died, all I saw was pain."

His smile lit up her world. "Then I met you. The moment I laid eyes on you in this very spot, I knew. You're who I've waited for to rescue me from a lifetime of loneliness. To show me love is worth the gamble."

His gaze roamed her face, stopping a split second longer on her lips before meeting her eyes again. "I love you, Megan Gentry. I know this is asking a lot, but please stay with me. I never want to see you go."

Megan couldn't stop the tears if she tried, nor could she deny he was offering everything she wanted on a silver platter. "I love you too, Aidan."

He smiled and started to lean forward, but she put a hand to his chest, stopping his forward progression. "You do believe me, right?"

That smile she loved, that turned her inside out, grew and he nodded. "I believed you the first time you said it. It scared me shitless. But now?" He laid a hand over hers on his chest and leaned in closer, their lips barely brushing together. "I want to hear it from these lips for the rest of my life. Say it again."

"I love you, Aidan Reynolds." Her arms twined around his neck and pulled him closer.

The words barely left her lips before his mouth covered hers, his arms snaking around her waist. In the distance, the sound of applause and whistling filled the air.

He pulled back and lowered his forehead to hers. "You know the family is about to descend on us. Let's untangle ourselves as quick as possible. I've missed you in my bed and in my arms. We have some catching up to do." His hands ran over her ass and pulled her impossibly close.

She ran her tongue over her bottom lip. "Only if you read me my rights."

He nuzzled her neck. "You have the right to scream my name…"

"AIDAN, you shouldn't have. Honestly. It's too much."

They'd just arrived home from his mother's house where they had a birthday party for Megan. He'd surprised her by arranging for Nate to be there to enjoy the festivities. The tears had flowed unchecked from Megan, who had missed her brother.

She'd never made it to Florida to run his bar, but Aidan had talked to Nate the day he professed his love to her in the middle of the road in front of what he thought was the entire population of Madison Ridge. Nate had told him if he could pull off the feat and win the girl, Aidan had his blessing and he'd gladly find a replacement.

Standing at the island in the kitchen, Megan turned the camera in her hands that Aidan had splurged on for her birthday. He came up behind her and wrapped his arms around her waist, dropping his chin to her shoulder.

"It was worth every penny I spent to see that smile on your face. I know you like the Polaroid, but now you can take the serious pictures you want."

"I still can't believe your mom gave me that photography job for the chamber. And then Emma setting me up with some weddings? It's been a dream come true." She set the pricey equipment down and turned in his arms, wrapping her arms around his neck. "I can't thank you enough."

"I have some ideas of how you can thank me." He rubbed his lips over hers, causing her to moan softly.

"Remind me to thank my brother for insisting on staying at the inn."

He chuckled and pulled back. "Agreed. But before we get too far down that road, I have one more thing for you."

"No. Nothing more. Getting my brother here and the camera? I can't take much more." She started to put her hands over her face, but he grabbed one and pulled her with him out the back door.

"Yes. I'm pretty sure you're going to like this one."

He hoped to God she did. His sisters and Emma had gushed over the ring he'd picked for Megan, saying it was perfect for her. For his Megan, he didn't go with a traditional solitaire. Megan had brought color into his world, and when he found a round sapphire solitaire with a diamond halo along the edge, he knew it was hers.

The box sat like a paperweight in his pocket.

"Aidan, where are you taking me?" Megan asked on a laugh as they went down the stairs and into the back yard.

He turned and faced her, her smiling face bathed in moonlight. A bead of sweat ran down his spine while his heart beat double time in his chest. God, she was beautiful. To think he'd almost let her go all because he was so scared to lose something before he ever had a real chance to have it.

"Close your eyes."

She narrowed her eyes at him and pursed her lips. "It's already dark out here. I can't see anything anyway."

Aidan rolled his eyes. "Please, baby? I really want to give you this present before I give you the one present you like on a daily basis."

She swatted at his abs with a grin but did as he asked. "Okay. Now what?"

Aidan took her by the shoulders and led her over to the small shed he'd spent the last few weeks working on. He opened the door and took her hand to lead her just inside the entrance. "Okay, stand there. Keep your eyes closed."

Aidan did a quick glance around, approving of the way the girls had set up the lighting in the shed. Outdoor lights were strung along the wall, giving the space an almost cozy candlelight setting.

He'd set it up with everything Megan would need to have a darkroom. A desk lined one wall with a chair and a new laptop where she could work on photos. Next to it was a storage cabinet that held all the materials she'd need to develop film and all of her equipment she used when taking the wedding photos or other photo shoots. Along the wall was a long rectangular table with trays where she could develop film for those shots she decided not to do digital. Rope with clothespins hung above it stretched from one wall to the other to hang the pictures to dry.

He knew this because he'd just hung four notebook paper-sized photos with one word on each.

Turning back to the woman who'd changed his life, he blew out a breath and patted the ring box in the pocket of his slacks. "Keep your eyes closed."

"I am."

With his free hand, he took hers and pulled her in front of him so when she opened her eyes, she'd see the most important question he'd ever asked in his life. He leaned down, his mouth at her ear. He had to stop himself from kissing the sensitive skin beneath the lobe that made her squirm.

"Open your eyes."

When she did and read WILL YOU MARRY ME spelled out in pictures, her gasp echoed in the small space. "Oh my God. Aidan."

She whirled around, her eyes wide, her lips parted. He cleared his throat and blew out a breath. With it, all of the nervousness left his body. Because the next words he said were true and pure.

"Megan, I love you. It's as simple as that and yet those words feel inadequate for how I feel about you. I never saw you coming, but as soon as I saw you, I knew. Even though I fought it every step of the way until I knew I couldn't fight it anymore. I've told you this before, but it bears repeating. You rescued me, Megan. And for that, I will be eternally grateful. Even when you're driving me crazy with your messes."

"Oh babe," she breathed out, tears in her eyes.

He pulled the box out of his pocket and opened it. "Megan Gentry, will you do me the honor of being my wife?"

She covered her mouth with her hands, her eyes glued to the ring. "Oh my God, Aidan. It's gorgeous."

"You like it?"

"I love it."

"Wanna wear it?"

She laughed through tears and held out her hand. He slid it on her ring finger, and his shoulders relaxed when it slid on perfectly. She stared at it for a moment before looking up at him and wrapping her arms around his neck.

"Yes, I'll marry you." She looked around the small room that he'd turned into her darkroom. "I can't believe you did this for me."

She brought her gaze back to him. "I can't wait to wake up beside you every morning, fall asleep on your chest every night, have your babies. I can't wait to begin our life together."

Something deep in his soul sighed, and peace washed over him.

He lifted her up, cupping her ass as she wrapped her legs around his waist. His hand cupped the back of her head and tangled in her hair, bringing her mouth to his, sealing the deal with a kiss, soft and sweet.

"And we're just getting started."

Thank you for reading **WRECK ME**! Want to see what happens next for Aidan & Megan? Get access to their bonus scene by signing up for my newsletter.

Flip the page to read about book one in the Madison Ridge spinoff series, Unexpected Forever. This Charley and Nate's sexy, accidental pregnancy, best friend's brother romance.

Unexpected Forever: A steamy, accidental pregnancy, age gap romance

When I meet my best friend's baseball star older brother, our chemistry is out of the park.
And for one night, he shows me more pleasure than I thought possible.
But two months later, life throws me a curveball in the form of two pink lines.

We couldn't be more different.

He's a newly retired future baseball Hall of Fame contender, his handsome face rakes in millions of sponsorship dollars.

I'm launching my dream career as an event planner and thus far, my biggest accomplishment is carrying twenty shots of tequila in a bar without spilling a drop.

From putting together a crib to managing my weird cravings, Nate insists on being involved in our accidental family. I'm falling for him, and even though his emotional scars run deeper than his physical injuries, the way he brushes his lips over my forehead makes me wonder if he could be falling for me too.

We may have started as a one-time thing, but now I want our unexpected forever.

Preorder your copy now!

Turn the page to see where Madison Ridge all began with Shane and Emma's story in Trouble Me: a steamy, workplace romance.

trouble me:
chapter one

BURGERS AND BILLS

EMMA TWISTED her lips into a semblance of a smile as she served Jimmy, her last customer, his usual heaping plate of cholesterol disguised as a double burger and fries. Maggie's Diner served the best burgers in Madison Ridge, or so she'd heard. She'd never been able to bring herself to try one after smelling grease all day long.

Once back behind the counter, Emma breathed deep and pulled the mortgage bill out of her apron pocket. Once upon a time, avoidance came easy. She'd learned to evade any situation that exposed her vulnerability. But avoidance was a safety net she no longer used.

She ripped the envelope open like a bandage off an open wound and forced herself to focus on the bright red all-capped letters that made her stomach churn. The amount in bold was much larger than she anticipated. So much so her vision momentarily blurred.

Emma tapped a finger on the Formica countertop, her mind calculating her bank balance. Even if she could liquidate the last two pieces in her fine art collection tomorrow, she'd never make enough to pay the past due payments and save the family estate. Not by a long shot.

Winning the lottery wouldn't hurt.

Hell, no. Gambling had been her father's main vice and look where it had landed him.

Emma blinked back tears and shoved the letter into her apron, along with the thoughts from her mind, when Jimmy shuffled up front to pay his bill.

She punched the check total into the register and waited while he pulled out his wallet. "It's getting late. Vera's going to wonder where you've been."

Jimmy grunted as he handed over a twenty. "Nah. She's at some artsy wine and painting thing tonight. Probably not thought of me once."

Emma chuckled. "After forty-something years of marriage, I seriously doubt that's true."

With a work-worn hand, he waved away the change she tried to give him. "Nah, you keep it."

Emma's smile was genuine in spite of her fatigue. "Thanks, Jimmy. See you tomorrow."

He waved as he walked out the door, the bell above the front door ringing in his wake. As she set about the mindless task of refilling ketchup bottles for the next day, dread tightened her chest like a vise. She needed to nail her job interview tomorrow. The operations director job at a local winery was the only job in town that paid anywhere in the vicinity of what she needed.

Emma slid her hand into her apron and rubbed the white chip she kept with her. The surrender chip was the hardest to earn and held more significance to her than her bronzed two-year chip. As she did several times a day, Emma recited the Serenity Prayer silently in her mind. The pills and booze had stolen so much from her. Her family's estate would not be one of them.

A winery was not a good place for Emma, but she needed the job. She was out of choices and out of time.

When the diner was empty, she bused Jimmy's table and dared to dream about a hot shower and fresh sheets. Just getting off her feet sounded like a heaping slice of heaven.

The bell announcing another customer rang, sounding like a siren in Emma's ears. Yanked back to reality, she had to bite back a groan. Mentally, she'd already clocked out for the day and was at home, in bed. But she shook out the ache in her feet and plastered on her best fake smile.

Turning to greet the customer, "hello" died on her lips. Even in the dingy surroundings, the man filling the doorway stood out like a beacon in a storm-darkened night. He glanced around the empty diner, his chestnut-colored hair glinting under the harsh lighting.

When her mouth and brain caught up with each other, she managed to say, "Sit anywhere you like."

He stared at her for a few heartbeats before he muttered, "Thanks."

In spite of herself, her sleepy lady parts sat up and noticed him even though a frown marred his full lips. His moves were slow and deliberate, like a panther stalking its prey, settling into a booth at the back of the place.

With a heavy sigh, Emma pressed a hand to her lower back and stretched. Standing on her feet for long periods was difficult after she'd broken her back two years ago. She moved a hand to rub the puckered skin on her upper thigh, one of the more visible scars that reminded her of darker days.

Most of the time, she was laser-focused on the future. But every so often, the past would reach out and bitch-slap her. Right now, her tired ass was just ready to get home and curl up in bed with a pint of chocolate ice cream.

Squaring her shoulders, she walked around the L-shaped counter toward her just-stepped-out-of-a-Ralph-Lauren-catalogue customer. She pulled out her tablet and pen as she approached him. Mystery Man perused the well-worn, plastic-covered menu, snapping it closed when she walked up to the table.

"Hey, I'm Emma. What can I get you?"

When he looked up and met Emma's gaze, her lips parted, her eyes widening of their own volition.

Holy hell.

Long, dark lashes framed intense cerulean-blue eyes that reminded her of the South Pacific Sea. They seemed to bore right into her soul when he looked at her.

Damn. The man had sex appeal in spades.

He blinked at her then glanced down at the menu, rubbing a hand across his strong jaw. "How are the burgers?" His voice held a husky quality that made her tingle in all the right places.

Prying her tongue off the roof of her mouth, she kicked her brain into gear. "They're the best in town. You won't be hungry when you finish."

While he figured out what he wanted, she studied him from under her lashes, pen hovering over the notepad. A lock of dark hair fell over his forehead and the thick, rich mane held a slight wave that all but begged her to muss it up. One side of her mouth quirked up. Women paid good money for the hair color this guy was born with.

"I'll take a cheeseburger with fries and a soda."

She bit her lip in an effort not to smile. The hot mystery man must be an out-of-towner. All the locals simply referred to a soda as "Coke." "What kind of soda?"

"Coca-Cola, please."

Yep, definitely a tourist. She nodded, not bothering to write it down. "Will do."

He put the menu back behind the napkin dispenser, dismissing her. When she returned a few minutes later with his drink, he'd lost the navy blazer. His crisp, white button-down shirt accented his broad shoulders, causing her heart to flutter. She'd always been a sucker for that classic male physique. "Here ya go. Your burger and fries will be up in a few."

He muttered an absent-minded "thank you," his attention focused on the phone in his hand.

Emma frowned and walked away. He may be hot as sin but he had all the social skills of a grizzly bear. Not that it mattered to her as long as he left a tip.

While she worked to ready the diner for closing, she kept an eye on the level of his drink, but otherwise left him alone. When Bud, the night cook, popped the bell and called out, "Order Up!" she grabbed the plated food and headed toward her definite last customer of the day.

She was locking the damn door this time.

"Here ya go."

Her customer moved back so she could put down his plate, his focus still on his phone. Irritation flared and weaved its way into her voice. "Need anything else?"

"No." His tone was brusque, putting her teeth on edge. She spun on her heel, but only made it a couple of steps before he called her back.

"Yes?" She tried to hide the aggravation in her voice. She wasn't expecting him to fall all over her or anything. He was way out of her newfound league. His clothes and demeanor screamed money and power. These days, hers screamed desperation. But was it too much to ask for a little courtesy? Eye contact, or a "thank you" she didn't have to strain to hear?

She walked back and leaned a hip against the edge of the table. Her body hadn't been her own for the last two years, and the longer she stood on her feet, the more it revolted. All she wanted to do was get this guy out of here and go home.

He looked up with the intense blue eyes that she tried to ignore. "Can I add a slice of pie to my order?" he asked.

"We have apple, peach, and cherry."

"Hmmm." He tapped his finger on the rim of the turquoise-tinted coke glass. "Peach, please."

"Okay. Be back in a few."

"Thanks." One corner of his mouth lifted in a half smile that was obnoxiously heart-stopping. She could only imagine what his full-on smile would be like. Angels probably broke into song. A ping from his phone diverted his attention and she was subtly dismissed.

Her teeth clenched until her jaw ached, and she barely resisted the urge to stomp back into the kitchen. With jerky movements, she sliced a piece of pie and slid it onto a plate.

Emma closed her eyes and pinched the bridge of her nose. She needed to get a grip. She was overly tired and didn't need a man she would most likely never see again to get under her skin. Blowing out a deep breath, she pasted a smile on her face and sailed out of the kitchen to his table.

"Here's your peach—"

As she moved to set down the plate in front of him, he lifted his glass up to his mouth. Plate and glass collided, sending a shower of Coke all over his very white, very expensive shirt.

Click here to order Trouble Me

Thank you so much for reading WRECK ME. It means the world to me that you took a chance on my book! A review on **your favorite retailer** or Goodreads would mean the world to me and makes a HUGE difference for new indie authors like me!

30 Days Until "The End": An Inspirational Guide to Finishing Your Novel in 30 Days

If you're looking for humor, positivity, and a swift kick to your flagging motivation, Eliza Peake's inspirational guide to completing a draft in thirty days is a must have.

get a sneak peek of all things eliza!

If you'd like to be a part of my street team where you receive access to ARC's first, join my Elite Street Team!

If you like to talk about books, hot guys, and general fun stuff in a drama free zone, join my reader group, Eliza Peake's Reader Group. We have a fun group going and growing all the time!

author's note

Dear Reader,

Thank you for reading *Wreck Me!* I hope you enjoyed Aidan and Megan's story!

I really enjoyed spending time with this two. Aidan may be the baby brother, but he's got that hero thing down cold having been a military guy and now a sheriff. And while all of the Reynolds children were affected their father's untimely death, Aidan was hit especially hard with trying to be the man of the house at a young age. It really shaped the man he became.

He's also got a bit of a dirty side to him that was a surprise! And Megan was a great match for him. Sunny to his broody and willing to push the boundaries and show Aidan her appreciation for all he did for her.

Needless to say, I think they both won.

If you liked *Wreck Me*, would you consider leaving me a review? I can be found on Goodreads, Bookbub, and and **all major retailers.** Reviews are like gold to us authors and we appreciate them more than you know.

Happy Reading!

Love fearlessly and live intentionally,

Eliza

acknowledgments

A huge thank you to my editors, Happily Editing Ann's, for making my words shine as always. And keeping my timelines straight!

To Julianne Fangmann making this beautiful cover! Your ability to take a bunch of pics I send and make it a cover never ceases to amaze me. Nor does your patience with me. Thank you for being AMAZING!

To Kelly Fletcher who always wants to read whatever I write. How did I get so lucky to find you girl?

To the Harlots Author group for being an awesome, smart group of writers with so much knowledge, lead by our fearless leader Melanie Harlow!

To Wildfire Marketing for all the help with my promo on the book. Thank you for getting my name out!

To Spotify for having a huge source of songs I could choose from to put me in the mood while I wrote this book.

To my family, especially, my husband Mr. P, my daughter, and my sister for being my biggest cheerleaders, for keeping me organized, and most of all for being patient and listening to me when I babble about these stories.

And to MY READERS, my Peake's Pirates!! These stories are for you! Without you guys, my words would never make it out there. I love you all and grateful for each and every one of you!

about the author

Hey y'all! I'm Eliza and I write steamy, all the feels romance full of heart, heat, and humor. My heroes are swoony alphas, my heroines are strong and audacious, and family is at the center of it all.

I'm a proud mom and a Southern girl who can bless a heart with the best of them. I live with my very own book boyfriend, a snoring dog, and a sassy cat.

In my downtime, I read all the panty-melting romances I can get my hands on, drink coffee by day, wine by night, and indulge my woo-woo side as often as possible. I'm also hopelessly addicted to tacos.

I dream of retiring to the beach someday where I'll continue writing sexy romance stories to my heart's content and taking sunrise and sunset walks in the sand, thinking of my next book!

Join my newsletter, The Sneak Peake, to get updates on all sorts of shenanigans, exclusive content, and news on books and appearances at http://elizapeake.com/subscribe/

Find her at www.elizapeake.com.